# Fighting Words: Bruisers, Brawlers, & Bad Intentions

**Edited by: Scott Blackburn**

ISBN (Paperback): 979-8-9951341-0-7
Cover art by: Christopher Jennings

www.leonardoaudio.com

# Table of Contents

I

# A Note about Fighting from the Publisher

**Quick** question for you ... Have you ever been in a fight? Do you remember it? Did you win? Did you lose? Did you hurt your face? Did you break a knuckle?

When we decided as a publishing company to roll out a few story collections this year, as a former boxing coach, combat sports was the first topic that came to mind. I've always been fascinated by fighting. The physical and psychological aspects of it. And how objectives, obstacles, and real-life stakes affect performance and outcomes.

Where did that fascination begin? Growing up, it was known that my father was literally the toughest guy in my town for a long while. But I, unfortunately, took after my mother, both physically and emotionally, at least in my early stages of life. Petite and smiley. A nervous, timid, and frail child, I'd do whatever I could to avoid physical combat and debate.

I remember at 7 years old, being forced to fight Craig from up the street in a neighbor's front yard, as his 10-year-old brother Rich acted as referee. (Was the fix in? The setup was there, but I'm pretty sure they didn't need it. And we're all very friendly today.)

As a 13-year-old eighth-grader (and quite underdeveloped compared to class peers) I was instigated by a shitstain of a gym teacher to fight my good friend Mike (who happened to be twice my size). That fight lasted a few hours through several locations in the city to avoid oncoming authorities. I remember it being utterly grueling, and finally getting cracked on the left temple to end it, then the moans from the onlookers, and staggering home after, alone. Wallowing in my spiraling thoughts. Then all the snickers from classmates the following day. Kids can be cruel, as we know.

Then, just a year later, I was passing by a schoolyard in my neighborhood when I saw a group of guys picking on a developmentally-disabled teenager. It was too shitty to let it continue. While just trying to slow them down a bit, one of the punks started with me, pushing and jostling me around—since I was a skinny kid who hadn't hit the weights yet. Out of nowhere, I belted him with a left hook that shook him up. But I was even more stunned than he was. I had no idea where that punch came from. (And for those keeping score ... no, I didn't "win." Not really. I let him off the hook, which is my MO.)

But what was it that allowed me to toss that punch, and connect? And why—I distinctly remember—had I not been nervous at all? Was it because I was defending someone else, instead of just myself? Was it because I was finally maturing physically and able to handle myself?

I learned the hard way, through my early years of being bullied and then flipping the script and becoming a Head Doorman of the largest nightclub in LA, that I don't have that hungry, visceral "killer instinct" to inflict pain on other people. At that nightclub, I helped break up a triad gang fight in our venue that spilled out onto our front foyer. I was able to subdue two assailants who were attacking members of our internal security team. One guy somehow got hold of an umbrella and was swinging it down onto the security guy's head, who was cowering in a corner with no way of escape. I ran over and instead of striking him in the jaw and knocking him out, I picked him up and threw him over our security fence. Why that choice? Why not blast him into the next century? That was also a situation that I can recall in great detail. And again, maybe because I was defending other people and not myself, I was calm as a cucumber.

Why do we remember such incredible detail, frame-by-frame of some of these moments, and then others fly right by, and you're just trying to recall what you did on autopilot? When is it purely instinctual, and when is it an active choice? And does your training lead to you developing instincts, or do we revert to our genetic coding under certain conditions?

My only bad night working that door was coming to the defense of another doorman at our upscale club room on the same premises, and being sucker-slapped by one person, and then wrestling someone who was 50 pounds heavier than myself while I wore wooden-soled shoes. It was an upscale event, and Barney, my General Manager, asked me to wear nice shoes, and those were the only ones I had. Above all else, I soon learned that no matter what, when you're working the door, you need traction. Another risk-averse lesson. Always wear rubber-soled shoes at a nightclub door. That fight ended with me getting tossed into a metal fence head first, by three guys, then getting pounded in the back of my head with a cell phone.

I remember not feeling great mentally for a month after that. I'm guessing a mixture of depression and concussion symptoms. (I didn't get checked out.)

As a teenager, I developed a bloodthirsty love for boxing. I can thank my dad for planting that seed when together, we would watch Marvelous Marvin Hagler fights in the 1980s, and then the resurgence of Lowell's Micky Ward in the late '90s. I would watch both the ESPN and HBO fights with my dad every chance I got. Those are some of the memories I hold dearest.

I also started dating my future wife in my teenage years, and her brother, Richie "The Mountain" Lamontagne ended up becoming a regional Cruiserweight champion in the '90s and 2000s. I'd often watch him train and spar, and I learned a ton from him and another friend, Middleweight "Dangerous" Dana Rosenblatt, while I worked out alongside them at World Gym in Somerville, Massachusetts.

Then, fast-forward to the start of college. I put on 50 pounds of muscle, and started training hard in boxing. I wanted to find out if I could be like my future brother-in-law. I would take the Green Line from Boston College all the way to Sullivan Station. A 90-minute ride. (No smartphones then. Just my CD Walkman skipping all over the place.)

What usually happens when someone tries to do something that they truly were not destined to do?

Nothing good. But the important thing to state here is whenever I tried to step it up and spar good fighters, I'd freeze up. I couldn't execute what my coaches implored me to do. I couldn't duplicate all the drills and combinations that were trained into me. Why?

Just after my Boston College graduation, I got a job working for US Senator Ed Markey when he was a Representative in Congress. (I was a Political Science major.) That's when I first got the itch to pursue boxing as an actual fighter. I started sparring in earnest, and would take some licks from better fighters, but thankfully most of them "carried" me to help build me up. I'd head into the office with a nice shiner or facial bruising after a night of good work, and I'd get all the strange looks, since I wasn't transparent about my training regimen. I didn't blame them for those looks. They had no idea. No one at that office expressly told me to stop, but it didn't look great when I was publicly speaking on behalf of Ed at various City Halls, looking like I got worked over at the docks for my wallet and keys.

My dad had some wonderfully blunt advice when he got wind of my wishes to be a boxer. He pulled me aside one night after I came home from my night job at the gym, and said to me, "Hey kid, truth is, you're never gonna be a champion. If you're not gonna be that, why do it? Why take those punches? You're already in college." Words of sage-like wisdom. I was the only person in our immediate family who was capable of receiving a college education. It was practical advice. (My dad was a common sense machine. I miss him and his advice dearly.)

I tried once more, in my late-20s, when living in LA and establishing an acting career. This was when I was working the door at that nightclub. I figured since I wasn't living in Boston anymore, I could reinvent myself in certain ways. Pursuing being a fighter was also a cool thing to talk about. It opened doors. Agents liked the notoriety it brought, and the possibility of more press and potential days on set as a stunt guy or working with fight choreographers. The primary issue was I kept getting hurt in training, mainly dealing with two bad shoulders (which is not good when your job is to throw punches). I was too brittle. I was also finally realizing that I wasn't very good. Serviceable and driven, but not athletic or fast enough to elevate my skills in the ring.

In the third round of a smoker fight (a non-sanctioned amateur bout) on a card that I put together at Crunch Gym in LA where I was the head boxing trainer, my buddy Andre (a former Canadian amateur champion) blasted my nose halfway across my face. Final attempt, complete. About a thousand hours of sparring under me, but never to carry a USA amateur passbook.

I can say that as an upper-echelon "boxing casual", I've experienced some really cool stuff. I've worked a pro corner with legendary trainer Goody Petronelli. I've been cast to play "Jesse" James Leija (in an unfortunately never-made movie). For a few years, I was a boxing commentator and popular podcaster on the Stick n' Move podcast (long before the recent podcast boom). I've refereed a charity boxing match, and I helped choreograph boxing scenes for the early Marvel movie Daredevil. I've had the honor of being part of the athletic trainer team in both professional and amateur boxing camps. And as a recreational boxing trainer, I worked my ass off to get great at working mitts. It's a skillset that's helped a nice chunk of MMA fighters improve their hands for the Octagon. I've even held mitts for actors Sam Rockwell, Josh Holloway, Eliza Dushku, and a bunch of other well-known TV and film actors and personalities. Is that leaving a mark? No, of course not. But it sure has been a fun ride. I can carry a nice conversation about boxing and MMA. It sometimes comes in handy.

Profuse thanks go to editor, Scott Blackburn, whose wrangling and macro editing skills were top notch. A wonderful teammate. Glad we could work together again, amigo. I want to personally thank all our terrific authors who participated in this first run. Your stories are engaging, visceral and memorable. They're a pleasure to publish, and I sincerely hope we did them justice with our audio performances. Regarding those performances, thank you so much to the audiobook narrators for putting in the prep work and delivering choices that best reflect the authors' intent. Absolute kickass auditory storytelling.

Thank you Melissa DeJesus, Maren Detlefs, Chris Jennings, Krissy Barnes, and the rest of the Leonardo Audio team for putting this together. Terrific work all around. And thank you Dad, for planting those seeds. Wish you could experience these stories with us.

Chris Ciulla, Perennial False Starter,
Founder and CEO, Leonardo Audio
"Your Story, Told Right"

# Saint Bullethead

## by Nick Kolakowski

### 1.

**The first** time I saw David Wilson, I thought: *Now there's a guy who's gonna get his ass kicked.* His body looked like a couple balls of clay mashed together, his eyes wide and scared as he stripped down to a too-tight pair of red nylon shorts. I figured he would last five, maybe ten seconds against anyone who could brawl—back then, I didn't know anything about the .32 bullet that cored out a chunk of his brain or the power it gave him.

Wilson stood shivering in the sickly fluorescent light, the other fighters circling him like wolves, sniffing his weakness. This weekly battle in the underground parking garage on 34th and 5th was a dozen guys going to war two-by-two. It was run by Wall Street guys who trained hard at a gym downtown, guys who wanted to prove they could smash a nose into a face like it was nothing. They bet big money on themselves, with all kinds of crazy side wagers: ten thousand on who would break a bone first or a Rolex watch on a knockout. The audience was reliably insane; a couple of dozen fanatics clustered around the parked cars, yelling themselves hoarse over the smack of flesh on bone.

# 2

Wilson was the first fight of the night, a paid warm-up, and the sadist putting together the roster decided he should face off against Brian O'Malley, a wealth management VP at Goldman Sachs who paid real MMA guys to train him every weekend. O'Malley was built like he had taken every steroid in the world.

At these fights, my job was to take bets and handle the cash and prizes. I'm 300 pounds and solid as a brick shithouse, bench four hundred without a sweat. I would've done the NFL proud if a bad tackle hadn't wrecked my left knee and ended my college career. The knee also meant I'd never make it as a fighter in the ring, but I still had worth as a bouncer, enforcer, or simply the scary-looking guard who holds a million in cash while a bunch of dudes break their knuckles against other dudes' jaws. Even though I minded their money, these Wall Street guys never liked talking to me. In their eyes, I was just a dumb animal.

Right at the start, though, Wilson zeroed in like a torpedo and chatted me up. "You're the only one here who doesn't have a vested interest in me getting beaten to a pulp," he said before the fight and laughed.

I chuckled at that. I was supposed to keep stony as a statue, beware of anyone trying to get too close, but I could tell he wasn't any kind of threat. "You want to bet on yourself?" I asked. "Take a dive early?"

He laughed again. "I want to bet on myself to win."

"That's your right as a proud American, but the odds are a hundred to one," I said, doing the math in my head. "You want to lose money *and* some teeth? You were coming out ahead with that fee they're paying you."

"I'm sure," he said and pulled a warm wad of cash from his pocket. "This is everything they were going to pay me, a thousand bucks. Think these guys can afford it if I win?"

I looked him over again and noted the jagged scar in the corner of his mouth, the oversized dent behind his ear. "Hey, it's your ass," I said, sticking out a hand. "Gimme."

Five minutes later, Wilson stood inside the seething circle of fight aficionados as Brian O'Malley charged at him, fists balled, ready to kick his ass.

And something amazing happened.

Like a light going out, the fear left Wilson's eyes. He stood straighter, his spine stiffening, his hands closing into fists.

For the first time, I noticed his scarred knuckles and sturdy wrists.

Now I thought: Oh shit, he fooled us all.

O'Malley wasn't the type to play with his prey: he charged across the space, fists high, ready to crush. I knew from previous nights that he liked starting off with a couple of fierce kicks to the abdomen, jostling his opponent into letting their guard slip, then grappling them to the pavement, ground and pounding them to death.

Wilson took a hard knee to the abdomen that knocked him onto the balls of his feet—a heavy hit that should have lit up his every nerve like a Christmas tree of agony. Except Wilson's face barely twitched. He jabbed twice at O'Malley, much faster than I expected, tapping the bigger man's nose and jaw.

If Wilson meant for that move to drive O'Malley back, it failed. O'Malley swept forward like a wave, grabbing Wilson's wrist, and slammed him flat to the concrete.

*Ooof.*

From there, O'Malley swept his legs around Wilson's scrawny left arm and levered his body up, locking Wilson into an armbar.

A trained fighter can slip free of an armbar without breaking their limb. It takes knowledge, practice, and a little luck. Wilson clearly had none of those things. He thrashed and struggled but refused to tap out, and O'Malley punished him for it by torquing the arm harder, harder, harder. The crowd went apeshit.

"Just tap out," I muttered under my breath. "It's not worth the limb."

Except Wilson wasn't in the mood to quit. He bucked like a dying deer and—*pop*—his arm exploded, his radius bone stabbing through the skin.

O'Malley jerked back, startled, his face spattered with Wilson's blood.

O'Malley's grip loosened, and Wilson slithered free, stood, and lashed out with his right foot as hard as he could, smashing O'Malley's jaw to pieces. O'Malley flopped back, unconscious.

The parking garage fell silent enough to hear the fluorescents humming overhead, the blood dripping from the tear in Wilson's flesh. Wilson examined his exposed bone as if it were a mildly interesting insect before pressing it back into his arm with the heel of his other hand. He swiped his shirt from the side mirror of the

Honda, where he'd draped it before the fight, and used it to tie off the wound.

As he walked toward me through the stunned crowd, his head held high, his shoulders back, I felt something strange in my guts, like my stomach had turned into a stone heavy enough to drop through me to the ground. Later, I imagined people in ancient times feeling the same thing as they witnessed a saint perform a miracle or an angel descend from heaven—not a sense of transcendence, but dread at something too powerful for them to comprehend.

Wilson stopped in front of me and stuck out his good hand. "Put 'er there," he said. "What's your name?"

I shook his hand carefully, like his other arm might fall off. "Sherman," I said.

"Solid." He grinned, revealing front teeth smeared with blood. "I want you to be my manager."

## 2.

The way Wilson told it, he was buying cigarettes at his corner bodega when a dude in a black hoodie walked through the front door and shot him through the back of the head.

*Bam*, no warning.

Wilson didn't smoke unless he was drinking, and he'd just polished off a six-pack of cheap beer in his apartment with plans to suck down at least three cancer sticks on a long walk to The Barrel, one of the few bars in his rapidly gentrifying neighborhood that stayed open past midnight. Wilson had broken up with his girlfriend a few days before, a real depth charge to his soul, and overloading his body on sweet nicotine and alcohol seemed like a good idea.

Anyway, the police never found the guy in the black hoodie because the bodega's one security camera didn't have a good angle on the door, and they assumed the shooting was a case of mistaken identity. Sure, that could be it, or maybe the guy was jacked up on something, planned to rob the bodega, popped in, got scared, and fired off a shot before running. "I never even heard the gun," Wilson told me. "One second, I'm paying, and then, blink, I wake up in the hospital."

If the shooter had managed to hit the back of Wilson's skull at a diagonal, piercing both the right and left hemispheres, Wilson would have coded right on the bodega's dirty floor. Instead, the bullet skipped straight across the part of Wilson's brain that controls pain—he couldn't remember its name, just that it was something multi-fucking-syllabic based on Latin, its acronym ACC. An inch later, that speedy chunk of metal skimmed the little nugget that helps regulate adrenaline and some other body chemicals, then punched out his mouth, taking three teeth with it.

The police pried the smushed bullet from the wall behind the register and one of Wilson's teeth from the bodega worker's shoulder. That bodega worker ended up in therapy for PTSD. Getting splashed with a customer's blood will do that to a guy, especially if he's a teenager who's only worked the register for a week.

The EMTs had Wilson at the hospital fifteen minutes later, and the burned-out ER docs discovered something very cool: the bullet had carved a gazillion-to-one path through their new patient's skull, leaving the most critical stuff—his ability to walk, talk, act like a normal person—pretty much intact. Sure, a bunch of other brain structures were permanently out-of-order, but for the folks at Mercy Hospital, any patient who left the ER still breathing counted as a big win.

When they kicked him loose from the hospital after a month, Wilson took up a fierce smoking habit. He'd burn up a pack-a-day, easy, on top of downing a case of beer. He tried all the shit that frightened him—skydiving, ocean swimming, heroin. He maxed out his credit cards to travel to Spain so he could run with the bulls. Nicotine and alcohol are great, but there's no high like surviving a bullet to the head. When you know there's nothing except a void on the other side of the curtain, why worry about anything? Why not push your body—your scarred, itching, twitching, alive-but-not-quite-right body—as far as it can go, like an amusement park ride made of meat?

And a high like that costs money. Lots of money.

Wilson was never good at much, he told me. He was always one of those guys you hire when any warm body will do: ringing up purchases, making deliveries, clicking the same button repeatedly. He liked to read, but he was always too lazy to apply himself in school or line up a dumbass cubicle job. When he was shot, he was working as a content moderator, which means you sit in front of your laptop and delete the most horrible crap the internet can show you, all for slightly more than minimum wage. This job is worse than death, he used to joke with his coworkers.

The job didn't come with health insurance, either.

Guess the size of his hospital bill.

If you answered, "Enough to buy a house," you're right.

He needed lots of money to pay that down, too, because he was sick of the bill collectors calling him at all hours, guys with thick accents who threatened to ruin him forever.

You can't always trust an origin story, but the way Wilson put it, he was drinking in a tiki bar on the Lower East Side when he saw UFC fighting on television. A pair of guys in the octagon, sweating under the bright lights as they smashed each other to bruised beef. The closed captioning informed him those guys would make millions for one night's work.

Wilson couldn't fight—the last time he threw a punch was in middle school, maybe? But as he sat there, holding his sweating-cool glass to the prickling, reddened scar on his face, he knew he could *take* a punch better than most people.

Because of that bullet, he had no sense of pain. A truck could run over his foot, and he'd only feel it as a slight tugging.

He needed to take a few self-defense classes and then find a fight that paid, like one of those underground brawls he thought he'd heard about, people yelling and throwing wads of cash at two fighters in a ring.

He hit the worst drinking establishments until he found a rough-looking bartender with scarred-up knuckles, and he flat-out asked the guy to direct him to a bare-knuckle boxing match.

*I told him I was gonna kick everyone's ass, and I did it in a snooty British accent*, is how he described it to me.

*Hey, I was drunk.*

The bartender stared at Wilson like he was a cockroach speaking Urdu, then snorted and said:

*You ain't no fighter.*

When he described this to me, Wilson raised his left hand so I could see the big white dot in the middle of the palm, a tense knot of scar tissue.

*I grabbed that little knife he was using to cut lemons*, Wilson said, *and I slammed it right through there, pinned myself to the bar. And I told him: I'm a damn fighter.*

The bartender directed him to his first fight.

## 3.

By the time I met him in that parking garage, Wilson had fought ten underground bouts, losing his first seven. On his eighth fight, trading blood with a tattooed Russian in Brighton Beach, he began to develop a technique. These guys he was going up against always assumed that a kimura or an armbar would lock up their opponent for good, that the pain and the threat of a broken limb would be too much for any human to resist.

Not Wilson, though. Squeezed in his rival's grip, he would push, push, push until his joints popped from their sockets and his bones cracked, allowing him to slip free. He always had his follow-up attack ready to go, a flurry of punches or kicks to the head, and three times that had been good for the knockout.

A week after I met him, as we sat on a bench in front of a brewery near his apartment, I stated the obvious: "You might not feel pain, but you're getting hurt."

He raised his arm, still in a cast from his battle with O'Malley. I was drinking beer, but he was swigging handfuls of pills—steroids and vitamins and herbs an old lady swore would heal his body faster—with sips of whole milk from a carton. "No shit," he said. "But I also heal quickly. I always have. I get my ass beat, but most of the time it's just bruising."

"Yeah," I said. "But if you can't feel pain, how do you know something's not broken inside? You could have something busted in your liver or your kidneys. Brain bleed. These guys you're fighting, they're no joke."

"I'm still shitting okay for now." He chuckled and slugged more milk. "And if that changes, well ... at least I'm dying on my feet."

I had nothing to say to that. We sat and watched as the subway entrance across the street vomited commuters, sad people marching in lockstep with their office clothes and shoulder bags, their heads down. So many of them would do anything to avoid even the briefest pain, to live in nonstop comfort, and that made me admire Wilson even more: he might have been a loser and a weirdo, but when fate handed him a golden ticket, he decided to do something hard and messy, even if it wasn't the smartest play.

# 11

"I have a question," I said.

"Shoot."

"Why'd you ask me to be your manager?"

He popped a monster pill. "You know it's hard to find an underground fight with a big payout. Like, retire-for-ever sort of big."

"Yep."

"The first time I saw you, you looked like a guy who knew his way around this whole fight world. That you could find me more money quickly."

"Well, good news on that front because you're already building a rep, which means more dudes want to fight you," I said. "I just heard about a fight in a month down in Coney Island, this garage? It's real heavyweights. You could make ten thousand, easy. Maybe more. But can you heal in time?"

"Probably not," he said and pulled out his phone. Swiping it to life, he tilted the screen so I could see a webpage. "But I want to do this. It's in two months. You see how it's going around the web? We could be set for life, baby."

I skimmed the page's garish colors, the title blinking with pink neon over a photo of a bloody fist wrapped in dirty gauze. I'd known about it, sure, and dismissed it as a stunt, a prank—at worst, something that might kill a lot of people. "You're crazy," I said. "You'll come home in a bag."

"Hey, I stepped outside my front door and almost ended up in a bag," he said, returning his phone to his pocket. He offered me the serene gaze of a graveyard angel. "Let's do it. I want to see how many lives I have left."

## 4.

Before I go further, I should bring up Brent Baker, known to the broader world as the Fantastic Majestic, the first influencer ever to hit 100 billion views on YouTube. Every week, Baker spent millions of dollars on the world's most outrageous challenges. I always liked the one where he had nine people buried alive for a week, nothing in the coffin with them but a bottle of water and a breathing tube, with a brand-new Porsche for whoever endured without losing their mind.

Baker made a fortune off that kind of stupid stuff.

Still, it was an arms race with the other online titans out there, and he was losing badly to the spectacle freaks also spending big money to ram fire trucks through bounce houses or live inside a replica White House for a year. So, he came up with a new plan, a really dumb one —but given the amount of dumb people in the world, those kinds of plans earn you a lot of eyeballs.

In his video announcing the project, Baker stood waist-deep in an infinity pool, jabbering at the camera like a ferret jacked on heart-attack levels of caffeine. "When I was a kid, I used to blow all my money at this arcade down the block, okay?" he said, jabbing his fingers on phantom buttons. "And my all-time favorite games were 'Street Fighter 2' and 'Mortal Kombat,' okay? Like, I spent every quarter I had on ripping out other fighters' spines. It was absolutely sick. I had all the combinations down, I wanted to be the fighting champion of the world ... "

As he spoke, the camera rose into the air, revealing a wide lawn behind the pool, where two dozen men and women in black GI uniforms pumped their feet and fists in unison. Beyond the lawn, a warm ocean lapped at a narrow sliver of bone-white beach. Baker now spoke in voiceover: "And now that I've got more money than God, I decided, okay, I'm never gonna be champion of the world because I faint when I get cut even a little bit, but I can host my own tournament of fighters, okay? Fighters from all over the world, of all fighting disciplines, all of them going head-to-head ... "

The scene cut to a giant orb of transparent plastic, filling rapidly with bundles of hundred-dollar bills, as Baker's voice rose to a shrill scream: " ... for prizes totaling *ONE HUNDRED MILLION DOLLARS.*"

Baker's contest came with one rule: no rules.

No holds barred.

No moves banned.

Fighters could smack the groin, gouge out an eye, bite a throat, get their fingers in their opponent's hair, and yank. Even death wasn't a big deal—if you happened to snap a rival's neck, well, that's why Baker was hosting this contest on a tropical island he'd bought a few years ago, outside any regular country's jurisdiction.

"I sent in that one YouTube clip," Wilson told me. "From when O'Malley popped out my arm bone, and I hit him in the head?"

I remembered the video: some rando in the parking garage had managed to rack up a couple of thousand hits by posting his smartphone footage online, only for the Wall Street guys to ban him from their little fight club for life. They didn't like the idea of the cops sniffing around their fun.

"Okay," I said. "But I thought you wanted me to be your manager. Recommend fights, that kind of shit."

"I do," he said, holding up a hand, "but you're moving too slow—"

"I'm trying to get the right fights." I pointed at his busted arm. "Which means getting you with the right fighters. Dudes who won't kill you, know what I mean?"

He shrugged. "Here's another way to think about this. If I get in, you're coming along with me, which means you're getting a tropical vacation. I probably won't win, and what is this guy saying about fighting to the death? I bet he's just trying to get engagement. I do some fights, I get knocked around, I win one of the smaller prizes—which is still, like, a million—and we go get drunk on the beach ... look, that's something memorable. That's living."

I thought about what passed for my own existence. Managing a bar a few nights per week. Bouncing at the rock club a couple blocks from my house every other weekend. Holding the money while a bunch of idiots worked out their octagon dreams in parking lots and alleys. And I had to admit, Wilson made some good points. The thing about "no rules" is that it sounded like a bunch of hype. And I liked the idea of lying on a hot beach with a cold can of beer in my hand, watching the sun sink into the ocean.

A few days later, Wilson texted me:

THEY TOOK ME!! I'M IN!!!!!

Looking back, it was like getting excited about a bus hitting you.

## 5.

The tournament was first class all the way: Baker's island had once belonged to a drug kingpin, a good buddy of Escobar's who turned the place into a waypoint for cocaine trafficking *and* a nonstop orgy.

This enterprising Columbian had built a marble palace in the jungle two hundred yards from the beach, and Baker had poured money into renovating the ruins into the world's biggest mancave. The vaulted spaces were thick with cigar smoke, the pool was choked with dozens of bikini-clad groupies jittering to a nonstop lineup of Baker's famous DJ friends, and the fighters had anything they wanted—sports massages, doctors, trainers, unlimited food and liquor and drugs. You could probably get a raw zebra steak if you asked one of the red-suited minders nicely.

Baker had ordered a caged octagon built on the beach at the asphalt tip of the old traffickers' runway. A matrix of cameras wired to an overhead grid broadcast each fight to the world. A squadron of doctors would try to patch together the wounded.

# 16

We shared the flight down with a bunch of MMA fighters I'd seen brawl so many times onscreen. They bumped chests and growled at each other, hungry to hurt. I recognized David Eagan, who fought prelims or main card for a gazillion UFC events until they booted him out for drug use.

The moment we arrived at the mansion, I spotted a sumo wrestler from Japan, 400 pounds of man-mountain, downing twenty shots of top-shelf whiskey in a row.

A little later, Wilson told me he glimpsed an extravagantly tattooed woman from some snowy country who practiced Viking death pummeling, whatever the hell that meant. "Maybe I should ask her out," he joked, "after she turns my head to a paste."

There was a nutso feral guy from Siberia. His teeth sharpened to points—he scared me. A pair of former Special Forces guys, muscled up and wired for death, freaked me out even more. They'd snap Wilson's neck without thinking twice about it.

Wilson fixated on the figure dressed from head-to-toe in black, stalking the shadows as the pre-fight party ramped up. He was shorter and lighter than virtually anyone else on the roster, and everyone gave him some distance. "Where the hell did they find a fucking ninja?" Wilson asked me, his voice tinged with awe.

"He's probably a joke," I said, trying to calm him down, but in my heart of hearts, I suspected that guy was probably the deadliest one of all. You don't walk outside dressed like that unless you're ready to take on anyone who makes a joke about Snake Eyes from G.I. Joe.

# 17

The night before the fight, we walked down for a look at the octagon, which swarmed with workers doing last-minute preparations. A wide table on the south side of the structure would fit the three announcers who'd call the blow-by-blow, including Baker. "How're you feeling?" I asked him.

Wilson had a huge Cuban cigar burning in the corner of his mouth. He wasn't wearing a cast anymore, but his arm looked thin and weak. "Good," he said. "But I got a confession."

"You don't want to do it?" I laughed, trying to make a joke of it, but part of me would have been fine with him deciding to tap out—I didn't want to fly back to the States with him in a bag.

"Nah. But I didn't tell you the whole story of how I got in." He chuckled. "You think they'd put me on a roster with these people, with my record? With how I look? No, I showed them my pain thing. I sold myself as a freak."

"How?" I asked, giving him a quick scan. There were no wounds visible, so he hadn't repeated the knife-through-the-palm trick that had so effectively convinced that bartender.

He slipped off his right shoe. He wasn't wearing socks. His pinkie toe was missing, the stub covered with a red-spotted bandage.

"You fucking idiot," I said. "You need all your toes to balance."

He shook his head. "I needed to lose a toe on camera to show how badass I am. I told them I could be a serious spoiler, keep things entertaining." His voice rose. "It's a

$100,000 if you survive the first match, remember? And you get twenty percent. That boosts our lives for a while. It's not like you have to do anything."

He was right. I felt guilty about that fact, but he was right: all I needed to do was stand there and shout advice he probably wouldn't use as a ninja or a Special Forces guy or similar badass turned him into a pile of broken flesh with some bone bits mixed in. And if he won a few matches? Well, we might become a little famous after that—maybe we could leverage that into more money, endorsing painkillers, *something.*

## 6.

The ninja went out in the first round.

That surprised me. If I'd bet cash, I would've put every cent on him. I guess you can't trust a costume. The guy was paired against one of the Special Forces dudes, and he spent his first twenty seconds in the octagon doing all kinds of spooky-crazy poses, crouching down and throwing his arms out and twirling his fingers. The Special Forces guy—his name was Donovan, he'd done a decade in Delta Force and wanted to do something that paid more than eighty grand a year—walked up and kicked the ninja in the right thigh hard enough to numb the leg, and then he stomped until our black-clad friend stopped moving.

The weirdos and ghosts that Baker had collected because he wanted a real-life version of "Street Fighter" all went out early. I could tell the nerds in the crowd were disappointed because they'd grown up on a steady diet of kung-fu and superhero movies, where the fighter with the strangest powers usually triumphs. Those of us who'd actually lived real lives, though, knew that winning a fight often comes down to one thing: who hits hardest, fastest, and without a shred of remorse.

For his first fight, they put Wilson up against the sumo wrestler, a gentleman named Raiden Risuke. When Raiden entered the octagon, the structure shuddered beneath his weight. Each of his palms looked big enough to swallow up Wilson's head like a baseball.

"Coming down here," Wilson whispered to me as I finished wrapping his hands, "might have been a mistake."

"Now you tell me," I said. "Look, do you want to quit? You'll catch massive shit for it, but that won't matter once we're back on the plane."

He shook his head. "No."

"Okay," I said. "Then my best advice is just use your speed. Try to get behind him or on his flank and ... "

"What?" Wilson asked. "Scare him with some bad language? I punch him, my whole arm's just gonna sink in."

A loud buzzer from the speakers overhead signaled the match would begin in twenty seconds. We were out of time. "You'll figure it out," I said, slapping him on the shoulder. "Stay loose."

"Right," he said and entered the octagon, where Raiden was pounding the floor with his fists, mugging for the crowd.

The bell rang, and Raiden charged. It was like watching a freight train made of sweaty flesh—despite his size, he barreled across the small space in what felt like a fraction of a second, his arms spread wide to grab.

Wilson wasn't particularly quick, but he managed to step aside just in time, leaving Raiden to barrel into the fence. Wilson scrambled backward across the space, his guard up, his eyes flicking over his opponent for any kind of opening.

Raiden spent a few seconds gesturing to the crowd, which roared back, cheering what they probably thought was Wilson's imminent splattering. Then he spun on his heel, snorted loudly, and charged again at Wilson, who had backed against the opposite side of the octagon.

Wilson dropped his guard.

He wants out of this tournament, I thought. Too bad he didn't decide that *before* stepping into battle. Now Raiden will probably hurt him so bad we'll need a stretcher to get him on the flight home ...

Raiden moved even faster than before, a huge blur beneath the big lights, his fingers grasping for Wilson's neck...

Wilson stepped aside.

Raiden crashed headfirst into one of the support beams holding the octagon in place. With a hideous groan, the structure tilted, and for a delirious instant, I thought it would capsize atop the announcer desk, where Baker and two other meatheads—professionals to the bitter end—were still narrating the match even as they stood and scampered back. Raiden collapsed on his face as the octagon crashed back down, sand blasting from gaps in the flooring.

Wilson kicked the sumo giant in the head for good measure, but it was pointless: the dude was out cold. The next morning, I learned that a handful of online betters had actually placed wagers on Raiden knocking himself out, at 20,000-to-1 odds, and won a fortune. None of that mattered in the moment, though. The crowd went nuclear as Wilson turned to grin at me, his skinny arms held up in triumph.

## 7.

Baker's people had remade the tile-walled basement of the mansion into a nightclub, complete with leather couches, laser lights, and a brightly lit bar serving top-shelf liquor. The music was loud enough to make the old drains in the middle of the space hum, and I didn't want to think about the horrible things that had probably taken place down here during the Cocaine Island years. Wilson and I found seats in a far corner where we could sip our absurdly expensive whiskey in relative peace.

A lot of people had put money on Raiden to win. That's the only reason I could figure out why everyone was so cold to us after we left the octagon. And the funny thing was, it didn't really affect me at all. I was used to rejection in life, from the NFL scouts who looked at my busted knee and laughed to the over-entitled jackasses who tried to start fights with me when I was bouncing.

But Wilson, I could tell it affected him—he was expecting something like the final scene of "Rocky 3," a crowd of cheering people lifting him onto their shoulders. Instead, everyone cleared a path for us as we made our way from the octagon to the mansion.

"That was wild," he said after we retrieved our whiskies.

"You were very lucky," I offered. "That guy could have steamrolled you. But we're up a hundred grand, right, no matter what happens?"

"Yep, a hundred grand," he said.

"That's pretty good," I said. "Maybe we should quit while we're ahead. And look, I won't even take my fee. I'll just consider this a nice vacation. We can be home by tomorrow morning."

"What if I'm on a lucky streak?" He winked. "C'mon, dude, I've never had anything like this happen to me in my life, and I never will again. It beats skydiving or anything like that."

"That's the thing about luck," I said. "It runs out. I don't want you getting killed."

"We all owe a death." He sipped and pointed across the space. "Look, we have a very special guest."

The basement club wasn't nearly as fun or crowded as the rooms upstairs—maybe everyone else sensed the ghosts drifting around down here—but there were still enough people bopping to the DJ to make it hard for me to follow Wilson's finger. When I did, I was startled: Baker himself was standing in the doorway, his entourage oddly absent.

Baker locked eyes with me and marched toward us, batting away a few dancers who tried to touch him. Onscreen, he was the perpetually exuberant elf, high on life as he unleashed his latest pyrotechnics; off-camera, he had the air of a steely operator, the kind of guy who'd kill you without much thought. I'd knocked it out with some tough hombres in my time, but something about him made me hesitate and shudder.

He stood before us. "May I sit?" he asked. Maybe it was a trick of my ears, but I swore the DJ had lowered the music just enough for him to speak without needing to raise his voice.

"Of course," Wilson said, waving him onward.

Baker plopped on the cushion to our left and bent forward, his hands steepled. "Congrats out there," he said. "It was quite entertaining. Our viewership spiked for those thirty seconds."

"Happy to hear that," I said.

Baker nodded. "I had my analytics folks take some spot polls, do a little data mining from social media, and they found that Wilson here appeals very highly to a broad demographic. They see him as an underdog, a true hero."

"That's me," Wilson said and chuckled. "A true hero. Especially when I can pay the rent."

"Well, that's what I want to talk to you about," Baker said, leaning forward.

I wondered why he'd come alone. Where was the crew dedicated to filming his every waking moment? The friends and hangers-on we'd seen clustered around him upstairs?

"We're going to play around with the order of the next fights," Baker said. "We originally had you up against one of the UFC ladies, but we decided that wasn't exciting enough. We want you to fight one of the people the algorithm says will make it to the very end."

"Why?" I asked.

"I'm only telling you this because you signed one hell of an NDA," Baker said, wagging a finger at me. "Our traffic numbers are a little soft. My advertisers, they're getting uppity. So, I need an exciting match, and that means my freak who feels no pain—no offense—"

"None taken," Wilson said.

"—and we're going to pair him up with a real killer. I know it's asking a lot—you're probably the one contestant with the least amount of training here—again, no offense," Baker shrugged, "but if you somehow manage to win, I'll pay you an extra million, on top of whatever you'd earn in the standard pot. What do you say?"

"Which fighter?" I asked, wondering if they would pair Wilson against one of the Special Forces guys or that disgraced heavyweight boxer who'd chewed off a guy's ear back in the day. My biggest fear, that Wilson would be dismantled and left in pieces, hit me in the gut. We'd already survived hellish odds on that first match.

"I can't tell you," Baker said, "but that's the deal. What do you think?"

"We'll take it," Wilson said—almost shouting—before I could ask any questions. Then he gave me a side-eye, defying me to say anything in return.

It's not your body on the line, I told myself. You haven't known this guy for all that long. He gets hurt, especially because he didn't take your advice. That's on him, right?

No, I felt some responsibility, no matter what happened.

"Great," Baker said, standing. "Good luck out there."

He turned and left without looking back, disappearing into the wall of flesh, trembling to the bass from the DJ's speakers. I drained my whiskey and debated getting another, a double this time around. Before I could stand, Wilson said, "We're popular tonight."

I looked up. A trio of dudes approached us, hard-looking types with grizzled jaws and steely gazes. They weren't fighters, and I couldn't recall seeing them anywhere on the island. The biggest one, a bald-headed goon with a jagged scar tracing a line from his jaw to his left ear, took a seat beside us without being asked while his partners stood on either side of the couch, close enough to grab us if they wanted to.

"Coming to congratulate us?" I said, figuring I was fast enough to grab the guy nearest to me and slam him to the ground if it came to that. Wilson might have a chance with the scarred man, but that would still leave one guy free to do some damage. Baker claimed the only guns on the island were in the hands of his private security, but blades were very easy to hide.

"Congrats," the scarred man said in a deadpan voice. He had a faint accent I couldn't quite place, maybe from somewhere in Eastern Europe. "What you did was like a cartoon. Trip, fall, boom."

"We aim to please," Wilson said. "Well, the sumo guy aimed to please, I mean."

"What's your name?" I asked the scarred man. "Who do we have the pleasure of addressing here?"

"My name isn't important," the scarred man said, leaning forward. "What is important is that Wilson here loses his next match, or something very bad will happen to him. Do you understand?"

The music hummed the drains and bounced off the tiled walls. I realized I was holding my breath. I exhaled loudly and said, "Excuse me?"

"I know you feel no pain, but trust me," the scarred man said, his lips peeling back from yellow teeth. "We will have ways of making you regret your whole life if you do not take a fall. You won't leave this island alive. Very simple thing. Do you understand?"

"Let me guess," Wilson said. "If we tell Baker or anyone else, we're also dead, correct?"

"Correct." The scarred man turned to his compatriots. "See, these are smart boys."

"We hear what you're saying," I said, which seemed like the most neutral possible statement I could deliver. Meanwhile, my mind was scrambling. What the hell was this?

"Good." The scarred man stood. "Lose or die." Gesturing for his goons to follow him, he disappeared upstairs.

Once they were gone, Wilson exhaled loudly. "What the fuck was that?"

"Exactly what it looked like," I said. "They're betting big on your opponent, whoever it is."

"You believe them? About killing us?"

"We can't afford not to take them seriously." I marveled at how steady my voice sounded. I wanted to stand, to get us out of here, except my knees felt like jelly. I'd faced down so many threats in my life with a smile, and yet those guys had freaked me out. A predator always knows when it's in the presence of a larger beast.

"God," Wilson said. "I need a new drink."

"So do I," I said. "But good news, and no offense, but your chances of winning the next fight were already low."

"Everyone keeps telling me 'no offense,'" he snapped, "right before they tell me I'm too weak to make it. But I'm here, aren't I? I've gotten this far. And those guys clearly think I can win if they're threatening us."

"Look, we can't afford to be stupid."

"Baker said there was a bonus if I win the next round."

"You can't spend that if you're dead."

"Maybe we can come up with a plan."

I sighed. "The best plan is to just take a tumble. We need to be smart about this."

Wilson levered himself upright, swirling his empty glass in the air. "I'm going for another drink. I'll see you at the next fight, okay?" And he stormed off, weaving only slightly from the alcohol. Part of me wanted to chase him, but my legs still refused to work. I kept thinking about the scarred man saying, *You won't leave this island alive.*

I had no idea what to do.

# 8.

I didn't think Wilson had much of a chance against a sumo wrestler, but I definitely knew he had no hope of winning against Ivan Sabenin, a mixed martial arts fighter who'd spent time fighting professional bouts all over the world, including a few in the UFC before he was banned for gouging out an opponent's eye in front of a sellout crowd. Ivan was a pillar of muscle, every inch of his skin expensively tattooed, his eyes black and cold as river stones.

It was a relief, as much as I hated to admit it. This guy was going to turn Wilson into paste. And yet, as Wilson's manager, it was my professional duty to give my fighter the best advice possible.

"Ivan will fight dirty from the jump," I told Wilson as we prepped. "His opener will be something illegal because he figures none of the other fighters here are ready for it."

"How do you know that?" Wilson asked. His face was pale, his hands cold as I wrapped them.

"I'm just guessing," I said, "but I watched a bunch of this guy's fights on YouTube."

"What's my strategy here? Do I just fall down like you want me to?"

Yep, just flop down, I almost told him. Get on the mat and hope he doesn't do you permanent damage. Your chances of winning this match are almost zero, but *our* chances of dying if you succeed are one hundred percent.

Since last night, when he'd fled to get more whiskey and never came back, Wilson had done his best to avoid me. He texted me throughout the day that he was getting a massage or a bite to eat or a B12 injection from one of the creepy nurses lurking around, but whenever I showed up at his location, he'd already left—if he'd ever been there in the first place.

I wondered if he thought he could really win. If his victory against the sumo guy had gone completely to his head.

I wondered if he thought he'd never be killed.

"Whatever I want doesn't matter," I told him. "I'm just trying to give you the best shot at survival, which means doing whatever you need to do. It's no rules in there, remember? This guy's also pretty smart. He knows you don't feel pain, so I guarantee he's just going for the knockout here."

The buzzer sounded. Wilson climbed into the octagon, doing his best to fix Ivan with a hard stare. For his part, Ivan paced his half of the space, flexing his hands, snarling through bared teeth—if he was trying to intimidate everyone, it was working.

The opening bell rang, but neither man charged. Too many fighters in this tournament had opted for maximum aggression from the jump and regretted it. As the winners ascended the ranks, they became more strategic, wary of what their opponents could do, especially if they'd never encountered a certain fighting style before. Ivan was more strategic than I gave him credit for.

It pissed the crowd off, though—they hadn't flown all this way to watch a couple of dudes tiptoe around each other.

Wilson snapped first. Instead of waiting for Ivan to come to him, he charged across the space, leaping into the air at the last second, his right fist raised over his head like he planned on bringing it down in a drop punch. As Ivan raised his forearms for the block, I spied his feral smirk, like he couldn't imagine even a stupid amateur being this obvious.

Except Wilson had other plans. As Ivan blocked the inevitable blow with his stony flesh, Wilson's left fist darted from below, socking the Russian in the jaw.

It wasn't a hard blow, but it was enough to drive Ivan onto his back foot. Wilson landed in front of him and switched to his next move: digging his fingers into Ivan's eye sockets. Except Ivan was ready for that, his huge hands clenching Wilson's wrists.

Wilson tried to kick, to extract himself, but Ivan neatly swiveled to the side so Wilson's foot bounced off his flank. Ivan lifted a thrashing Wilson into the air, the tattooed tigers on his massive forearms writhing as he strained.

I had no idea what I'd do in that position. Ivan outweighed Wilson by 100 pounds and had probably spent ten thousand more days in the gym. This whole thing was stupid. I was about to watch my friend—and yes, by this point, I thought of Wilson as my friend—get destroyed.

Ivan hurled Wilson to the floor hard enough to shake the octagon. At the announcers' desk, Baker shouted in what sounded like a blood frenzy.

As Wilson groaned and spat blood, Ivan knelt beside him, gripped Wilson's injured arm, and twisted as hard as he could. The Russian had clearly done his homework, or maybe he had just recognized the pale limb as an obvious weakness.

Wilson grunted as the bone exploded again through half-healed skin.

In the crowd to my left, someone groaned and passed out. I felt ready to heave up my own guts, but I kept my eyes locked on Wilson because I owed him my witness. And while I'd never confess this to anyone, a small part of me felt the warm rush of relief at the sight of that horrific wound because it meant this was over—we were safe from those guys who'd kill us.

With a roar from his deepest soul, Wilson rose up, twisting around as he did so, and rammed his jagged bone through the Russian's throat.

Ivan fell back, his open mouth geysering blood, his eyes bulging, as Wilson levered onto his knees, bringing his broken arm down again and again like a knife into the man's neck and stomach.

The crowd shrieked like the world's largest teakettle. A cheer started in the darkness, building as it jumped from person to person until hundreds of mouths roared in unison: "*BULLETHEAD ... BULLETHEAD ... BULLETHEAD ... BULLETHEAD ...* "

I didn't know they'd given Wilson a nickname.

Wilson stood, slick as a newborn, his bad arm dangling loose, the bone gleaming under the hot lights. His eyes found mine, and I recognized the same expression as after he'd done in O'Malley: triumph like a drug high.

And it finally clicked for me.

Wilson wasn't fighting for the money, not even in the face of all those expenses.

He wasn't fighting for the thrill despite all the other insane things he'd done since waking up in the hospital.

No, here was a guy like so many guys, who'd spent his existence as a loser, lurking at the edges of things—and now he was a winner, the quiet center of the screaming crowd, the focus of a million eyes online, remembered forever.

For Wilson, that was worth more than his arm: it was worth his life.

A platoon of orange-vested doctors crashed into the octagon with their medical kits and portable defibrillators. Four of them fell beside the Russian and slapped quick-clotting bandages over his seeping wounds while another two readied to shock his heart back to life. Another three worked on Wilson, tightening a tourniquet over his upper arm.

I couldn't see anything beyond the nearest row of screaming faces, of course, but I knew they were out there, no doubt biding their time. Baker had hired amazing security, big mercenaries in bullet-resistant vests, their shoulders heavy with strapped submachine guns—if anyone tried anything stupid near the octagon, they would only have a second or two to regret their decision before those guys blasted them into a blood mist.

No, if I had to guess, I'd say our scarred friend bet we'd try to slip away and hide until we could find transport off the island. He'd want to do us quickly, messily, with fewer people around, which meant he'd likely take his shot on the small road cut through the jungle between the octagon and the mansion or even inside the mansion itself. I considered finding Baker or one of his people and revealing the whole setup, asking for help, except I was already out of time: Wilson had climbed from the octagon, surrounded by doctors and security guys clearing a hole through the crowd.

I rushed over, the scrum parting to let me through. I was mouth-to-ear with Wilson, so close his warm blood spattered my shirt. "What now?" I asked.

"You worry too much," he said, his voice raspy, like a broken part of his chest was squeezing his lungs.

"Nobody's ever accused me of that before." I peeked above the doctors in front of us. We were almost through the crowd, the dark jungle looming beyond. I was sure our killers were waiting for us there, sweaty fingers on triggers, ready to send a message.

Wilson chuckled and coughed a little blood. "No, you've done good. You're winning, too ... "

"What about those guys?" I almost shouted. "The ones who said they'd—"

The treeline lit up, strobic, flickering like lightning. The audience behind us stampeded. The doctors hit the sand, hands over their heads, while the guards dropped into their shooting stances, their rifles sweeping the dark. I dipped, trying to carry Wilson to the ground with me as gunfire tore through the humid night. Despite his wrecked body, though, Wilson had enough strength to haul me upright. He was grinning now, his face lit by the crossfire hurricane so it looked like a skull.

"Relax, you wimp," he said. "You think I wouldn't tell Baker someone's messing with his game?"

I could tell it was two groups shooting at each other in the jungle. Faint screams told me that one side was losing badly. I spun around and saw Baker beside the octagon, surrounded by his grim-faced security. Baker offered us a hearty thumbs-up.

"We're all good, bro," Wilson said. "I'm like a god now."

I felt that same burst of awe as when he'd first approached me in the parking lot. The sense that I was in the presence of the unknowable, something larger than myself, more than capable of shattering me at any moment. Saint Bullethead, I thought. Our patron saint of the downtrodden and the hurt. Come save us in the ring. Come save us from our dull lives.

# Where the River Breaks

# by L.S. Goozdich

## PORTER

**Porter tasted blood**. It filled his mouth fast, coppery and thick. His gaze had drifted. A mistake that his opponent made him pay for. The jab found him before he saw it coming, stole his air, left him open for the uppercut that snapped his head back. His gloves, white a second ago, ran red as he wiped his mouth and stumbled to his corner.

Sully was there with a bucket.

"Rinse your mouth, kid." The short man slipped between the ropes, eyes sharp as broken glass. "What are you doing looking off into the gym? Something more important than the fight in front of you?"

Porter shook his head. "I was just—"

"Don't finish that. I know what you were doing. Don't do it again. Comport yourself like a man. Stay focused on what's real. Not that private war you've built in your head with Danny."

Porter nodded and spit blood into the bucket.

"That's a lot," Sully muttered. He grabbed Porter's chin, turned his head, and pried his mouth open.

Then his eyes yawned wide.

"What is it?" Porter asked.

Sully didn't answer. He scanned the ring, head darting, searching. Then he bent, plucking something from the mat. Under the gym's hot lights, the tooth gleamed—white and red.

"Shit," Porter said. "My mom's gonna kill me."

Sully's eyes narrowed. "Fifty push-ups, Porter. You know the rules."

Porter groaned but dropped to his knuckles. Plenty of time now to watch what had stolen his attention in the ring. Danny Carter. Slinging his bag over his shoulder, he headed for the door.

"See you, Coach," Danny said.

Sully nodded. "Alright, Danny. Good work today."

**DANNY**

Outside, the June heat lingered. Sweat ran in rivulets down Danny's face. His legs wanted to walk, not run. That was the voice of the coward; his father had told him that. And that lesson stuck.

Danny Carter would not be a coward. Not today.

He ran.

The night smelled of cut grass and warm pavement, the scent of a town settling into sleep. Danny ran with steady, measured strides, past darkened windows and rust-bitten mailboxes, past porches where flags hung limp in the still air. Porch swings sang under the weight of weary souls. Working class men and women holding back tomorrow with cold drinks in their hands.

Danny could have used one of those drinks. His mouth was dry, and his lungs burned, but he didn't stop. His father wouldn't have stopped.

At the corner of Pine and Jackson, he slowed. The house sat there, quiet and worn, waiting for him like an old dog too tired to stand. The cruiser wasn't in the driveway anymore. It hadn't been for two years. A wind chime his mother never took down stirred weakly as he passed it. The porch steps creaked under his weight.

Danny let himself in. The screen door whined, and the main door clicked shut behind him. It was quiet. It was always quiet now.

Inside, the kitchen light burned low. The smell of onions and gravy still clung to the air. A plate sat waiting on the counter, wrapped in plastic, fogged with steam. Beside it, a note in his mother's looping, tired script:

Danny, late shift again. Eat while it's warm. Love you, sweetheart.

His stomach clenched, and not from hunger.

Danny peeled back the plastic wrap, sat at the table, and ate in silence. The clock on the wall ticked, steady and slow. Seconds dragged themselves by at a painful pace anytime he was in the house. Especially when he was alone. Danny wished he could just stay at the boxing gym. That's where he felt okay. That place was more like home to him these days.

Outside, tires rolled lazily over asphalt. He tensed. Not her car. Not yet. Not for a real long while. He hated her working nights. Hated the thought of her out there, moving through the world, tired and alone. One day he would be something. He would be somebody, and then his mother wouldn't have to sacrifice to keep them afloat. He was going to make sure of that.

After silently eating his meal, Danny rinsed his plate, left it in the sink, and headed for his room. The walls still held pieces of the past—his father's badge in its case, a folded flag behind glass. Things meant to honor a man who had left the house one morning and never came back. Mementos that he had to face. Pieces of a history Danny tried never to speak of.

Danny sat on the bed, rubbing his hands together, knuckles still raw from today's training. The house groaned with a humid summer breeze, and he could hear the wind chime as it whispered in the dark. He lay back, hands behind his head, staring at the ceiling.

Sully had told him he needed to push off the canvas. As if you're launching a spear, he had said Feel the weight shift, let it roll up through your legs, your hips, your torso, and finally, snap it out through your fist. A punch isn't just about the hit; it's a chain reaction. Those words were all he could think about.

The ceiling acted as a blank canvas before him; he tried seeing it in his mind's eye. He pictured the weight shifting— heel to toe, coiling like a spring. The energy rolled up his legs, twisting through his hips, winding tight in his torso. He saw himself launching the punch—not just throwing it, but driving it, the force snapping out through his fist like a whipcrack.

Again. And again. He saw that punch planting itself square on the jaw of Porter Reyes.

Danny watched this on a loop for hours. Until his eyes grew too heavy, and he had to let them shut.

# 39

## PORTER

Porter Reyes was up before the sun.

His jaw ached, the empty space in his mouth pulsing with a dull throb. He ran his tongue over the gap where his tooth used to be, and the reality of it set in all over again.

*Shit.*

His worry was not the tooth, but his mother finding out about the tooth.

He rolled out of bed, cracked his neck, and got to work.

Morning was for movement. His feet slapped against cold tile as he shuffled to the bathroom, splashed his face, and stared himself down in the mirror. His lip was split. His eye had the faintest smudge of purple creeping in. But it was the missing tooth that got him. It made him look different. Rougher. Like a fighter who had been at it a little too long.

Like his father.

Porter swallowed, gripping the edge of the sink.

He had been too young to really remember the fights. His mother never talked about them. Not in detail, anyway. Just warnings, clipped and bitter—*fighting chews men up and spits them out*. But other people filled in the gaps. Coaches. Old gym rats. Even Sully when he was in the mood.

His father had been good. Not great, but good. Fast hands, mean left hook. But that only got you so far. Good didn't pay the bills. Good didn't keep the lights on.

So, he took fights he shouldn't have. Fights for men with thick wallets and mean streaks. Fights with no weigh-ins, no gloves, just money exchanged in parking lots and back rooms that were thick with smoke and lies. And when the fights stopped paying, he found other ways.

Porter dragged a hand down his face.

The image of his father was pressing heavy on his chest. It was hard to breathe.

He had his father's hands—he'd heard that before. Long-fingered, knuckles squared, built for breaking things. He had his father's nose too, before the fights took it.

But he wasn't going to have his father's story.

He wasn't going to end up in a cell, waiting for the years to end him like a slow-working poison. Wasn't going to be the man whose name turned people quiet. Wasn't going to be the shadow walking the edges of his mother's eyes.

He exhaled, shaking it off, forcing the thoughts away.

He had work to do.

Morning was for movement.

Roadwork first. Five miles in the breaking dawn, the sky bleeding soft pinks and golds over the rooftops. The early air smelled sweet, like honeysuckle and stale rain. The sidewalks were empty except for him. He ran with his mouth closed. The gap in his teeth felt bigger when the wind hit it.

Back home, the heavy bag was waiting. Same place it'd always been—hanging in the garage, leather cracked, the stink of old sweat soaked into it. His father's bag. Porter rolled the wraps over his knuckles, yanking them tight. No music, no crowd, just the sound of his breath and the chain creaking above. He stepped in, weight shifting, launching punches—heel to toe, through the hips, through the shoulders, all the way out. The bag jumped, rocked back, came swinging back for more. So, he gave it more.

He kept swinging, driving his fists into the bag, feeling the sweat running hot down his back. Three minutes ended a while ago. Porter didn't care. The round was through, but he had more in him. He liked fighting through the end of a round. Liked fighting through exhaustion. Through pain.

Instead of stopping, he picked up the pace. His punches had more behind them. This was an act of defiance to Porter. He would not stop. He didn't go looking for easy ways out of anything. The easy way is what put you behind bars. The easy way killed your honor and eventually your soul.

To keep thoughts of his father at bay, Porter threw an onslaught against the bag. Uppercuts, hooks, overhands. Nothing but power. The world had shrunk to nothing but breath and leather—until his mother's voice cut through.

"Porter, school starts in an hour," she called from the doorway.

He exhaled hard, letting his hands drop, the bag swaying gently in front of him.

The smell of coffee and frying eggs drifted in from the kitchen as he made the walk.

He wiped his face on his sleeve and stepped toward the table. His mother stood at the stove, moving like she always did—quick, efficient, already dressed for work. She didn't look up.

"How many miles?" she asked.

"Five," Porter said, sitting, breathing deep.

She nodded. "Good. You should be hungry then. Eat before it gets cold."

She set a plate down in front of him—scrambled eggs, toast, sausage. It smelled like home.

And then she turned.

It was then she saw.

Her hands went to her hips, eyes narrowing, cutting like switchblades. "Jesus, Porter. Open your mouth."

He hesitated, but there was no fighting it. He parted his lips, letting her see the damage.

Her breath came out slow, measured. Not mad—something worse.

"Goddamn it," she muttered, rubbing a hand over her face. "I told you to wait until we could afford you a new mouth guard before you got in that ring again. Damn it, Porter. You need to learn to listen."

Porter slapped the table in frustration. "I know."

"We don't have insurance. What do you want me to do? Tape that tooth back in your head?"

"I don't want you to do shit. It's fine. Leave it."

She ran a hand through her hair. "Eat your breakfast and watch that mouth."

She turned back to the stove, shoulders tight. Porter picked up his fork, but the food tasted different now. He wasn't hungry.

The house remained quiet except for the scrape of silverware on plates and the ticking of the old clock on the wall.

Nine hours until boxing.

**DANNY**

Danny focused on his breath, keeping it steady and measured as he crossed the fifteenth minute of shadowboxing. His bedroom—cramped, familiar—became the ring. Lateral steps took him toward the TV stand, the video game console, the cluttered desk in the corner. A pivot sent him back along the length of his bed. But that wasn't what he saw.

What he saw was every opponent who had ever put him down. Every fighter who had made him doubt, made him question whether he had it in him. They were there, waiting in the dim light, their faces twisted by memory—half-formed, half-forgotten, but always felt. Like ghosts of old battles, revenants clawing their way out of the past.

They closed in, these phantoms of his failures. Their punches came in echoes—mistakes looping, replaying, demanding to be answered. But this time, Danny was ready.

That hook to the body that stole gold from him in second grade? Blocked, countered, erased. The shoveling uppercut that had put him on his back two years ago? Slipping past him now, missing by inches.

He wasn't a kid anymore. He wasn't the same fighter who took those shots, who hesitated, who froze. He tightened his guard, kept his head moving, kept his feet light. This time, he dictated the fight.

His breath was getting away from him. He tried to reel it in, slow it down, but it kept slipping, just like everything else. The room was too small. The walls pressed in. The floor felt like it was getting unsteady beneath his feet.

And then he saw him.

His father.

Not as a ghost, not as some half-formed memory, but clear as day, standing just outside the ring of shadows, watching. The same way he always had. Silent. Unmoved. His head low, not shaking, not scolding—just disappointed.

Danny's stomach tightened. It was worse than anger. Worse than anything his father could have said. That quiet, that stillness, that look that told him everything he needed to know.

His chest burned. His hands shook.

*Get it together, Danny!*

The past circled him, throwing its punches, reminding him of every failure. Every time he came up short. Every time he hit the canvas and looked for his father in the crowd, only to find him already turning away. His heart pounded, he tried to keep his hands steady. He had to make them stay steady. The past was going to keep swinging. Danny just wasn't sure if he had an answer for it anymore.

Finally, having had enough, he sat on the edge of his bed, his body caving in like a weight vest had been thrown over his shoulders. His hands hung between his knees, knuckles shaking from trying to break those ghosts that never bled. His breath was shallow, tight in his chest. He stared at the floor, but all he could see was his father's face, the way it looked past him, through him, like Danny was just another fighter who couldn't go the distance.

He let himself fall back onto the mattress, staring at the ceiling, at the cracks and the peeling paint. His room had never felt smaller. The walls weren't walls—they were ropes, pressing him in, leaving him nowhere to go but down.

He needed out.

The gym. The smell of sweat and leather, the sound of the bags, the weight of the gloves on his hands. That was home. More than this place could be anymore. More than this room that still felt like a kid's room, filled with trophies that didn't mean a thing.

He checked the time. Too early. There was a whole day ahead of him. The thought of going to school came and went. He didn't have it in him today.

He shut his eyes and willed himself to sleep, just to make the hours pass faster. Just to get to the only place that ever felt like it made sense.

That evening Danny got to the gym before even Sully. The place was locked up tight, the windows fogged from yesterday's sweat. He dug into his bag, found his keys, and let himself in.

The heat struck him like a right cross. Sweltering and dead, the air clung to him like an old, damp coat. Sweat prickled through his blonde hair before he even set his bag down. The air was dead, heavy with the ghosts of a hundred workouts. He wiped his forehead with the back of his hand, backed out, and grabbed the old rock they used to prop the door open.

It wasn't much, but sometimes—if the evening was kind—a breeze would fight its way inside and offer something that felt like salvation against the warmth. Danny wasted no time. He pulled the jump rope from his bag and got to work. *Clip-clap. Clip-clap.* The rope slapped the scuffed wood, setting the beat. A rhythm. A song. Like jazz—unpredictable, electric.

He floated through double-unders, dipped into squats mid-air, crossed and uncrossed his hands in a blur. No pattern. No plan. Just movement. His body found the music, and he let it dance.

Danny's breath was getting sharp now, the rhythm of the rope faltering as his arms burned and his calves screamed. Sweat poured down his back, hot and steady, like a faucet left running. His lungs pulled for air. His feet caught sluggish on the floor.

*Snap.*

The rope smacked against his shin, leaving a bright, stinging line.

He sucked in a breath, wiped the sweat from his eyes, and started again.

*Clip-clap. Clip-clap.*

Pain doesn't mean stop. Pain means push harder.

Ten minutes in, and the voice came creeping toward him. The one that always did. The one that started soft, almost reasonable.

*You can slow down. Take a breath. You've done enough.*

He gritted his teeth and pushed harder.

Dad wouldn't quit.

That thought alone sent something sour through him. His father had been the strongest man in Danny's life. A fighter to the bone. A fighter in the way he lived. In the way he protected people. In the way he stood until the very end.

Danny went faster.

If you want to be half the man he was, stop whining. Stop trying to quit.

His legs burned. His chest ached. The jump rope was slick in his hands, but he didn't stop.

Because the man who took his father away was still breathing. Still living. His son was out there too—Porter Reyes, the one everyone thought was going places. A real fighter with a real future.

Danny clenched his jaw, his feet moving so fast now they barely touched the ground.

Win. Or be nothing. Win or have no future.

His lungs were on fire, but he wouldn't stop.

The back door groaned open, and a gust of cooler air slipped in. Danny didn't stop. Didn't even look. He knew it was Sully. Knew the old man was standing there, watching, probably with that same unreadable look—the one that left you guessing, approval or disappointment?

Danny pushed harder. Rope snapping. Feet hammering the wood. His whole body thrumming like a live wire.

If he stopped now, if he let up even for a second, that voice in his head would turn on him.

*Not good enough. Not strong enough. Not him.*

He swallowed back the burn in his throat, kept his arms tight, his shoulders loose. Faster. Lighter. He wanted to feel weightless. Wanted to disappear into the movement, into the work, until there was nothing left but the rhythm and the fight.

"My word, kid. You come straight from the pool?" Sully gave his shaker a lazy swirl before taking a swig.

Danny shook his head, still fighting for breath. "No, sir. Just working."

"A little too hard, maybe. Get some water." Sully tipped his chin toward the fridge.

Danny let the rope fall, hands on his head, lungs aching as he walked to the fridge. He grabbed a bottle, twisted off the cap, took a long pull. The cold ran through him like a second wind.

"You been alright, Danny?"

The boy nodded, sweat slipping off his chin, spattering the floor like rain.

"Well, I heard you haven't been staying consistent with school," Sully said.

"Yeah."

Sully chuckled. "Always a chatterbox, you." He finished his shake and wiped his mouth with the back of his hand. "How's getting caught up going?"

Danny shrugged. "Same as ever."

Sully eyed him. "That science grade where it needs to be?"

Danny hesitated, then took another swig. "It's getting there."

Porter Reyes stepped through the open door. He didn't announce himself. Just walked in like he always did—like he belonged, like this place was his as much as anyone's. Sweat had dried to salt on his skin, the last traces of roadwork still humming in his muscles. His hoodie sagged off one shoulder, wraps snug around his fists.

Danny didn't look up. He didn't have to. He could feel Porter's presence the way a fighter feels a punch coming. He took another sip of water, slow, measured, then set the bottle down and rolled his wrists, shaking out the stiffness.

Sully, leaning against the ring ropes, gave Porter a nod. "There he is."

Porter dropped his bag by the wall. "Would have been here sooner, but I had a few extra miles in me to-day."

Danny let out a breath through his nose, picked up his jump rope, and started swinging it again. The soft clip-clap filled the gym. Sully's eyes flicked from one boy to the other, examining the sour look each had plastered on, before he sighed.

Porter stepped to the far side of the gym, never breaking Danny's gaze. He pulled a rope from the pile, the leather cord coiling in his grip like a snake waking from sleep. A quiet current ran between them, unseen but unmistakable, pulling them into its flow.

The first slap of Porter's rope against the floor cut through the quiet. Clip-clap. Clip-clap. Danny's rhythm faltered for half a beat before he adjusted, matching the tempo. Neither spoke. Neither needed to. The duel had begun the moment they met each other's eyes, the ropes carving the challenge into the heavy air like a silent declaration of war.

Sweat beaded on their brows, muscles burning with each hop, each twist, each double-under. The ropes sang in counterpoint, a rhythm of war. The floorboards caught their weight and gave it back. Their breath grew thinner, but neither let it show.

Faster now. The pace quickened, neither willing to fall behind. Danny's lungs screamed, his calves begged, but he didn't stop. He wouldn't. Across the gym, Porter's jaw tightened, his own body protesting, but his pride roared louder.

Sully stayed quiet, leaned against the ring, simply watching. He said nothing. He'd seen this before. The language of fighters, of boys too proud to back down, too wounded to say why they couldn't. The ropes kept turning, the battle waged on in silence, all as the air grew hotter around them.

Sully let them go on for a while, but finally he said something under his breath, a tired sound that came from years of knowing when to step in.

"That's enough," he called. "Enough of the rope, boys."

They both stopped, muscles taut and breathing heavy. Sully stepped forward, rubbing the back of his neck.

"You two, always going at each other in some way or another. Always battling with your egos." He shook his head, but his eyes were steady. "Young men with too much pride. You're fighting the wrong fight, boys."

Porter and Danny exchanged quick glances, but neither said a word. Sully flicked a hand toward the ring.

"Get in the ring. Shadowbox. Move around. And I've had about enough of this mean mugging between you two." He clapped a hand on the rope, his voice taking on that dry edge that told them it was time to focus. "Get to work and stay focused on what matters," he said.

The ring was small, but the space between them felt like the size of a continent. Porter and Danny circled, eyes never leaving each other, every movement a challenge. The sound of their feet scuffing against the canvas was a soft beat, their personal battle drum for the rising tension. There was no room for softness, no room for anything but that steady pulse of challenge and rivalry.

Porter stepped forward, crowding Danny's space, his footwork cutting the ring into tighter quarters. He was a silhouette, a quick flicker of motion, a man shaped by too many solitary nights beneath harsh gym lights. The space between them shrank until it was nothing but heat and breath.

Danny shifted, a clean pivot, his fist brushing against Porter's shoulder, a test, an intentional nudge. The kind of nudge that said, *I'm here.*

Porter reacted instantly, stepping into him, closing the gap, a little too close, a little too aggressive. It wasn't just the quiet that charged the room; it was the way their eyes met, a clash of intent, a calculation in every motion. They moved, danced, shadows in a struggle of pride and power.

One moment, Danny's foot found Porter's heel, tripping him just slightly, and Porter was right there—nose to nose, chest to chest, a sneer pulling at his lip. The gap between them felt razor-thin, each breath a silent prelude to the inevitable.

Sully watched, standing just outside the ropes. He could see it in the way their shoulders were tense, the way their jaws were set. This wasn't about form or technique anymore. This wasn't about boxing. This was a battle for something deeper. There was a uniquely adolescent hunger in both of them, a hunger to prove they were more than their fathers' ghosts, more than the weight of history and blood. But the weight of that hunger was heavy, like iron, like chains. Neither of them knew how much it slowed them. How greatly it held them back.

Sully watched Danny get too close. Porter sent him back with a shove. Without a word Danny's fist shot forward, fast and sharp, a jab meant for more than Porter—aimed squarely at the world that had backed him into this corner. The world that gave him this bottomless pit of anger.

Porter took the hit, a flash of pain, but it didn't show. He stepped back, eyes hard, teeth clenched. He didn't let it slide; he responded, closing in again. The fists were flying now—quick, heavy, unrelenting.

"Enough!" Sully's voice cut through the chaos, deep and loud, reverberating off the walls of the gym like a gunshot. The boys froze, momentarily caught in the grip of the sound.

"That's enough, boys," Sully said again, this time with more weight behind it, his hands held up like a referee stepping into the center of a fight. Danny's breath was ragged, chest heaving. Porter's fists were still clenched, ready, but the fire in his eyes had dimmed just enough to hear Sully's words.

Sully didn't wait for either of them to speak. "Step into my office. Now."

It was even hotter in Sully's office, a compact furnace closing in on them like a clenched fist as the door closed behind them. A fan rattled uselessly in the corner, achieving very little. The hum of a neon sign outside cast a dull, flickering glow through the window.

Danny and Porter sat like caged dogs, sweat drying on their skin, shoulders still tight. Neither looked at the other.

Sully leaned against the desk, arms crossed. He didn't rush to speak. He let the moment hang, heavy as a verdict, waiting for them to feel the weight of it. Then—

"You two ready to talk and listen?" His voice was controlled and even. "Or should I step outside, let you tear each other apart first?"

Neither said a word. Danny's teeth ground together; his breath slow but shaking. Porter's hands stayed balled, fingers digging into his palms.

Sully exhaled and shook his head. "This crap between you two, I've had enough. I really have. I'm not watching it another day."

"Danny started it," Porter said.

"You're the one who crowded me in the ring," Danny retorted in a shout.

"Knock that off. This pointing fingers back and forth ain't what we are doing here."

Porter shifted, his chair creaking beneath him.

Danny just stared at the floor.

Sully pointed at both of them. "You want to blame somebody, let me grab a mirror. I'll show you who you can blame."

More silence followed.

"Now, look," Sully started again. "I'm not blind and I'm not a fool. I know the history here. But you can't blame the storm for how you steer the ship."

"What's that supposed to mean?" Porter said.

"It means you two don't get to point back at your fathers as the reason you're constantly at each other's throats. I think you both understand that your fathers did what they did thinking it would leave you something better. Maybe what they did was wrong. Maybe what they did was right. But none of that is the point."

Danny lifted his head, eyes dark and burning. "What is the point then?"

Sully let out a weary sigh. "The point is you get to decide what comes next. You're not the past. Neither of you are. You ain't your old man's mistakes Porter. And you ain't your old man's badge, Danny. You're your own people."

Sully's eyes flicked to Porter, who looked away.

"You think you owe something to their fight? That it's yours to finish?" Sully shook his head. "It's not your fight, boys. And if you keep trying to carry it, it's gonna break you both."

The quiet wasn't peace—it was a loaded thing, thick with all the words they'd swallowed and all the moments that had brought them here.

Sully pushed off the desk. He clapped his hands together, breaking the silence like a hammer on glass.

"So, it's high time you let each other off the hook." He pointed to the door. "You're going to train together tonight. Partner drills only, and if either of you so much as looks at the other sideways before training's done, you're out of here for a week."

He opened the door.

Danny and Porter stood, slow and stiff. They didn't speak as they stepped back into the heat of the gym.

Sully watched them go, shaking his head.

He muttered something to himself, then sat back down.

The fan rattled on.

They started with a simple jab-catch drill. One man fired, the other parried. Rhythm, control, timing. That was the idea.

But Porter was putting too much behind his jab. Danny felt it, the weight, the intent. So, he sent one back a little firmer. Just enough to let Porter know.

Porter caught it, squared his stance. His next jab came harder, faster. Smacked Danny's palm with enough force to send a jolt through his arm.

Danny answered.

*BAM.*

A jab that landed more like a cross, snapping Porter's head an inch back. His feet shifted—more reaction than intention.

"Chill out," Porter muttered.

"You started it," Danny shot back, keeping the drill going.

"I didn't do shit." Porter's jab came quick and stiff.

Danny's hand ached, but he didn't show it. "Keep your voice down. I'm not getting kicked out of the gym because of you. I swear." His jab was harder this time.

Porter smirked. "You swear what? What are you gonna do about it?"

"Nothing," Danny said, resetting. "Because I got a fight coming up, and I know how to control myself. Luckily, I had an old man capable of teaching me that."

"You'll do nothing because you're a coward."

Words had a way of cutting past the guard.

Danny moved before thinking. His right cross came off the jab, precise and sudden. Porter reeled, but his instincts took over. He stepped in, twisting into a hook.

The drill was gone. The fight had begun.

Sully was on them in a heartbeat, faster than a man his age had any right to move. His voice cracked like a whip— commanding, final.

"Enough!"

His grip was iron, his shove a command, the trained motions of a man who had spent years stepping between pride and regret.

Danny staggered back, chest heaving, knuckles burning under his gloves. Porter wiped his mouth with the back of his hand, eyes still focused.

"You wanna act like a couple of street punks, go do it somewhere else," Sully barked. "Not in my gym. Not on my time."

Neither spoke. Their breathing filled the space, hot and ragged. Sully wasn't looking for words anyway. He held out his hand, palm up, expectant.

"Keys."

Danny hesitated. So did Porter. Sully's stare bore into them, there was nothing they could say. Not anymore.

"I am not asking," Sully said.

Reluctantly, Danny tore his gloves off and dug into his pocket before slapping his key onto Sully's palm. Porter did the same, slower, jaw tight.

"You're done. Both of you. One week. You wanna come back, you do it with your heads on straight. Otherwise, don't bother."

The boys muttered curses under their breath, shoving gear into their bags, their movements charged with frustration. Sully watched them closely.

"I suggest you two look each other in the eye. Say what needs saying. And for whatever can't be settled with words—you settle it with gloves on. Because you will not bring this back into my gym."

Outside it was getting dark. The summer air remained thick, the asphalt still holding the sun's fire. As Danny stepped into the parking lot, a group of boxers strolled in, fresh and laughing, oblivious to the storm rolling toward them.

One of them clapped Danny on the shoulder. "Yo, Danny—"

Danny barreled past, shoulder stiff.

Porter was right behind him. "What the hell was that?"

Danny kept walking. Porter caught up, shoved him hard. The group stopped, eyes darting between them, knowing things were about to get serious.

Danny didn't answer. Just put a hand on Porter's chest, shoving him back, trying to walk on.

Porter's voice cut through the night. "A fucking coward!"

He wasn't talking to Danny anymore. He was talking to the others, making sure they heard; he was sure Danny did too.

Danny stopped cold. Anger was bubbling inside of him. Then he turned, closing the space in a blink, grabbing Porter by the shirt. His voice was raw and tight. "I told you—I got a fight coming up. Now I can't train. Look what you did!"

Porter didn't flinch. "Who hit who?"

Danny's hands shook, his pulse hammering in his throat. He swallowed it down, shoved Porter back hard enough to make him stumble.

"Friday," Danny said, voice shaking. "You and me. We settle this." His fists balled tight. "Winner gets to come back to the gym. Loser turns his key in and finds somewhere else to train."

"Careful what you wish for," Porter said.

Danny was already walking away.

The fight for the gym started that night.

Darkness swallowed the city whole, streetlights buzzing like hornets, throwing long, mean shadows across the pavement. In his basement, Danny worked the heavy bag—old, cracked leather, swinging from a rusted chain bolted to the rafters. Short, brutal hooks. A straight right that shook dust from the ceiling. Sweat slicked his skin. The only sounds: his fists and the drum of his own pulse. Mom was gone, another late shift.

Across the river, Porter ran. Sneakers pounding asphalt. Night air biting his lungs. He passed the gym, but he kept his eyes locked ahead. No more looking over his shoulder. His intention was on what lay ahead. He'd carve his own name with his own two hands, leave something behind that didn't stink of someone else's sins.

Danny had his own ghost to outrun, whispering about duty, about honor, about how much blood it took to be a good man. He ran at dawn, feet slipping on dew-slick grass, lungs burning as he did hill sprints.

Porter lifted cinder blocks in an abandoned lot, arms trembling. At night, he worked a speed bag in his garage until his shoulders went numb. Danny swung a sledgehammer at an old tire, each strike ringing like a bell in the dark.

This wasn't about a gym anymore. Wasn't even about the fight. It was older, deeper. A wound too stubborn to close.

The clock ticked toward Friday, and they'd be ready.

The morning of the fight came like any other day. But they both knew it wasn't.

From different parts of town, they watched the same sun claw its way over the rooftops, burning off the night. The air felt different—thick, charged. A tension with weight, with teeth, something rising between them like a leviathan from deep water.

Tonight, they would stand toe to toe.

Tonight, they would finish a fight that started long before either of them threw a punch.

When dusk settled over the city in bruised purples and deep reds, the baseball field at Center Park sat empty. The dirt infield hard-packed, the grass gone brittle from summer's last heatwave. A single set of floodlights flickered, casting long, broken shadows.

Porter got there first. He stood near the pitcher's mound, hands on his hips, gloves hooked onto his waistband. The place smelled like dust and rusted chain-link. He rolled his shoulders, shook out his arms. His body was loose, ready. His mind was a different story.

Danny arrived minutes later, walking in slow, purposeful strides. His gloves hung from his fingers, swinging with each step. He stopped at the edge of the infield and took in the scene—the battered dugouts, the outfield fence with curling advertisements, the empty bleachers. A place where kids chased fly balls. Tonight, it was a ring.

Neither boy spoke at first.

Danny pulled on his gloves. Tightened the laces with his teeth. Porter did the same.

The wind cut through the field, carrying the distant sound of traffic, the occasional bark of a dog.

Finally, Porter exhaled, rolling his neck. "We doing this or what?"

Danny met his eyes. Nodded once.

No bell. No crowd. Just two names, two histories, and a fight that had been waiting to happen since a bullet bit skin two years ago.

They touched gloves, setting things in motion. There was no turning back now.

Danny moved first, sharp, testing. A swift jab that Porter slipped, answering with a hook that glanced off Danny's shoulder. No feeling out. No wasted movement. They'd both trained too long for that. They had been studying the other every day for years.

Danny feinted, then drove a right hand into Porter's ribs. Porter grunted, bit down, came back with a left that caught Danny on the cheekbone.

Then it really started.

Porter pressed forward, throwing in tight combinations, his gloves popping against Danny's guard, testing for gaps. Danny planted his feet, fired back—hooks that made Porter's ribs groan, a right cross that snapped his head to the side. The field echoed with the dull thud of leather on skin.

Danny had a brawler's instinct. He fought like he had something to prove, something to protect, like the gym itself was stitched into his skin. Short, brutal shots, head down, always pressing. His father's voice was in his head, the way it had always been.

*Stand your ground. Keep your hands up. Don't let him see you hurt.*

Porter fought like a man trying to carve himself out of stone. Every punch was the strike of a hammer, shaping something new, something that didn't belong to his father. He'd spent his whole life shrinking away from his name, the whispers, the weight of a crime he never committed. And here, in the blood and breath and rhythm of the fight, he was free.

Danny caught him with a right that clacked his teeth together. Porter spat blood into the dirt. Then he smiled. His missing tooth loud against the blood.

Danny saw it. Something changed.

He thought he knew Porter. Thought he was just his father's shadow, a thief looking to take what wasn't his. But Porter wasn't running anymore. He was standing and trading, eating shots, firing back, proving he belonged.

Danny respected that.

Porter ducked under a hook, drilled a left into Danny's gut, then a right upstairs that sent sweat flying from his jaw. Danny staggered, legs wobbling for a half-second before he found his balance.

Porter had figured Danny would crack sooner or later. Most guys did when the fight dragged past pain and into something deeper. But Danny wasn't most guys. He took the shot, let the hurt settle, then rose like it hadn't touched him at all. He didn't fight like someone desperate to hold onto the past—he fought like someone willing to bleed for the future.

And Porter felt something shift.

This wasn't about names anymore. Wasn't about fathers or history or who owed who what.

This was about him and Danny and the war they were waging right now.

And Danny wasn't going anywhere. Porter respected that.

The fight slowed, not out of exhaustion, but because they were no longer fighting out of hate. No longer were they burning with rage.

They fought because it was in them. Because they were born for it.

The next exchange was brutal. Danny rocked Porter with a right hand that sent him stumbling. Porter sucked in a breath, forced his legs to hold, then came back with everything—three punches, fast, precise, the last one landing flush on Danny's temple.

Danny fell to one knee, blinking against the stars in his vision.

Porter stepped back, breathing hard. Waiting.

Danny exhaled slow, wiped his glove on his shorts, then pushed himself to his feet. He looked at Porter, really looked at him, and nodded.

Respect. Earned the only way fighters know how.

Danny lifted his gloves. Porter did the same.

Danny moved first, slipping a cross and firing back—a one-two, sharp, clean, and full of bad intentions. Porter barely stayed upright. His legs wobbled, but he bit down, pushed forward, ducked under the next barrage, and drove an uppercut straight into Danny's side.

A perfect shot. Deep. Buried in the liver.

Danny buckled. His body locked up, breath stolen, knees giving before his mind could stop them. He fought to stand, muscles screaming, willpower alone dragging him toward his feet. But his body wouldn't listen. Not this time.

He knelt, gloves digging into the dirt, head bowed.

Then—he let go.

Tears slipped free, mixing with sweat, dripping into the grass.

Porter watched him, chest rising and falling, hands still curled into fists. Then he let them go too. Stripped off his gloves and reached out.

Danny took the hand and got to his feet. He nodded. No words. None were needed.

Danny bit his glove free, reached into his pocket, and laid the key into Porter's palm. A deal was a deal, and Danny was going to be a man true to his word.

Porter stood there, holding it, breath fast and hard, watching as Danny turned away. He walked to the dugout and sat heavy on the bench, elbows on his knees, head in his hands.

Porter looked down at the key. Then back at Danny. He rolled his jaw, flexed his fingers. His knuckles were raw, split in places. His ribs ached where Danny had dug in shots that would've dropped lesser fighters.

A long beat. Then Porter stepped forward.

Danny felt him before he saw him. He closed his eyes a moment, wiped the sweat from his brow, and sat up.

"Hell of a fight," Danny muttered.

Porter nodded. "Yeah." He looked at the key in his palm, then held it out. "This isn't mine."

Danny frowned, eyeing the key. "No, man. You earned it."

Porter shook his head. "I can't take that place from you, Danny. That's not what this was about."

Danny held his stare for a long moment. Then, finally, he took the key back. Rolling it between his fingers, he felt the weight of it.

Another silence.

Danny exhaled through his nose, a ghost of a smirk on his lips. "Didn't think I'd cry in front of you, though."

Porter gave a half-smile, flexing his sore hands. "Didn't think you'd hit that hard."

That got a quiet chuckle from Danny. A small thing, but real.

Porter sat down on the bench next to him. Neither said anything for a while. Just two fighters, bruised, breathing, feeling the last of the fight fade into the night.

Finally, Danny nodded toward him. "You think you could teach me to box like that?"

Porter looked at him, considering. Then he huffed a laugh. "If you teach me how to get my hook like yours."

Danny nodded again. No more words needed.

The night stretched quiet around them. Two boys who had fought like enemies sat like brothers.

And for the first time in a long time, the past didn't feel so heavy. For the first time in a while, there was something like peace in the silence between them. They could hear nothing but the river moving nearby the way it always did, carving its path, swallowing what came before.

# Pure Wrath

## by A.M. Adair

**The antique motorcycle** rumbled like a caged animal. The 2075 Harley Davidson was a hybrid power throwback to the Fat Boy of old. It'd been extremely popular in its day. Only those who'd achieved Level One could even dream of having something like it. Then again, only those who knew their bikes would see it for what it was. To most, it was just an odd-looking motorcycle. But it was more than just a conveyance to her. Time on the bike helped keep her grounded.

Calm.

Focused.

At peace.

Pulling into the diner's parking lot, she caught sight of a couple watching her. They were openly staring, making it easy to see their vice ranks: 32 and 35. They were both Level Three, but they looked young enough to have a chance to make Level Two before being locked in. She wished them well, even though they were being a little rude. She knew the motorcycle was drawing their attention, but it still made her uncomfortable. Her athletic build, full-face helmet, and leather riding gear hid her identity well, but the anonymity was temporary. It was only a matter of time before someone reacted to her. Reactions were inevitable. The only question was how.

As she turned off the bike, Bryana Union paused. She tended to avoid being out in public to prevent provoking responses—particularly the negative ones. But today was her father's birthday, and she had a promise to keep. Swinging her leg over the back of the bike in one fluid movement, she dismounted and removed her helmet. Her short, dark hair held streaks of gray that fell around her face, framing it, and the number 10 on her cheekbone. A scar bisected her left eyebrow. Another streaked across her chin and lower lip.

Hanging the helmet on the bike's handlebar, she removed her jacket and placed it over her seat. The blue of her shirt enhanced the color of her eyes, giving them an almost violet hue. She walked toward the diner's front door, leaving her gloves on. Hooking her hair behind her ear, she made a mental note about how long it was getting. She'd have to cut it soon to stay in regulation. In the space between where her hair fell and the collar of her shirt, her code chain was just visible, as required by the High Council.

Bryana rubbed her gloved hand across the back of her neck absently. She couldn't feel them, but she knew the numbers were there. 0-0-10-0-0-0-0. It was an accounting ... and warning for all the world to see about who she was, boiled down into seven categories—pride, envy, wrath, sloth, avarice, gluttony, and lust. The total of her chain, 10, was tattooed on her cheekbone. Showcasing her status within society. She didn't like it but accepted the wisdom of the High Council and the law.

Vice cataloging and virtue training had brought humanity back from the brink.

After the Final War ended in 2099, those who survived were broken, traumatized, and cynical. Fear of the new millennium was rampant. People barely trusted their own families, let alone any form of governance. Activities and occupations that had once represented truth and freedom were synonymous with manipulation. Former leadership positions were seen as gateways to repression and greed. The world learned the hard way that no one was immune to corruption; therefore, anyone seeking power was doing so for personal gain.

Faith was the last hope for the survivors, but even that was crumbling—the divides between the various religions and sects spawned ever-increasing collisions of violence. Extinction seemed inevitable. That's when the First Council presented a miracle. A Priest, a Rabbi, and an Imam put aside their differences for the salvation of humankind and discovered a way to catalog an individual's susceptibility to the seven deadly sins. A sequence of tests that reveal true character and looked inside a person's heart and mind to get to their truth. Every sin was graded on a scale of 0-10, with 0 being the best possible result. They instituted tattooing the results on the face and neck of the individual as a mechanism to help the world rebuild trust and a sense of community.

It worked.

What started with their small circle of followers grew and grew until it became the way of the world. At age 21, everyone received their first test and a biochip.

Their test results dictated what type of virtue training and level of society they would be assigned to. Virtue training was a way for people to better themselves, to get a handle on their vices, and to become the best version of themselves. As they improved, their quality of life and opportunities also improved.

The biochip kept them honest, regardless of their status.

Level Three (<42) was filled with young adults still making the mistakes of youth and those whose proclivities toward their vices were too ingrained to be trained out of them. Consequently, it was the largest group. They were monitored constantly and could only be trusted with positions that minimized the impact on the community if their vices got the better of them. Level Two (<28) was management personnel, security, and other positions of trust and authority based on the results of their code chain. Level One (<14) was where Council members were selected. They were the most virtuous and least sinful and, therefore, the only ones worthy of positions of governance. Everyone was retested every seven years, allowing them to potentially move to the next level until they were locked into their code at age 49.

At 49, your vices were considered permanent.

Then there were the Others, the individuals who never reached Level Three. The Others were the most dangerous, treacherous, and unrepentant members of society. They were kept in containment and underwent intensive rehabilitation training. To avoid becoming a drain on society, they were only given two chances to reach Level Three and move on. If they didn't, they were eliminated.

Bryana's hand clenched, the well-worn leather of the glove tightening across her knuckles with ease. She disapproved of the killing. But she couldn't argue with the logic or the proven results the system had produced. It was a harsh reality, but things had been so much worse before. They couldn't go back. No matter what the cost. Her hand unclenched and gripped the door handle of the front entrance to the diner. She took a deep breath and focused on calming her emotions and clearing her mind.

Today would be a good day. It had to be.

"Welcome to ... " The teenage girl who greeted her stood awe-struck. Her name tag said: Mary. She didn't have a tattoo yet, so she was a mystery, but Bryana knew the look on the girl's face all too well.

"Thank you. Could I sit in the back corner if it's not too much trouble? Please?"

Mary blinked a few times and, with a slight shake of her head, seemed to snap out of whatever thoughts had gripped her. Blushing, she cleared her throat before responding. "Of course. Please follow me."

Bryana smiled and followed Mary to her familiar corner booth—so many memories. Most of them were good. Sliding onto the bench with the wall behind her, Bryana noticed the updated menu projected in front of her. *Seems like they've changed a few things.*

Scanning over the content, she relaxed when she saw what she had come for.

"Have you dined here before?"

"Yes. Many times."

"We appreciate your patronage. In addition to our traditional human-centric restaurant experience, we've recently updated our service to include the universal contactless option, should you prefer it."

One thing her father had loved about this place was that he felt connected to other people, regardless of their level. It was one of the few places left that hadn't implemented standard automation, let alone the latest technology. He'd sworn that he could tell the difference between a pecan pie made by human hands and one created by a cybernetic. It'd made every visit a different experience. Even if he always ordered the same thing.

Bryana glanced at the empty seat across from her and sighed.

*Time changes everything, whether we want it to or not.*

She tried to hide her disappointment but failed. When she looked up, she saw Mary appear close to tears, having automatically assumed the blame for her customer's displeasure.

"I, um, can call over the automated concierge now if I've somehow offended you." Mary sounded like she'd been scolded.

"You haven't offended me at all. My apologies. I didn't mean to cause you distress."

Mary tried to smile, clearly still unsettled. "Would you prefer a different server?"

Bryana felt a tinge of guilt. Mary was young, but this reaction wasn't the girl's fault. The number 10 on Bryana's face was a force all its own, and this poor child was being crushed under the pressure of living up to its expectations.

If only she knew the truth.

Bryana was about to offer more reassurance when movement caught her attention. Two burly men stood from a booth on the far side of the diner. Their eyes shifted from Bryana to Mary and back, but their menace and intent were as clear as the number 41 on each face. Bryana sighed, shaking her head.

"Mary ... may I call you Mary?"

"Y-yes?"

"On my oath, you have done nothing wrong. My thoughts were somewhere else. I was looking forward to coffee, pie, and old-fashioned service. But now, I need you to walk away."

"I don't understand."

"Please. Don't ask questions. For your safety, go to the back of the restaurant. Now. Take as many of the other patrons as you can."

Mary took a couple of hesitant steps backward, confusion slowing her movement. Her next move put her right into the path of the 41 twins. The taller of the two men slid a beefy arm around Mary's waist, pulling her into his body. She stiffened, her eyes going wide. A 2X brand marked the forearm of the man holding Mary trapped against him.

Bryana's jaw clenched as she battled with the demon starting to claw its way to the surface. That brand meant Mary's captor had barely earned Level Three on his second try—and he was proud of it. He'd cheated death, locked in his number, and was now free to embrace his vices. It was a vulnerability in the system that, if left unchecked, threatened everything.

"Well, well, well. Looks like we have fucking royalty here, Bro." Tall 41 said.

"Doesn't look like much to me."

Her vision sharpened, and everything but the men and the girl faded.

*Not today.*

Bryana flattened her hands on the table, pressing down, counting to herself as she drew a deep breath and then let it out at the same pace. "You need to stop this. Let the girl go and leave. Now. You do not want this fight."

The men laughed.

"You trying to scare us, your holiness?"

"No. I'm trying to save you."

Anger colored the brute's face. Mary whimpered as he squeezed her tighter. "Fuck you. You think you're so high and mighty that you can say or do whatever you want, and we're just supposed to bow down to it."

"No. I don't."

Tall 41 put his mouth next to Mary's ear, intentionally making contact. "What'd this bitch say to make you cry, baby girl? Let me guess, she's too good for some nobody to touch her food, right?"

"N-no. It was my mistake."

"Don't fucking lie to me."

"I-I'm not."

Tall 41 threw Mary to the ground, his leg raised to stomp down—

A gloved fist connected with his jaw, knocking him off balance. Stumbling back, he never saw any of the vicious hooks that fractured his ribs, but his screams made it clear to everyone in the diner that he felt them.

Bryana grabbed his hair, using it as leverage to pulverize his face, striking over and over. Blood spurted from his nose, and his lip split in half as a broken tooth cut through the thin barrier of flesh. In seconds, his body went limp, hair ripping out from the root as he crashed to the ground.

Ducking under a wild haymaker from Short 41, Bryana countered with two shots to the body and an uppercut that snapped his jaw. Pressing the attack, she grabbed the back of his head, propelling it down into her waiting knee. There was a satisfying crack, and he collapsed. Blood covered his face, the point of origin lost in the crowd of contusions. Grabbing the back of his shirt, she propelled him headfirst into the side of the booth.

A hand grabbed her ankle, and she yanked her foot away, pivoting midair to stomp down on Tall 41's fingers. Joints cracked, and he shrieked. Bryana didn't stop. He curled into a ball in a vain attempt to protect himself. She stomped on his already compromised ribs again and again, her leg like a piston gaining speed.

"Stop! Please!"

Bryana whirled around to face the speaker. Her vision tinged red at the edges, hands balled into fists, ready for their next target. Mary recoiled, cowering in surrender. Her terror is palpable. Bryana's eyes darted around the diner. Patrons huddled together—blood. Two men sprawled on the floor, one barely breathing.

His wet gasps a macabre soundtrack to a living nightmare.

It happened again.

Shame hit like ice water poured over the inferno that had been her rage moments earlier. Bryana looked at herself. Streaks of blood crisscrossing everywhere. She knew without needing to check that none of it was hers. Bowing her head, she used her breathing exercises to put out the last embers. Her control returned, leaving only guilt.

*I'm so sorry, Dad.*

Looking at Mary, she asked, "Have you called it in yet?"

"N-no, ma'am."

"Please do. I'll wait for them." Mary doesn't move. Bryana's guilt intensified as she realized the girl's fear was anchoring her to the ground. "It's the law, Mary. I do not, and will not, hold it against you. I promise."

Bryana held her hair up as she turned and kneeled on the floor, showing her code chain clearly to the girl. A tentative step, followed by a gasp, let her know when Mary saw where her 10 came from.

*At least she knows I'm not a liar.*

Slowly getting to her feet, Bryana kept her hands open and away from her body as she moved to the door. "I'm truly sorry this happened. Please let Vice Control know I will be waiting outside for the Assessor."

Back in the parking lot, Bryana shifted her jacket to the motorcycle's handlebars and sat on the seat, resting her hands in front of her, palms up and in plain sight. She closed her eyes and waited for her judgment. Most people feared the Assessors. For Bryana, it was just another day. She'd been in this situation more times than she could count.

The guilt weighed on her regardless. She hated hurting people.

It'd been almost four months since her last incident. The longest she'd gone yet. She took a moment to allow herself a little solace in the fact that she was going longer periods of time without losing control. Her father had been right. The program was working. She just needed to be patient and stick with it.

A humming sound alerted Bryana to Vice Control's arrival. Seconds later, a convoy of four vehicles, each formidable but deceptively sleek with a liquid mercury-like coating, coasted to a stop within feet of her. Doors opened in unison, and a dozen Enforcers, wearing the same blue as her, poured out. The team leader, a bulldog of a man, recognized her immediately. He barked orders to the rest of the team and then approached her. His eyes narrowed, wrinkling the 15 on his face, when he saw the extent of the blood splatter.

"How bad, Chief?"

"It's bad, Bishop. Are the medics en route?" As if to answer her question, a red emergency medical cybernetic pod detached from the trail vehicle and moved toward the diner along with several Enforcers.

"Personnel are standing by to flash in if the bot can't handle it."

Bryana shook her head. Those men might be terrible people, but didn't they at least deserve to have someone, a human someone, with them in case they didn't make it?

Bishop removed a square, black-framed device from his pocket, the transparent surface in the center iridescent in the sunlight. Knowing the procedure by heart, she pulled off her gloves, exposing her monstrous hands. Scars like a patchwork quilt covered her enlarged knuckles and branched out like spider's legs along her fingers and down the back of her hand—indisputable evidence of her long history of violence.

She despised looking at them.

Bryana held her right hand out to Bishop, steady as a rock, as he scanned her chip. The screen swirled and then turned blue, revealing an image of her and her code chain. Below that was Bryana Union, Level One, Regional Chief of Vice Control.

Bishop didn't need to verify that her tattoos matched the chip; he knew what they would say, but he did it anyway, sticking with protocol regardless of the fact that he was investigating his boss. She was grateful it was him. Bishop may have been a Level Two, but his temperament was precisely what an Enforcer should be, which is why he was her second-in-command.

"Who's the Assessor for this?" she asked.

"Someone I haven't met. Name's Westmore."

"Another new Assessor? That's the fourth one this year."

Bishop shrugged. "They say most Assessors burn out within a few years. Being both judge and jury takes a toll. That's why they get to transfer to the Capital to be with the High Council after their service. It's a reward for carrying so much weight on their shoulders."

A spot in the middle of the parking lot began to glow as if on cue. Bryana turned and closed her eyes, seeing the bright flash of light through her lids anyway. Looking back, she saw a handsome man in dark sunglasses and a tailored gray suit. He was younger than she expected, but the 7 on his cheekbone left no doubt in her mind who he was. For several years, she'd noticed a trend with Assessor selection. They all had the same code chain breakdown: 1-1-1-1-1-1-1. She'd asked a previous Assessor about it when she'd picked up on the pattern and was told that having some low-level personal insight into each deadly sin made for more effective Assessors.

It'd made sense at the time. But something about it didn't sit right with her anymore. If nothing else, the Council should be looking into what was causing the higher turnover within the Assessor ranks. She'd have to bring it up at the next meeting as part of her quarterly report.

With a nod to her, Bishop called over one of the newest team members to watch her.

*Jones?*

Bryana made sure she didn't move or say anything as Bishop left to brief the Assessor; she didn't want to make the kid guarding her too nervous. She watched as Bishop handed Westmore the scanner with her information for him to review. As Bishop spoke, Bryana saw Westmore's eyebrows rise, and then he took the sunglasses off and looked over at her. She didn't look away.

The Assessor's expression didn't change, but something about how he looked at her made her skin crawl.

Something isn't right.

Bishop finished briefing Westmore and then escorted him inside the diner. It felt like an eternity before they came back out. When they did, Bryana braced herself for what was to come. Lucky for her, Bishop didn't make her wait.

"They're both alive, but it's too early to say what damage will be permanent."

She nodded, but her gut twisted.

*At least they're alive.*

"Chief Union. I've heard so much about you. I'm Assessor Westmore. I wish it were under better circumstances, but it's a pleasure to meet you finally," Westmore said. He held out his hand, and she hesitated before shaking it.

*Is he serious?*

"I've reviewed the footage and confirmed the sequence of events with the citizens inside the diner. I've also verified that both men involved in this altercation were 2Xers. I am ready to rule that you effectively neutralized a vice spike and active threat to the citizenry. You may return to your duties. Thank you for your service."

Bryana hid her surprise. While she hadn't expected significant consequences, there was usually some form of reprimand. She deserved one. "Sir, my actions were more severe than required. You can see from my file that I've been suspended for increasing lengths of time after each incident. I submit myself for a minimum two-week suspension."

Westmore looked surprised. "Are you questioning my judgment, Chief Union?"

"No, sir. I'm critiquing my handling of the situation. My predisposition to violence cannot be seen as acceptable or encouraged."

"Interesting."

"Sir?"

"You believe your actions are something to be ashamed of. From what I see, you are the pinnacle of what our society needs. Purity."

"I'm afraid I'm not following you."

Westmore turned to Bishop. "Give us a minute." Bishop nodded and, with a glance at Bryana, moved off. Once he was gone, Westmore said, "For decades, the High Council has been keeping a record of how our way of life has evolved. And the data is conclusive. Progress has stagnated. Advancement beyond Level Three is in decline. Worse still are the numbers of people making it to Level Three in the first place. As it is now, people have a fifty-fifty shot at being purged from society. And it's only a matter of time before the scales tip and there are more Others than those capable of rising above how they were born. We've hit a crossroads."

*This can't be happening.*

Bryana's mind spun with the implications. None of them were good. "There has to be something that can be done."

Westmore smiled, and the hair on the back of her neck stood on end.

“That’s where you come in. The High Council needs to gain more insight into why vices are surging if they are to prevent our way of life from crumbling. What better way than by relying on those whose vices are not diluted by competing urges?”

“So, you’re hoping people with only one vice will help bring understanding? Then what?”

“We’re looking for more than just understanding. We’re looking for ways to apply it. And to that end, we need the very best of the worst, so to speak. You are pure wrath. It made you the obvious choice to lead this region’s Vice Control, and you’ve excelled here. But now we need you. The High Council needs you.”

“I’m honored, sir. However, I’m compelled to point out that just because I’m a zero in the other categories doesn’t mean I’m immune to vice. I’m just not predisposed to it. Given the wrong circumstances, everyone is capable of sin.”

Westmore smiles. “I’m aware. You pointing it out does nothing but validate that you are exactly what we are looking for.”

Bryana stood at attention, trying to ignore the unease creeping through her. “I serve at the High Council’s discretion. If this is what is needed of me, I’ll do it. May I request time to serve my suspension and turnover with a replacement?”

Westmore studied her a moment. “What do you do while on suspension?”

“I run myself through a program my father designed to help me stay in control.”

He seemed to be considering his words before speaking again. “I heard about his passing. You have my condolences. He served as an Assessor longer than anyone else and wrote many of the guidelines we still use. I assume he stayed here to be with you when he retired?”

“He did.”

“This program he designed for you—would it be possible for me to see it?”

*Why?*

“Yes, sir.”

“Great! I will be at your place tomorrow morning at nine. Now, if you'll excuse me, I need to report my findings and initiate the nomination process for your replacement.”

Bryana inclined her head and clamped her mouth shut. She watched Westmore strut back to the center of the parking lot. Anxiety made her feel jittery, but she couldn't figure out why. The news he'd shared had been alarming, but it didn't explain her reaction.

Something was off.

The air around Westmore began to glow. This time, she didn't turn away. Westmore put on his sunglasses and smiled at her. Then, he was gone in a flash. Purple spots filled her field of view as the residual effects from watching the flash lingered. Her eyes watered, and she blinked to clear them. Bishop returned to her side.

“Everything okay?” Bishop asked.

“I honestly don't know. How's everything inside?”

“The 2Xers are being stabilized, and the patrons are being escorted out through the kitchen to stay out of the way. We have their contact information and will follow up with them within the next 72 hours."

"Good. I'll return to my residence for my two-week suspension."

"Chief, if I may?"

"What?"

"You've already been out of the office for two months. I don't want to appear dismissive. I know how close you and your father were. But we need you, too. Could you delay your suspension until the department is caught up administratively? We can only do so much without your final approval."

Bryana wanted to kick herself. "I'm sorry, Bishop. I know my absence has been a burden. And you're right. I have responsibilities that can't be put off. Particularly now."

"What do you mean?"

"They are nominating my replacement, and I want to ensure that everything is ready for the transition."

"Wait, what? But you were cleared to return to duty. I heard it myself."

"The High Council has another position they need me for."

Bishop settled a little. "What position?"

"Some type of consultant for the High Council. I'm not clear on the details, but that doesn't matter. Right now, the priority is getting everything in order."

"How much time do you think you have left with us?"

"Not sure about that either. Identifying candidates and submitting the nominations can happen relatively quickly. But whether they choose to accept the position is another matter entirely."

"Yeah. It's not exactly an easy life."

"I'll head into work now and get started. It'll also give me a chance to pack up my personal effects."

Bishop's brow furrowed. "Don't you think it may be better if you went home first?"

Bryana glanced at her blood-covered clothes. "I have extra clothes and toiletries in my office. I'll get cleaned up there."

"Chief, you don't need to rush this."

"I understand your concern, and I appreciate it. But I've been gone too long already, and this is a fluid situation. I'll go home and start my suspension as soon as I finish."

"But it could take days."

"All the more reason to start now."

Bryana had difficulty getting out of bed, but her fatigue was a blessing in disguise. After 20 straight hours, she'd finished everything waiting for her at the office and then went home. Work and exhaustion had provided her a reprieve from thinking about what had happened the day before. She'd only slept a couple of hours, but she needed to be as ready as possible for the visit from Westmore.

Bryana felt restless despite her exhaustion.

With coffee in hand, she set her hand wraps on the kitchen counter. Her knuckles were slightly swollen because she hadn't bothered to ice them, and they'd taken on a grotesque shade of blue-black. She looked around the first floor of her home. The kitchen was connected to her training area. There were no separate living or dining spaces; every available inch was dedicated to her program. Aside from a bathroom, nothing on the first level was enclosed. Switchback stairs led up to the loft on the second level, which functioned as her bedroom and library.

She placed her hand over the electronic tablet in front of her. It contained all the details of her journey to control her rage. It had been her father's life work ... and her last hope. She was about to turn 49. Her vice was permanent; the final test would make it official. They had both known it, but her father never stopped believing she could learn to rein it in. The process they had spent decades refining was getting results. For the last several years, she had been following the same routine. What had started as an experiment had become so much more.

Now, she needed it.

Buzz.

Bryana pressed a button on the console beside her, and a heads-up display projected an image of Westmore waiting to enter through her front gate. She released the gate lock and observed him strut into the courtyard. A surge of irritation shot through her.

Breathe.

Setting the coffee down, she moved to meet her esteemed guest. She opened the door before Westmore could knock. "Good morning, sir."

He smiled. She didn't buy it.

"Good morning. Thank you again for allowing me into your home and agreeing to serve the High Council."

"Of course, sir. It's an honor to serve."

Westmore walked in as though he owned the place, but his pace slowed as he moved into her training area. Heavy bags, speed bags, automated strike pads, weights, and cardio equipment surrounded an old-fashioned boxing ring.

"Interesting décor choices."

"It may seem odd, but most of my spare time is devoted to my training program."

"Explain that. Did your father come up with a new virtue training curriculum?"

"No. I've been through every course available. If anything, the training amplified my vice."

"So, what is it that you do instead?"

"It's probably better to show you," Bryana said as she retrieved her hand wraps from the counter. With lightning-quick efficiency, she wrapped her knuckles, the motion instinctual. Once finished, she picked up the tablet and handed it to Westmore. "This has everything: how we started, modified, and, I think, finally found a program that's working."

"Uh, forgive me, but given what I saw yesterday, what makes you think it's working?"

Breathe.

"Because I'm in control more often and maintaining it for extended periods of time. When I was younger, anything ... everything would set me off. Maybe things could have been different if it had just been a bad temper. But it wasn't. And the physical violence escalated the older I got. Until we refined the program to the one I've been using for years."

"Could you demonstrate it?"

"Yes, sir."

Bryana inclined her head and moved to the first section of her circuit. A seven-foot mirror that defied gravity hovered over a magnetic field in the floor. She centered herself, and an array of choices lit up around her image. She stretched, limbering up and mentally preparing herself. Then, she selected the first icon. The mirror shimmered, and a rapid sequence of images—angry, violent scenes—flashed before her. Her pulse jumped, and her jaw clenched.

She pressed the second icon—more images, this time victims and the aftermath of violence. Her body tensed, fists clenching so hard her fingernails dug into the permanent grooves in her palm.

With the third icon, a three-minute timer appeared, and dark, pulsating music started playing. Bryana moved to her next station: cardio. Setting the resistance on her simulator to soft sand, she took off at a steady jog. The modified gravity conditions weighed down her feet, heightening her agitation.

A sound like nails on a chalkboard cut through the music, and the simulator stopped.

Bryana jumped off and rushed to the heavy bags. The timer on the mirror started the three-minute countdown again. Jab-cross combos evolved to include variations of hooks and uppercuts. Bryana wailed on each bag as she weaved between them, her muscles burning.

Time.

Free weights.

Time.

Speed bags.

Time.

Strike pads on a human form illuminated in various sequences, requiring precision and focus through combination after combination.

Time.

Bryana returned to the mirror. The timer sat frozen at zero. Sweat streamed down her body, and every muscle protested, but the worst was yet to come.

She selected the fourth icon, and a new series of images flowed across the surface in front of her. Nightmarish depictions of the worst of humanity assaulted her. Horrific abuse, mass murder, genocide, nuclear war ... then the words: "The choice is yours."

Bryana selected the final icon and turned away from the mirror. The sound of boots marching and children crying replaced the music. She put on a thin, gray, full-body suit and pulled the hood over her head. Then, she put on gloves and glasses and stepped into the boxing ring.

A hologram of a man appeared in front of her, snarling, holding a knife.

Bryana stood still. Arms at her sides ... waiting. The image feinted left, then right. Bryana didn't move. When the lunge came, she twisted out of the way. Her computerized opponent attacked over and over. Bryana ducked, dodged, and danced away from every attempt, never engaging.

Then the round was over. Silence fell as Bryana took a knee. Her chest heaved from the exertion, her muscles screamed, and her mind reeled. Waves of emotion washed over her: anger, sadness, fear, acceptance, and then ... hope. Her breathing slowed, and she stood up.

Clapping reminded her that she wasn't alone.

Westmore approached the ring as she removed the biosensor suit. "Where did you learn to do all that?"

"My father accessed the combat archives. The video records allowed the program to break down the movements and we experimented with different methodologies. I've been through regimens of everything we have on file, but we discovered the more pugilistic variants channeled my anger more effectively and gave us the best results."

"That was an impressive workout, but I have no idea how that supposedly helps you."

"Think of it as a desensitization. The program's AI intentionally triggers me with the images it chooses. Every detail is designed to heighten my agitation and increase my rage response. Running with restricted movements and hitting the heavy bag gives me a physical release valve; the weights tire me out, and then the speed bags and targets force my mind to focus. So, when I get to the final test, I've already dumped a ton of emotion and energy. That gives me a chance to practice control."

"Is that why you didn't fight the hologram?"

"Yes. Last week was the first time I was able to make it through the entire round."

"Is it the same every time?"

"No. The program is constantly evolving. It's linked to my biochip and adjusts the stimuli to trigger a response."

Westmore looked at the tablet with newfound interest. "And all of your father's work is on here?"

Bryana felt uneasy. "Yes, sir."

"Do you think it could be replicated for the other vices?"

"My father thought it might be possible."

"Might?"

"He believed only those who genuinely wanted to change could handle the immersion training. For anyone who wasn't committed, it could transform them into monsters."

"Is that why it's working for you? You're committed to the process?"

"That ... and I'm already a monster."

Westmore smiled. "You're not a monster. You're a gift."

Bryana's skin crawled. She hid her reaction by grabbing a towel and wiping her face. "Did you have any more questions, sir?"

"Please, call me Damion."

"Sir?"

"Damion. It's my name."

"Uh, yes, sir. It's just highly unusual."

"Well, you and I will be working together a lot, and I would like us to be friends."

"Okay. Damion. Uh, may I ask what we will be doing?"

He smiled again. This time, Bryana felt the urge to punch him. Luckily, her training program had done its job, and she held back. However, the sudden feeling was disturbing, nonetheless.

"In due time. For now, I want you to rest up. A transport will be here at the end of your self-imposed suspension to take you to the High Council. I will arrange for your accommodations to mimic what you have here."

"Yes, s—Damion."

"May I make a copy of your father's program? I want our experts to review the data and get their thoughts on other possible applications."

NO!

Bryana clenched her jaw. She backed away as casually as possible to avoid revealing her internal struggle. Placing the kitchen counter between them, she fought for control.

*What's wrong with me?*

Her father wouldn't have hesitated to give his work to a fellow Assessor, let alone one working directly for the High Council.

"Whatever the High Council needs."

"Good!" Westmore connected a small white device to the tablet. Seconds later, it flashed green, and it was over. He set the tablet on the counter, apparently oblivious to the danger he was in the closer he got to her.

"This may be the key to our future, Bryana."

She dug her fingernails into her palms. "My father hoped as much."

The strain in her voice broke through his fixation with the program. He was close enough for her to see his eyes dilate as his fight-or-flight instinct sent alarm signals to his brain. “Well, I’ve taken up enough of your time. I’ll show myself out.” He retreated to the door quickly. “Thank you again for your service. We’ll see you soon.”

The second the door locked behind him, Bryana went to the mirror and started the program again. She could barely lift her arms by the time she reached the speed bags. Her legs felt like mush, and she stumbled repeatedly. But her mind was clear again. She pushed through the final rounds much slower than usual but didn’t stop. The action allowed her to concentrate on her conversation with Westmore. She was determined to figure out what had set her off.

When she entered the ring to test herself against an opponent, the program projected an image of Westmore. Confused, she waited to see what the hologram would do. The image didn’t attack; it just watched her. The expression on its face triggered her again. But this time, she was worn down enough to fight the feeling. The answer hit her harder than any opponent ever could.

Vice spike.

She’d spent most of her adult life as a part of Vice Control. Her ability to sense a vice spike was almost supernatural and had never failed her. But now, she doubted herself. How could it be possible? While no one was immune to sin, an Assessor’s proclivities should have been negligible and shouldn’t have set her off.

Something was very wrong. Westmore was lying.

When the program ended, Bryana hobbled back to the kitchen counter instead of taking a knee. Practically collapsing onto a stool, she grabbed her tablet, hands and arms shaking so badly she could barely pull up the main screen.

Everything looked in order.

She ran a query to see if anything had been accessed or modified. Only one thing popped up: her trigger parameters. Every detail her father had used to train the AI engine on what would set her off was cataloged. Bryana tried to calm her mind, but she was struggling. Westmore had said they needed to be able to study each sin in its purest form. Her triggers would inevitably come up as a part of that. If nothing else, then for everyone's safety.

So why didn't she believe him?

Two weeks flew by. Bryana was waiting out front with two duffle bags for her transport to the Capital. When it arrived, it wasn't what she expected. A sleek white helicopter was almost on top of her before she realized it was there. It hovered a foot off the ground, the synthetic pilot effortlessly navigating inside the confines of her courtyard. The door slid open. She picked up her bags and jogged to the waiting transport.

An empty but luxurious white leather interior greeted her. Bryana set her bags inside and hopped in. As she buckled herself into a seat, the door closed and locked. The helicopter took off, and the motion was so smooth that it was almost imperceptible. A screen lit up in front of her with the words, "Welcome, Chief Union." Below the welcome was the remaining flight time: 2 hours and 30 minutes. A compartment opened beside her seat with an assortment of drinks and snacks.

Bryana grabbed some water and settled in for the ride—and whatever awaited her on the other side. She looked out the window and watched her city fade away. The landscape transitioned into wilderness. Few remnants from the world before the Final War survived, but the skeletal remains of buildings and other structures that were no longer recognizable jutted through the green canopies of trees and seas of grass periodically—a reminder of what was lost.

For the most part, people stayed in one of the regional cities attached to the Capital by roads that were like spokes on a bike wheel. Nature had been allowed to retake everything else. Just one more way the First Council had tried to bring healing. Bryana knew people were living outside of the High Council's protection, choosing the harsh realities of the wild and the dangers it presented. From above, it looked so serene. But she knew it was anything but.

Life and death warred out there every day. And more often than not, death won. Nature was cruel, but it was no match for man. At least in the cities, the rules of their society kept man in check.

Didn't it?

Bryana wasn't so confident anymore. But she was sure that the answers were coming. And she needed to be ready.

"Welcome to the Capital, Bryana."

Westmore presented her with a small silver and gold insignia, just like the one he was wearing. The insignia was the crest of the High Council, and wearing it meant she acted with their authority. For a moment, she was overwhelmed by conflicting emotions.

"Thank you, sir."

"Damion."

"My apologies. Damion."

Bryana pinned on the crest, then shouldered one duffle and carried the other. Gently waving off the Level Two attendant, who scurried over to take them for her. Westmore didn't comment but did seem amused for some reason. She tried to block him out to avoid a repeat of their last interaction. Fortunately, her surroundings gave her plenty of distractions.

The city's gold and silver accents over its white construction made it look heavenly. Everything seemed to gleam or glitter in the sunlight, and it was so clean that even the air seemed clearer. It was beautiful. She was so taken with her surroundings that she didn't immediately notice that very few people were around. And of those who were, not a single one was a Level Three.

*Are we in a restricted area?*

"Why don't we start by getting you settled into your new residence, and then I can brief you on what we will be working on together."

"I would appreciate that."

Bryana followed Westmore toward a high-rise tower that seemed to go on forever. Inside, the granite floors, multi-story water features, and lush greenery made the foyer feel like another world. They stepped inside a glass-enclosed hover lift. Westmore called out residence 21, and the lift shot upwards, disorienting Bryana momentarily.

"You'll get used to the motion before too long."

She nodded, not trusting herself to speak.

On the 21st floor, they left the lift, and Westmore led her to an ornate door with a gilded frame. "This is the only residence on this floor, so you won't be disturbed." He touched the door, and a green light pulsed through the frame. The door opened.

Bryana wanted to ask who else had access to the residence and if she could control it but refrained. She needed to see what Westmore would reveal without her asking. Walking through the door, she was amazed to see an upgraded version of her training setup.

"We did our best to make this feel as much like home as possible. In addition to the upgrades, there was still plenty of space for us to give you a living room and dining area, too."

"Um, thank you."

"Of course! Now, if you're hungry, the kitchen is fully stocked. And if you would like to freshen up from the trip, I can come back later."

Bryana dropped her bags on the kitchen counter. "Actually, I would prefer to get started if that is an option."

Westmore smiled.

*I'm not going to like this.*

"I expected as much. Come with me." Westmore walked across her training area to the windows, and Bryana followed. As she approached, she noticed a smoke tendril rising from below. Once she reached the window, the source was impossible to miss.

Hundreds of feet below and about a mile away from her position, she noticed people moving in a clearing outside the city's walls. Thousands of them.

*What is happening here?*

"I'm sure you're aware that some people choose to live outside of our society. Have you encountered any of them before?"

"When I was a child."

"Well, consider yourself lucky. Their numbers grow every year, and so does their madness."

"What are you talking about?"

"What you're seeing is not a group of people choosing a different way of life, as I'm certain you've been told. That is a cancer that is tearing apart everything we hold dear. It isn't enough for them to live separately from us. Now, we're to blame for all their hardships."

"Are you saying they believe they've been forced into their way of life?"

"Yes. And they've grown violent. Those walls are only a couple of years old. They were necessary to keep the Deviants from stealing our resources and murdering our citizens."

Bryana focused on the movements of the people.

*Why are they congregating there?*

"I had no idea. Why haven't the regions been warned about this?"

"Some have. But the violence seems to be concentrated on the Capital, and we intend to deal with it before it spreads further."

"How?"

"By using the breakthrough your father found with you. His work has provided us with the blueprint to control our vices." A tone alerted Westmore, and he glanced at his watch. "Our ride is here. Come with me, and I'll show you what we've accomplished."

Westmore sat beside her in the luxury hover conveyance, typing away on his tablet, giving her time to sift through her thoughts. Nothing he had told her was outwardly alarming, yet she couldn't shake the feeling that she was missing something crucial. Something dangerous. For a moment, Bryana allowed herself to think about her father. He had believed deeply in their way of life and taught her to believe as well. She owed everything she was to him.

But what if he had been wrong?

The conveyance stopped in front of what appeared to be a massive, enclosed arena just inside the city wall. The smoke trail rising in the background told her they were near where she had seen the gathering of Deviants.

"What is this place?"

"This is our research facility. We have the latest equipment, the best security, and some of the finest minds in the world, all focused on dealing with our problem."

They climbed the stairs in front of the arena and entered a black granite and metal lobby. A mesh shield barred their path until Westmore approached, and it rolled out of the way. Inside was a cavernous space with a myriad of lab spaces and equipment she couldn't identify.

"What do you need from me?"

Westmore's smile took on a sinister quality this time.

"We've made an incredible breakthrough, thanks to you and your father. The data he collected on you was the key. It was of a vice in its strongest and purest form. And because of that, we now have a way to control wrath. It's only right that you be the first to be freed from sin."

Bryana stopped mid-stride, completely stunned. It took Westmore a few steps before he realized she wasn't still walking beside him. Even the self-satisfied smirk that slithered across his face barely registered. Could it be true? Could they help her finally be free of her vice?

"H-how?"

"Let me show you."

Bryana followed Westmore into a bustling office with Level Two personnel in white lab coats. None of them paid attention to the two newcomers; they kept working. The space practically thrummed with energy and excitement, and their enthusiasm for their work was contagious. She felt hope.

Westmore picked up an autoinjector, holding it for her to see. "Inside this is a new biochip. It's been upgraded with an AI program modeled after the one you use for training. The difference is that the algorithm in this biochip reacts to your body's responses and can send signals that alter them."

"So, when I start feeling angry—"

"The chip will calm you."

*It's too good to be true.*

Bryana fought to keep her emotions from overriding her thoughts, but the possibility that she could be free from her vice was all-consuming. It was something she'd believed was unattainable. Feeling overwhelmed, she leaned against the table to steady herself. The feel of the cool, smooth surface brought her focus to her hands. The scars on her hands stood out in contrast, made more grotesque by comparison.

"Is it ready to be tested?"

"We've already tested it. And the results have been remarkable. But because your vice is undiluted by anything else, we're not certain how someone like you will respond."

Bryana held out her hand without hesitation. But it wasn't her hand that Westmore wanted. He injected the new chip at the base of her neck without any preamble. Startled by the jolt of pain, Bryana instinctually braced for a rush of anger ... nothing. She felt a flicker, and then it was gone.

Westmore studied her, his self-satisfied grin growing with each passing second. She felt another flicker but no flame.

*Is it working?*

He must have anticipated her thoughts because he turned and beckoned her to follow him.

They left the lab and entered an enclosed area at the back of the arena. Metal bars twelve feet high buzzed with electricity as she walked past them. The only item inside the cage was a mirror, similar to the one she had at home. Westmore connected the white device he had used to copy her father's program to the mirror frame and exited, a transparent door sliding shut behind him. "For everyone's safety, I thought it would be best to test whether the new chip is functioning in a secure location."

Bryana agreed with the logic but still felt unsettled in a cage. Turning toward the mirror, she selected the first icon. Angry, violent images swirled across the screen. She could feel the pain and fear in them, but her anger couldn't take hold. Her excitement was growing, and even the tinge of guilt over being able to feel so thrilled while the images on the screen were still playing couldn't stop the emotion.

She hit the second icon. Once again, she could empathize with the victims, but her rage never manifested. Every flicker was extinguished before it could spark into a flame.

*I'm free!*

Tears welled in her eyes, but she didn't try to hide them. "Thank you. I-it's a miracle."

"Just the first of many. Now, all we need to do is find five more individuals with pure sins, and we'll be able to control them all."

Alarms shrieked in the back of her mind loud enough to break through and grab her attention. "Why just five more?"

Westmore looked at her like she was his new favorite toy. "Let me tell you a little story, Bryana. My grandfather was a member of the High Council, but more than that, he was a visionary. He saw the way things were going in society and was bold enough to do what was necessary to ensure a future for the best of us. He made the first moves to adjust the way we catalogue and assess people to give favor to those with exceptional minds and talent. What most people saw as the sin of pride, he recognized as a sign of greatness. I am pure greatness."

Bryana's pulse picked up steam, but all she felt was shock ... and sadness.

*No. It can't be.*

"My father continued my grandfather's work, making even greater contributions to our vision. High Council members and Assessors were hand selected based on intelligence and loyalty. Something that we eventually extended to the people in the Capital. They were disposed of if they didn't understand or accept their place in society."

Her gut clenched. "The Deviants."

"Yes. Some people decided life in the wild was preferable to what we are building here. But look around you. Our Capital is close to perfection. Only a fool would deny it."

"Why are you telling me this?"

"Because you are my gift to our new world order. While I develop the programming that will allow us to control all sin, I need assets to thin the herd."

"Excuse me?"

He rolled his eyes, speaking slower as though she was a child. "You're going to earn your keep by killing every Deviant old enough to question the authority of the High Council."

"Never."

Westmore sneered at her. "What makes you think you have a choice? That chip may keep the monster we both know you are at bay, but it works both ways." He pulled a small black remote from his pocket and pressed a button. Behind her, massive doors rolled open, revealing a horde of people being funneled toward her by an unseen force. Desperate, half-starved faces fixated on her and the crest of the High Council on her shirt. Their eyes dilated ...

She knew that look.

Turning back to Westmore, she watched as he pushed another button—

Bryana screamed as her rage surpassed anything she'd ever felt before. Her skin burned, her fists clenched, and her nails drew blood as they cut through the scar tissue into the flesh of her palm. The first wave of Deviants stopped feet from her, instinctual self-preservation making most of them pause. At least for a moment.

Three men, their anger radiating off them in waves, surrounded her.

"You. Don't. Want. This."

"You don't get to tell us what we want!" The first man yelled back.

The second man lunged at her. Bryana deflected the attack, throwing him off balance and sinking in a rear naked choke. The other two men started in for her, and she squeezed harder. Her victim sputtered, his flailing attempts to free himself slowed, and his compatriots pulled up short.

Movement caught her eye. Westmore was laughing!

*NO!*

Bryana slammed the man in her arms against the cage wall and observed as his body convulsed, collapsing to the ground while making contact with the metal bars. An instant later, she pivoted, seizing the man who had spoken to her and spinning him into the cage beside his friend. Both men were jolted in bursts as their bodies' resistance impeded the flow of electricity.

Snarling, Bryana ducked under a punch from the third man. Shooting in low, she drove her shoulder into his stomach and pushed forward with her legs. The third man desperately tried to keep his balance but fell backward into the cage. Jolts of electricity coursed through him and into Bryana, causing her new chip to pump more adrenaline into her body.

She climbed, using the man's body like a ladder, leaping to grab the top of the cage. Her skin burned, and a sharp stabbing sensation shot through her from the contact, but she didn't care. Bryana pulled herself up and over the enclosure with an ease that could only come from years of intense physical training. When her knees hit the ground outside the cage, they buckled, and she rolled through the motion. Coming to a stop, she saw Westmore smirking at her.

"I'm impressed. Your skills are outstanding. Maybe I'll keep you around after all." He raised the remote. "On a short leash, of course."

Bryana started for him as he pressed a button ... and everything changed in the blink of an eye. Her body began to shake from the adrenaline dump, and she felt a searing pain in her hands and legs. Tears fell freely, and she stumbled forward, barely catching herself as the horror of what this man and his family had done crushed her.

"That's better. Soon enough, I'll be able to make you feel however I choose. But for now, keeping you docile will suffice."

Bryana didn't move or respond as she closed her eyes, took a deep breath, and then let it out at the same pace.

*The choice is mine.*

When she opened her eyes, they were focused.

Calm.

Grounded.

She pulled the High Council Crest off her shirt and tossed it over her shoulder.

Westmore took a step backward, and she moved toward him. "What do you think you're doing?"

"My job."

"Your job is to do as I command."

"No. It's to deal with threats."

Westmore blustered. "I have no intention of letting you stop me. You'll have to kill me. And you don't have it in you anymore."

"Your mistake is thinking I need anger to do what needs to be done."

For the first time since she'd met him, Westmore looked shaken. She closed the distance between them, and he bolted. He'd only made it a few steps before she tackled him, sending them both crashing to the ground. The remote tumbled a few feet away. Air came rushing out of his lungs, and he gasped and coughed.

The sound of approaching footsteps alerted Bryana to the reinforcements. Flipping Westmore onto his stomach, she cranked his right arm behind his back and upward, using her knee to pin his hand between his shoulder blades. He screamed but couldn't move without causing himself pain.

She scanned the faces of the crowd around her. Fear and dismay permeated the group. Anxious glances at Westmore and then at each other told her everything. "You don't want to do this."

All eyes shifted to a woman with gray hair. A silver and gold crest on her lab coat. "Do you know who that is?"

"Someone who has been lying his entire life. Who has abused his position to enslave you and rob countless others of their lives."

"He's part of the High Council."

"Not anymore."

The woman appeared to agree ... then lifted a larger version of Westmore's black remote and pressed a button. The group around her tensed, and some shouted out. In an instant, they transformed, anger replacing fear. The gray-haired woman's expression remained unchanged. "Kill her."

*Westmore tested the chip on them!*

Bryana stayed low, rolling off Westmore and coming up in front of the nearest lab coat. The man lunged at her; she parried his punch and countered with a jab-cross that dropped him. Wild, erratic swings came from all directions as the mob attacked together. She ducked, dodged, and blocked as many blows as possible but still took some hits. None of the lab coats had training, but it didn't matter. Everyone has a puncher's chance, and they had the numbers.

She spun around, her backfist striking another minion, giving her a split-second to spot Westmore's remote. Diving for the device, she endured several kicks to her torso and someone yanking her hair. Grabbing the remote, she broke away and dashed toward the cage.

The Deviants she had fought inside the cage watched her from the other side of the door. One man leaned on a woman for support. All three were unsteady, still weak from their encounter with the electrified cage wall, but they were back on their feet again.

Bryana hesitated. Then looked each man in the eye. "This is your chance. Maybe your only chance ... to make things right. The choice is yours."

She used the remote and opened the cage door.

It only took a moment for the people in the cage to decide. Bryana could see their resolve. They didn't trust her, but they had nothing more to lose. It was time to fight.

If any distinct words were spoken, she didn't hear them above the roar of voices as the Deviants poured from the cage and clashed with the lab coats. Bryana pushed aside her guilt over the harm being inflicted. They were all just pawns in this game, but there was no other choice.

More light flooded the arena when the main doors opened, and Bryana spotted Westmore and the gray-haired woman fleeing. She immediately took off after them, shoving anyone who tried to stop her out of her way. Bursting out the door, she abruptly stopped when she realized a wall of people was standing in her way. Young, old, male, female ... it was like part of the city was frozen. Their eyes were vacant, unfixed, but they stood with a rigid stillness reminiscent of a synthetic. Each one held a makeshift weapon of some kind.

Westmore stood behind them with the gray-haired woman at his side.

"It's over now, Bryana. Too bad. You don't have what it takes to be one of us."

The gray-haired woman selected something on her remote, and the crowd started for her. The movements were sluggish and jerky, like they were forced. Human, but not.

*Mind control?*

"You may think you can fight them all, but, consider this: they're innocents. They have no control over what they're doing right now. Only a true monster would choose to hurt them to save themselves. Think about it. Would you be able to live with yourself if you killed an innocent?"

Bryana examined the remote in her hands more closely; each icon was crafted for Westmore's little game with her. She couldn't use it to stop the mind-control signal affecting these people or to shut down the anger coursing through the lab coats inside. She could only do one thing.

Bryana bowed her head, shifting her weight to kneel.

*Forgive me, father.*

She pressed the button to shut off her chip—the adrenaline already flooding her system hit her like a bomb blast as it funneled away from every urge except one—wrath. Her body shifted seamlessly from a kneel to a runner's lunge, and she sprinted through the crowd, barreling through bodies left and right as they mechanically stab, slash, and swing at her. Pain exploded everywhere.

She ignored it all.

Breaking through the crowd, her vision tunneled in on Westmore ... then shifted to the gray-haired woman. Bryana lunged and ripped the tablet from the woman's hands, knocking her to the ground in the process. Westmore jumped on her back, and Bryana slammed the back of her head into his nose. Screaming, Westmore stumbled backward, clutching at his broken nose, blood spilling between his fingers.

Bryana tore her attention away from Westmore, her anger making it hard to read the icons. The robotic crowd behind her inched closer. A rock sailed past her face; another impacted her hip.

*Focus, damnit!*

Finding what she needed, Bryana shut down the mind-control signal—and then the lab coat's rage. Around her, the crowd stopped. Confusion and fear ran through the group.

Glaring at Westmore, Bryana raised the remote above her head, ready to smash it.

"Stop!"

Bryana turned her glare to the gray-haired woman on the ground.

"That is the master control. If you destroy it, you destroy everything. Including the AI that can save you from your sin."

Bryana lowered the remote. Her shadowy reflection on the screen radiated intensity. Wild hair, blood flowing from her temple and nose ... eyes ... focused.

"So be it." Pivoting, she threw her entire body weight behind the swing as she bashed the tablet against Westmore's face. His head snapped around, and he dropped like dead weight as the shattered pieces of the remote showered around him.

"That choice was mine."

# Fight Club

## by David Moloney

**Officers reveled** in telling stories about brass and white shirts when they were mere mortals donning brown. There was something about their esteemed title now, the distance of time, how the orators and players were always depicted as far younger and stronger versions of their middle-aged, balding selves. Once mortal figures, the officers became victims of information distortion, and in so many retellings, had attained hero status, earned or not. This was especially true for Captain Dixon. Mike Menser had told Dixon's legendary story—about a fight club that started on Max in 2000, right after the movie of the same name came out—a pair of times to O'Brien in their few short months together: first, on a late weekend morning before chow, their clip-on ties draped over their laps, their feet up on the control panel; second, while standing together on the floor observing a fat, cross-eyed skinner washing his nuts in the curtainless shower.

Before cameras, before any eye-in-the-sky bullshit, Menser would editorialize. He usually had mint dip in his lip when in the control room. But, even when he didn't, he'd stick his tongue into his bottom lip to pad the void.

Today was a quiet Saturday—no brass, minimal radio traffic—which allowed the three officers assigned to Max some quiet hours in the unit's control room. Menser had a mint dip in his bottom lip and his boots up on the filing cabinet. Greenly sat with his hands cupped on his stomach, leaned back as far as he could in the old, cushioned desk chair, and manned the dormant control panel. The windows were tinted, and the light of the unit barely snuck in. The unit speakers were turned up, and the only sounds made were snoring and the *whoosh* of industrial toilets flushing. It was 1300 hours, and O'Brien wanted something to do, but instead he played *Tank Destroyer* on his phone.

Menser decided against letting the bubble stay quiet, and he blurted out, "O'Brien, did I ever tell you about the time I saw the captain fight an inmate down here?"

O'Brien looked up from his phone, and the way Menser exuded such enthusiasm that had been previously lacking made O'Brien shake his head and let him go on with it. Greenly had his eyes closed in a way one closes their eyes, but you can tell they're still awake.

Menser attempted to draw a loogie up his throat, but he couldn't crest it, so he withdrew the effort and swallowed, then began.

"The unit was full back then, always rocking, not like today with pussies that sleep all day. After the movie, you've seen *Fight Club*, right? The inmates got the idea to start their own. They were already on Max and weren't leaving anytime soon, so they started pairing up fights. Dixon would break them up right when they started. He didn't like the control it gave them. But I told him, I said,

'Let them fight.' He didn't agree. Dixon had a way about him. Even then, he knew he was going to be captain someday. He was quiet, like you, O'Brien. I see a lot of him in you."

O'Brien liked the compliment but wished it came from someone else.

"The fights happened so often that we were buried in paperwork. We couldn't get shit done. No tier time. Lunch barely fucking happened. I told Dixon it was safer than boxing. They had two referees, and it was definitely safer than a street fight. No weapons, no one allowed to jump in."

Menser let the story hang there for a moment. O'Brien thought about how it would have been a most humane fight for men who may not have seen a fight so civilized before. Menser was right about safety, but he missed the bigger point. The scheduled and regulated fighting lent them a humanity that they otherwise did not have inside the walls. But Dixon was hardwired into the policies and procedures, the training they were given during the in-house academy. *Strip the inmates of their individuality. Dehumanize them.* Menser couldn't see that Dixon wasn't against the violence and paperwork; rather, he was for something deeper, a conviction for maintaining the dividing line between the men in starched uniforms and the filthy offenders in orange.

Menser packed a can of tobacco in his hand and shoved a supplemental pinch of mint tobacco into his mouth. His speech changed slightly as he padded his bottom lip with his tongue.

"For some reason, maybe they wore him down, maybe he enjoyed the fights, whatever, Dixon started letting them go at it. He makes up his own rules. Each morning after a fight, he'd call them to their door grates, and he'd walk back and forth like he does, and he'd make up a rule like, 'No hitting in the face.' Or 'Stop when we say stop, or you're getting sprayed.' Then he'd pace some more and let them argue over the rule. But he wouldn't change it. He wasn't listening. He was thinking of the next rule, on the fly. I would just stand and watch. I was a rookie, and I liked fights. I liked rolling with those animals. Decent bangers, then. Woodsy, fucking Hammer, that dude Uzo. Real inmates."

Menser leaned forward and tugged at a bootlace, then spit into a Styrofoam cup. The dip juice clung to his fat bottom lip and hung like a rope to the cup. He pinched it off and sucked in the juice, then wiped his fingers on his brown pants. He'd been in shape once, but now his stomach stuck out and his shirtsleeves were too tight. He didn't shave like we were required to.

"He made up another rule. And this is what surprised me the most. He quoted straight from the movie, said, 'The most important rule is you don't talk about Fight Club.' And after he said that, the fucking place went nuts. Then, after making a promise to stop tinkering with the rules, he dropped his last one: he made the fights. He was ringmaster."

Greenly laughed, a short one, a sarcastic *ha*. He put his legs up on the panel and crossed them without moving his clasped hands from his belly or opening his eyes.

"You weren't there."

Menser spat again, leaned forward, and stared at Greenly. O'Brien had put his phone away and watched Menser squirm, fearful his story would be ruined or, worse, ridiculed.

Greenly, still unmoving, said, "You weren't either. Martinez was on the floor when it happened. He told me. You were up in the bubble spectating."

"Martinez lies. Bullshit, I wasn't on the floor. *He* was up here. Fucking Martinez." Menser spat again, but it didn't look like he had any.

"Keep going. I love this part," Greenly said.

Menser looked right at O'Brien like he wasn't telling the story anymore to Greenly.

"This cat Grieves, young kid, but he threw hands real nice, won the Golden Gloves when he was like sixteen. Dixon hated the kid, big mouth. Dixon pairs him up with the biggest dudes right down the line. Grieves was a buck thirty soaking wet. He had a wicked left, lung-shot. He started knocking guys down with his body hooks. No more face shots, so Grieves thrived in Dixon's concrete ring. Everyone wanted to fight him, then no one wanted to fight him. We'd pop the doors, and two fighters would come out. The spectators watched through the grates. Grieves never threw first. He'd bounce like a kangaroo all over and shit, dangling his arms. No one could hit him. Then he'd throw one left into the stomach, and that'd be all she wrote. *Boom*. One and done. Got to ten in a row at one point."

Greenly interrupted. "Grieves was a little bitch." He pulled his legs down from the panel. "Every time you tell this story, Grieves knocks down more guys. Martinez said he knocked down one before he fought Dixon, and it was the kid with the prosthetic leg."

"Where's Martinez now? That's right, fucking rotting on third shift. Martinez doesn't know his ass from his elbow. Grieves was a tough prick. You going to believe Martinez over me, OB?"

"It's your story. I believe you," O'Brien said. But O'Brien just wanted the story to end. He already knew how it did, and it wasn't worth filling their hungover silence.

"It is my story." Menser gave a long look at Greenly, who shook his head calmly, like he was too cool to care either way, like if Martinez were telling the story, Greenly would be doing the same thing.

"To make a long story short, the inmates start riding Dixon. We had to stop the fights if they didn't stop on their own. Dixon got rough like he wanted to play, too. He started digging elbows and arm-barring, and some of the inmates didn't like it. They started saying, if he's so tough, why doesn't he fight Grieves? And you know Dixon, he's got those cauliflower ears and he's strong as shit. I think he was excited at the thought."

The control room radio beeped. The officer in second-floor control notified them that an inmate was returning from court. O'Brien and Menser only had ten more minutes before they'd have to go back on the floor.

Menser positioned his clip-on tie and snapped the fastener over his shirt's throat latch. He continued. "And it was doable. Dixon and Grieves. We weren't writing reports. As far as the brass or anyone else was concerned, the fights did not happen. The inmates were perfect little soldiers during Fight Club. They'd shake hands and shower after and do their tier time. They got their aggression out on each other. I tell you, it was fucking healthy for them."

"Dixon doesn't say shit about the fight. He won't say yes or no. He clams up. Suddenly, he's got nothing to say. I'd watch him, and he'd seem the same, but there was something going on upstairs. Like he had already broken same major fucking rules and crossed the line, but fighting an orange shirt was dark side shit. After a week, we're standing out on the floor after a good scrum, I think it was Hammer and Holmes, and he starts telling me, out of nowhere, about how when he was a kid, his dad beat the shit out of him. How he started with belts and shoes, whatever in reach, and then when Dixon got bigger, it was straight fists."

Menser stopped to spit again.

Greenly turned to him with open eyes and said, "You've never said anything about Dixon's dad. This is new material." He smiled, and his white teeth, perfectly straight, stood out in the dark control room. His wife worked in Boston and was the breadwinner, like most of the officer's wives. Menser told O'Brien she had Greenly whiten his teeth and had him get braces a few years before their wedding. He played football at Penn State, and he could deadlift a tree trunk from out of the ground, but there was a reason why he was still in brown after all those years and why his teeth sparkled in the dark.

O'Brien had never heard this part, either. It was what made most of Menser's stories, at the very least, suspenseful.

"I never thought it as essential. I got to give you something Martinez can't, right? Because he wasn't there. I was."

This development interested O'Brien. He could see Menser, who was not a bright man, trying to build upon a one-dimensional war story by adding a theme, and O'Brien was curious to see if Menser was aware enough to tie it all together.

The office chair squeaked as Menser stood. He tucked his loose shirt in over his round belly. O'Brien reattached his tie as he waited for Menser to continue. O'Brien sensed Greenly was doing the same.

Menser leaned against a blackout shade. He continued. "Dixon tells me his dad took to wrestling him drunk at night. When Dixon got good and won States his freshman year of high school, his dad woke him up in bed that night and took him by the back of his neck in his boxers out to the front yard in the dark, and he slapped him a few times to get him into it. Dixon said he took his dad down in the grass. His old man worked in a lumberyard and landscaped and had these cuts and blisters always on his hands. He coated them in Blistex and swore by it. Dixon said he couldn't smell the booze on him. Rarely could. Or maybe he doesn't remember that for a reason. He smelled more like the menthol Blistex and wet wood. Said he'd never forget that smell. In the grass, he got hold of his dad and choked him until he was almost dead. He got quiet and looked up at the closed doors, and I could see his eyes changed like he got sad. And it was weird to see his face go to that shape. Then, after a few minutes of quiet, he said he could sometimes still feel his dad's hand on the back of his neck. Then he didn't talk about it again."

"Sounds more like a therapy session," Greenly said, but his tone had changed from mocking to sincere.

"Dixon wouldn't love the idea of you possessing this story of him getting all sentimental on the floor," O'Brien said. A booking officer radioed for the west wing elevator to be released. They only had a few more minutes for Menser to wrap up.

Menser also appeared to consider the clock and continued.

"He does a round and comes back and tells me he's going to tell the LT about Fight Club. He doesn't say why, and I don't tell him not to. I spent that whole afternoon and night sick to my stomach. I felt like I had committed a crime or something. I felt shitty for Dixon. He was a superstar here, and he fucked it up to let inmates bang on each other for fun because of some movie."

Greenly was silent and not smiling and watched Menser as intently as O'Brien had been. A toilet flushed, and the whoosh came through the monitor, and an officer called for a door on the second floor of the building over the radio. Menser relished in the moment, the stage, his tale at its crescendo, and he spat into the cup then went on.

"But Dixon doesn't tell the LT. The next day, I come on the unit, and it's O-six-hundred, and the whole unit's awake, talking about Dixon versus Grieves. Dixon never said nothing to me. At O-eight hundred, he takes his radio off and hands it to me. Then, his badge. I think the badge thing was more symbolic than anything, like he was just a man fighting another man, respecting Fight Club. He calls for Grieves's door, and Grieves comes out with his long arms hanging, and he's doing his kangaroo thing. Dixon is standing straight up like some old-timey boxer you see in black-and-white movies and shit. The inmates are cheering for Grieves, this white boy who's beaten all the blacks and Puerto Ricans. This was before the whites took over.

"Grieves must have had a tell, like in poker, or tipped his pitch or something, because Dixon hits him with a right, just below his eye, and Grieves falls over and sprawls out flat in the dayroom. If you blinked, you missed it. Silence. Nothing. No, 'Dixon cheated!' Or, 'Dixon broke his own rule!' It was just over. That was a wrap on Fight Club. Dixon beating Grieves like that sucked the fun out of it. "

Menser fingered the dip from his lip and dropped it in the cup as if to conclude his story with a disposable action. The men in the control room took the new addition to the story in. O'Brien thought it brave for Menser to tell something he probably never anticipated he'd ever tell. If true, the thing about Dixon and his dad was raw and sad, and picturing Dixon as a boy out in the yard wrestling his loaded old man was a lasting image, instructive even, providing O'Brien with a complicated picture of who his captain was.

Greenly spun the office chair when he heard the outer unit door click open. He released the control room's inner door and, without ceremony, Menser exited with O'Brien in tow.

They met the booking officer at the outer door and led the returning inmate onto the unit floor. O'Brien needed more practice with pat searches, so he didn't hesitate to order the inmate to the wall. As he made his way down the inmate's bony chest—palms facing in, thumbs pointed up—a feeling of intimacy overcame him, and he realized his body was out of position: his nose perched on the shoulder, chest against back, like a prom photo. When he recognized his awkwardness, he pretended to feel something in the breast pocket, then moved to the waistband. Another cozy moment as O'Brien ran his index fingers—one clockwise, the other counter—along the waistband. He had been entrusted with maintaining the safety and security of the jail, and he took it seriously, so he was surprised how flustered he was by this routine search, the closeness, and decided to focus on the movement of his fingers only to discover, upon completion, the motion was like drawing a heart in the air.

O'Brien rushed through the lower half, then he ordered the inmate to go to his cell. As he followed, with Menser close behind and breathing heavily, he had the urge to say something, anything, so he asked, "How'd court go?"

The inmate continued his slow walk.

"You don't ask him that," Menser said.

Once secured, O'Brien wanted to be away from Menser, so he broke from him and began to make a round.

"OB," Menser said.

O'Brien stopped in front of the metal stairs, and Menser shuffled over to him.

"Settle something for me," he said. He sniffed. "What difference does it make if I was on the floor or up there for that fight? Huh? I still would have seen it. And it still happened, so it doesn't fucking matter."

Menser walked towards the property closet. O'Brien continued his round of the unit, starting on the lower level. He passed the heavy doors, snuck a glance inside each cell, and counted sleeping bodies. As he walked, it occurred to him that there must have been a reason why Menser was so inclined to retell this story, even in the face of an unreceptive audience. O'Brien chewed it over as he wrapped up the round and headcount. As he rounded the mezzanine, he got eyes on Menser, who stood just inside the property closet's threshold, out of camera view, scrolling on his phone. O'Brien understood Menser had an unkind opinion of himself. It was in the way he blinked when thinking, as if blinking functioned like an engine starter. It was in the way he would take four bagged lunches, intended for the inmates, up to the control panel after chow. It was in his eyes. He told Fight Club. Expounded on particulars so he could build himself up. Make himself important. O'Brien could give him the satisfaction he so craved. As he observed Menser hiding in the closet, scrolling on the phone he wasn't supposed to have, he decided to never become the officer that Menser was. O'Brien's peers would never ridicule his stories. He would never eat lunch alone. The job would never break him.

O'Brien moved along the mezzanine railing, satisfied that he had come to an understanding. The dayroom smelled like bleach, and the chili the inmates had for dinner the night before. As he bounced down the metal stairs, he looked around at the dayroom tables and wondered where Dixon had knocked out Grieves. He weaved through the tables, investigating the past, searching for a clue that would reveal facts to bear witness to the record. As the inmates slept and snored, as Greenly dreamt in the control room, and as Menser looked for love on a phone app, O'Brien kept sniffing around and asking himself: Was it here? Was it here? Was it here?

# Conor McGregor was a Friend of Mine

## by J.B. Stevens

### 1.

**Hank didn't get** the punch mitt up in time.

Latisha's fist skimmed the top of the leather, caught him on the point of his chin, and everything went dark.

As his eyes opened, he saw the raw pipes that lined the exposed ceiling. "Was I out long?"

Latisha knelt to his side with her boxing glove on his shoulder. "Just a second. You got knocked out by a girl."

"You're not a girl—you're a fighter."

"Your brain okay?"

He smacked his skull. "Not much of it left." He closed his eyes and massaged his temples. The slight headache drifted away. The ringing in his ears, there since the war, remained. "It's basically useless."

"You always seemed slow. Come on. Let's work. I need that win, and we don't have a lot of time left."

He rolled over and pressed himself up.

The round timer beeped, the session began, and Latisha's glove slammed into her target. The impact caused sweat to fly off Hank's elbow, catching and refracting a bit of sunlight. It cut through dusty, damp air that smelled of adrenaline, old sweat, and cleaning products.

They moved together through the room, relaxed and familiar with one another's patterns. Hank knew it looked like a dance, and he loved it. All of his problems floated away, and he simply existed.

Latisha jabbed as Toto's *Africa* started up on the gym's sound system. She was a bit shorter than Hank and in above-average shape. She'd grown up in a rough part of Savannah with her mom and brother. Mom had worked as a hair braider right up until she passed.

Latisha punched.

Hank brought the mitt forward with a slap, and a satisfying *pop* echoed off the cinderblock walls. "Hands up, protect the chin."

She did as she was told, just like always. She was a quick learner and possessed an almost photographic memory for combative techniques.

Hank circled right, ignoring the pain in his foot—it bothered him on humid days. Latisha cut the angle and forced him to the left, her dominant side, just like they'd practiced.

"Good."

She dipped her chin and threw a straight right. *Pop.*

"Teep."

Latisha brought her rear knee up and jutted out the ball of her foot, catching Hank in the pad covering his belly button. *Pop.*

The kick sent him back two steps. "Good stuff!"

She bit down on the mouthpiece and circled to her strong side.

He loved preparing her, even if he didn't love the idea of her fighting for Sergio. "You sure about this?"

She nodded. "The bills keep coming. I'm running out of time. My whole life feels past due."

"Jab."

*Pop.*

Hank shifted positions. "Sergio's the shadiest promoter for a thousand miles. Hell, he's just a scumbag in general."

"Don't care. I need this," Latisha said.

"Jab."

*Pop.*

He lowered the punch mitt. "And if I refuse to get you ready?"

"I'm still taking the fight."

"Jab."

*Pop.*

He nodded. "I figured, but I had to try." Hank put his palms, one on top of the other, in front of his gut and pointed them to the floor. "Clinch, four knees, go!"

She faked a kick, stepped forward, and cupped the back of his head. Her forearms levered on his neck, pulling down his face. She shot four knees straight up, hard, lifting him off the ground, released the clinch, and stepped back, circling right.

He moved his hands. "Lead hook."

She slid an inch forward, rotated her core, and drove her fist toward his chin.

*Pop.*

Her tattoo, a half-man/half-spider thing, quivered.

Hank pointed at it. "Remind me, what's with the bug?"

"Anansi, he's a trickster from African folklore."

"Cool." He brought both mitts to his right, stacked on top of one another. "Switch kick."

Latisha's shin crashed into the target.

"Good stuff. How much is Sergio paying you?"

"We agreed on two hundred to show, two thousand to win, and he'll give me fifty tickets to sell—I get to keep the cash."

Hank's jaw clenched. The win money was way too high, and the fight was so close. She was being set up.

The wall clock beeped, and Hank dropped the mitts. "Let's get some water."

As she went to the fountain, Hank grabbed his bottle and sat on the wooden bench. She'd only fought MMA once, and it hadn't gone well. Her cardio was good, and her strikes were elite, but her grappling was as pathetic as Hank's love life.

Hank lowered the bottle. "Do you know the name of the opponent?"

"Not yet. But Sergio swore it's a fair fight."

"I'm sure he did." Hank shook his head. "Sergio's a promoter. He's here to build up his fighters, make a star, and sell tickets. If you're not the star, you're the victim."

"Doesn't matter. I got you on my side. Plus, the money."

"What about your day job?"

"I need more than minimum wage and free sandwiches. I'm tired of struggling. I want to be sitting on the beach back in Jamaica, sipping a fruity drink with a little pink umbrella in it."

"There're better ways to get there than getting punched in the face."

"For a kid from Yamacraw with a GED?"

"What about the military?"

"How'd that work out for you?"

His mind flashed to Baghdad. "Fair point."

Latisha nodded. "If you think of that better way, let me know."

"I will."

The front door opened, and Hank looked to the entrance.

Sergio stood there, backlit in the frame.

## 2.

Sergio always looked like he'd just glided out of a steam room. His hair, skin, hands—they always seemed damp. Between that and the tracksuit, he could have been an extra on *The Sopranos*.

As he strolled onto the mats, he raised his left hand. "My favorite fighter and my favorite has-been."

Hank grimaced. "Has-been?"

"I heard you got kicked off the force for attacking someone with a bird."

"I'm suspended, and I didn't attack anyone. I was chasing a fugitive. The situation got weird. A guy hunting with a falcon happened to be nearby. I used the available tools to get the job done." Hank pointed at Sergio's feet. "No shoes."

Sergio looked down. "Always clucking with the bossiness. I heard it was a vulture with a venereal disease. And the bird ran down a schoolteacher."

"From who?"

"Doesn't matter. I don't care. I come bearing gifts."

"What kind?"

"Easy money for simple work."

Hank frowned. "I've accepted your 'gifts' before. Fool me once ... "

"Sorry that you've made thousands of dollars off me for an hour of your time. You're a victim."

"There's still glitter inside my truck. I've cleaned it seven times."

Sergio rubbed the corners of his eyes. "Suck it up. Now, let's talk—back in the office."

"Fine." Hank gestured to the side of the training area. "Walk around the edge."

"Yes, sir. Captain Thomas." He stomped across the center of the mats, into the office, and took the seat behind the desk.

Hank followed. "Get out of my chair."

"It's not yours." He didn't move. "You're the help."

"Gustavo's letting me run the place while he's away, so it's mine." He leaned in. "Move."

Sergio rose and went to the other side of the desk.

Hank sat. It was warm. "What do you want?"

"I need something. Immediately. You need money, fast. Our interests have aligned."

"How do I know you'll pay?" Sonny Liston, a stray cat Hank was looking out for, jumped into his lap. "You stiffed me on my last fight."

"Incorrect. We didn't sell enough tickets. Conor McGregor was supposed to make an appearance—he's a friend of mine. That would've had attendance through the roof. When Conor chose to stay in Dublin and announced it on Instagram, things went south. You know how it goes. That Irish prick didn't want to come to Savannah for St. Patrick's. Anyone ever say you look a bit like him? Like maybe if his mama was Spanish?"

"I don't care about what McGregor does on vacation." Hank scratched Sonny behind the ears, and the cat purred. "I care about you not paying me."

"Go back and read your contract. It says, 'up to', not 'shall.' I paid you more than I could afford. I lost money. I did you a solid. You do this new job for me, and I'll pay cash now." He touched his pocket.

Hank rubbed his chin. If only someone would put Sergio in his place—teach him, you can't mess with people forever and get away with it.

Sergio sneezed. "It's a nothing gig. A few hours' work for good pay. Can you get rid of the cat?"

"I like Sonny more than you. The cat stays." Sergio's offers always included hidden strings. But he was late on the electric bill, and the clock was ticking. "How much are you paying?"

"More than your last four fights put together," Sergio said.

"What's the gig?"

"You know my nephew?"

"Jimmy, the drug addict?"

"Settle down—the kid has a problem. It's a disease. Let he who is without sin throw the first stone and all that. He's a good kid at heart."

"I remember the time he fixed the senior center bingo game and stole the prize. He's a peach."

"Mistakes have been made. Anyway, Jimmy has this lady he spends time with. Things went a bit sideways."

"I'm an out-of-work cop. I can't get her, or anyone else, out of legal trouble."

Sergio leaned back. "There's no getting out of this one."

"Is she locked up?"

"No. They were partying, and she snorted something spiked. We think it was fentanyl. She's in the back of Jimmy's car. They're parked outside the emergency room."

"What do you need me for? Get her inside."

"Jimmy has priors. I don't need him accidentally catching a new charge. His stupid ginger girlfriend—she loves smack. I need someone that's in good with the cops to walk her inside right now. That's all."

Hank bit his lip. If the girl needed help, and he got her help, he was doing something good. "They're already parked outside?"

"Yup. You go over there and say you want your hand checked out. Say it hurts on account of all the fighting. Whatever, make up a legit reason to be at the ER. You saw her on the curb, freaked out, and brought her in. You're a good Samaritan. However, if that red-headed slut is dead and—"

Hank slammed his fist on the desk. “Stop talking.” The cup of pencils jumped, fell, and rolled to the floor. Sonny darted off.

“Wow, wow, wow. Slow down, Wyatt Earp.”

“I’m not helping you with a corpse. You text Jimmy and order him to get the girl inside now, or I’m calling the cops.”

He sneered. “Over a junkie? You serious?”

“Get out your phone.” Hank stood and walked behind Sergio. “I’m watching you send the message, or you’re not leaving.”

“Dudley Do-Right over here.” Sergio didn’t move.

“I’m serious.”

“Fine.” Sergio typed out a message. “Get the girl inside. It’s your only play. Understood?” He sent it.

Jimmy texted back, “She’s not breathing.”

Sergio: “You’re not a doctor. Do the right thing before the pigs start oinking.”

Jimmy: “K.”

Sergio: “Promise?”

Jimmy: “Yeah.”

Sergio pocketed the phone and looked over his shoulder. “We good?”

“Not even remotely,” Hank said. “But I’ll let this one go.”

Sergio got up. “Again, sorry about the hawk with herpes.”

“Funny. Before you leave, what’s the name of Latisha’s opponent?”

“Can’t remember, but it doesn’t matter, girl’s a nobody. Latisha’s gonna mop the mats with her.”

"Sure. Now leave my office."

He smirked. "It's Gustavo's office."

Hank got up, grabbed Sergio by the collar, shoved him out, and slammed the door.

On the other side, he heard Sergio. "Latisha, come talk to me outside in my SUV."

Hank frowned.

"We talking about my fight?"

"And something else. You need money? I need a problem taken care of. I think you're just the lady for the job. You don't have any priors, right? You know that emergency room over by the Army base?"

"Yeah."

Hank jerked the door open and walked to the training area, but the gym was already empty. He went outside and watched the car pull off.

He texted Latisha. "Don't do him any favors. He will screw you."

A while later, she texted back, "I got this. See you at training."

He wanted to respond but didn't know what to say.

## 3.

Hank was on top of Latisha, dropping gentle elbows—just enough to keep her moving. The gym's air was sticky, and he was having a hard time finding his breath.

He threw a strike. "Move your hips. You can't push me off, but you can slide like a shrimp sideways. Use your core. Protect your face."

She crunched left, then right, and got her feet onto Hank's hips.

He gently tried to get back to top position. "Push me away and stand. Be ready to defend and throw that trailing uppercut."

She kicked him off and jumped up. He did a drop-step, going for a double-leg takedown. She unleashed a perfectly-timed punch, pulling back the power before taking out Hank's nose.

"Great work."

She circled right, taking a deep breath.

He faked a jab and went for another takedown. She mistimed her strike and ended up on her back with Hank to her side, chest-to-chest.

He started with low-speed overhand punches. She took a deep pull of air, got her feet on his hips, and shoved him off, immediately popping up into her fighting stance.

Hank tapped the mat. "I need a break. You taking one?"

Latisha pulled off her gloves. "No, going to jump rope."

She walked to the other side of the gym. She had a chance to go far, even into the UFC, and maybe win a belt. A lot more than he'd ever done.

Hank smiled—Latisha was breaking her family's pattern of squandering talent. She'd once told him that her mother had been a beautiful singer who'd developed throat cancer young due to a three-pack-a-day habit. Her dad was a superstar in triple-A baseball but never made it to the majors on account of the booze. And her oversized brother—he'd signed to play football for the Georgia Bulldogs, but before he arrived in Athens, he got high and lost an arm while screwing around with a train.

Hank sipped water and listened to the rhythmic slap of her rope hitting the mat. The round timer beeped. He set down his water bottle. "Let's work on your Thai clinch."

She walked over and went for her gloves.

"Leave them." He gestured to the center of the mat, and she came over. "Now, if your opponent tries to get in tight, what comes next?"

"Knees."

He nodded. "Only when her hands are occupied. Got to watch out for the takedowns." Hank stepped in. "Control my neck, break my posture, and slam your knee through my face like you're trying to touch the ceiling."

She palmed the back of his head. "Like this?"

"Exactly."

She gently threw two knees.

"Perfect. One of those sneaks through, and it's game over." He grinned. "Now, the easiest way for me to escape is dropping my hips low, and that sets up your guillotine."

"Guillotine? I'm not here to choke people. I'm here to knock them out."

"Everyone knows about your strikes. And they will try to avoid them. The blonde is going to try to get you to the ground." Hank put in his mouthpiece. "I'm gonna hit the double. As I come in, bump your hip a bit, make me think you're fighting the takedown. Then, when my head gets right up against you, my ear on your hip, cup my chin, and suck my skull into your armpit. Let me drive forward. Overhook my far arm, clasp the back side of your own hand. One foot in my hip, one over the back. Turn to your hip, arch, and wait for my tap. Ready?"

She got into her fighting stance. "Yup."

Hank lowered his hips and drove forward. His hands caught the back of her legs, and he put a cheek against her side.

She did exactly as he instructed, cupping the chin, overhooking and clasping her hands, then sinking the choke.

Hank tapped. "Good job."

She released. "Now what?"

"We practice the guillotine defense until it's second nature."

They drilled the move for an hour. When they were done, she could defend the choke in her sleep.

## 4.

Hank slid the grey metal chair behind the desk next to his. Latisha sat.

As she settled in, Sonny jumped into her lap.

"He likes you. You have a cat?"

"No. I always wanted one, though." The cat purred.

"Sonny needs a permanent home. You want to adopt him?"

She scratched behind the cat's ears. "He can't stay here?"

"Gustavo doesn't want hair everywhere."

"Why don't you take him?"

"With the day job, if I ever get back to it, I travel too much."

She smiled. Then her face dropped. "My landlord doesn't allow pets."

"Last time I dropped you off, cats and dogs were everywhere."

Latisha shrugged. "My neighbors don't care much about the rules."

"And you do?"

"When I have to."

Hank frowned. "What do you mean?"

"If I knew I wouldn't get caught or the risk was worth the reward, I'd break them. But not this time. I can't get kicked out."

"If things change, you'll give him a home?"

"Yes."

She grinned and rubbed Sonny's head.

Hank rotated the computer monitor so they both could see. Then, he went to Sergio's social media page. "They put out the first promo for your bout."

He clicked, and an image came up. The headline fighters, two local guys with good records, were at the top. Down below, on the third line, was a small picture of Latisha with her fists raised. Next to her was a pretty blonde in a wrestling stance.

"Look at her posture," Hank said. "We need to go over grappling defense again."

"Sergio swore it's a fair matchup."

"I'm sure he did. I trust him as far as I can throw him. What did he want from you the other day when you went for a ride?"

She hesitated, taking far longer to answer than normal. "I promised if I saw Jimmy trying to buy anything in my neighborhood, I'd call Sergio."

"That's it?"

"Yeah." She looked down and away. "I guess Sergio assumes since I live in the hood, I spend time around drug dealers."

"He's a jackass." Hank moved the wheel on his mouse, zooming in on the other girl's image. Her name was underneath in small print. "Sergio told me about some problem Jimmy was having with his Irish girlfriend. Sounded like a medical issue. Did he ask you to help with that?"

"Nope."

"Good. Be careful. He'll try to trick you."

She shrugged. "I'm pretty tricky myself."

Hank googled the blonde opponent. "She has a ton of wrestling matches."

Latisha leaned in. "She probably doesn't know jack about striking."

Hank wanted to say, *and you couldn't stop an outside trip from a geriatric cancer patient.*

He actually said, "You have an advantage on the feet, for sure. We need to keep her from grabbing you, maintain distance, keep outside—in punching range. Minimal kicks. Zero takedowns. You need a good game plan."

"And you can help with that."

"Yes, I can. You just have to follow it."

“I always do.” Latisha sat back. “Speaking of help, you don’t have a freezer, do you? A big one, with a lock.”

Hank turned away from the monitor. “That’s a weird question. No, why?”

“I need to keep a lot of meat fresh.”

“You get a side hustle as a butcher?”

“No. My brother bought a whole dead goat. He got a deal, and we need to keep it cold. You know us Jamaicans —love our goat.”

Hank pictured gigantic Demetrius, carrying the animal with his one arm, moseying by with his too-cool saunter. “When did he get out of jail?”

“About a week ago. The robbery charges were dropped. No one was home, no witnesses to the alleged breaking and entering. They can’t prove it was him. Anyway, about the freezer—”

“Hold up. Why does the freezer need to lock?”

“You’ve seen where I live. Can’t keep nothing.”

“I guess that makes sense. Either way, I don’t have a freezer, only the fridge. But if anyone mentions one, I’ll let you know.”

“Thanks, coach.” Latisha stood. “I need it, fast, before the meat spoils.”

“Makes sense. Don’t want things to go bad.”

“I hate it when things work out the wrong way.”

## 5.

Hank worked for the choke. His heels were on the inside of Latisha’s thighs. His arms were over one shoulder and under one armpit. He squeezed and held on, looking for an opening.

Latisha's heart rate was steady and smooth, slower than his. She controlled his attacking arm, the one over her shoulder, with both of her hands and tried to get her back flat on the mat on the opposite side—the correct technique.

Her grappling defense was coming along perfectly. He grinned—he was helping, moving her skills to the next level. There was no way anyone on the local circuit was going to get a choke on her. Her defense was too good.

He moved his right hand to her shoulder. "I found your opponent on Instagram."

"And?"

"I'm worried," Hank said. "She's a judo black belt, state wrestling champ, and pretty."

Latisha's eyes narrowed. "And I'm not."

"She's the type that Sergio can make money off of. He's trying to exploit both of you. I say we ruin Sergio's scheme. Hit him in the wallet with this fight."

She grinned. "I'll shave a few zeros off his bank account. You can bet on it."

"Great attitude. Remember the plan. Keep her on the outside, then jab her in the nose until her whole universe is your left fist. Make her bleed, suffer." He squeezed. "Now, escape my choke."

She got her back flat and twisted away from his choking arm.

Hank grinned. "Flawless. Where'd you learn that grip detail?"

"I watched that YouTube video you recommended."

"And you're already hitting the technique?" He tried to slide his right knee across her thigh and into full mount.

"Yeah." She pushed his leg and got to guard.

"Awesome." He threw some light punches. She raised her hands, underhooked her foot on his thigh, and swept him over—landing in mount.

She threw slow, gentle, arcing elbows. "Got you."

"Yes, you did." He tapped her on the side.

She stopped and jumped up. "And your winner is ... "

Flat on his back, with his eyes closed, Hank responded. "Latisha Johnson."

The bell chimed. "Grab something to drink. I'm going to top off Sonny's water."

When he returned, he grabbed his bottle. Under it rested three one-hundred-dollar bills. "What's this?"

She looked over. "Payment for training."

"Where'd you get this much cash? I thought you were hurting?"

"Sergio paid me for that thing with Jimmy, keeping him out of the hood."

Hank tilted his head to the left. He didn't want to take the money, but his mortgage was due. Add in the fact that his cop career was almost certainly over, and he could really use the cash. No, it wasn't right. He was here to help her, not the other way around.

He tried to give it back.

She smiled and pushed it onto him. "I insist."

He shouldn't, but he was becoming desperate. "Only this one time. No more, okay?"

"K."

As the bell rang and they moved back to the mat, the front door opened and sunlight blasted the dusty space.

Sergio walked in, wearing a Rolex and a gaudy gold chain. "Latisha." He raised a manila envelope.

"What?"

"Tickets and the rest of the cash for that favor."

Latisha took the envelope.

Sergio winked at Hank. "You messing around with any more of them seagulls with syphilis?"

"Funny."

"I thought so. See you later, Birdman." Sergio left.

She walked to Hank. "He is such a douche."

"That's why we're going to do everything we can to get your hand raised at the end of this."

She nodded and opened the package. There was a thick stack of bills and a wad of tickets.

Hank squinted. "That looks like a lot."

She closed the envelope. "He paid me in fives and tens, not hundreds."

"Oh."

Two rounds later, the bell rang, and he checked the wall clock. "It's time for my next client."

"Who is it?"

"Thaddius."

"That spoiled brat kid from the Ford plantation?"

Hank nodded. "Daddy says Thad is being bullied."

"They have bullies at Savannah Country Day?" She

pulled off her gloves.

"I suspect he's the bully, and I'm making him better at it."

"So the rich kid learns how to fight and be a more effective jerk?"

"Money can do amazing things."

"I wouldn't know." She took a drink. "But I hope to find out."

Before Hank could answer, Thaddius walked in.

Hank waved him over. "You want some tickets to Latisha's upcoming bout? Maybe you buy some for your friends?"

Latisha laughed and walked into the women's locker room.

"Pay for some local cage fights?" Thaddius sneered. "I went to the last UFC in Atlanta. Do you really think I'm going to waste my time watching a GameStop cashier beat up a Walmart stock boy?"

Latisha called out from behind the closed door. "I'm a sandwich artist—you judgmental prick."

Thaddius scoffed. "Exactly. How about this? Give me ten tickets. I sell them at a huge markup to idiots at my school and split the profit with you."

Latisha opened the door. "Fine." She opened the envelope and gave him ten. "You'll do just about anything for cash, won't you?"

"Yup."

# 6.

Debi's, a Savannah breakfast institution, smelled of fried bacon, the table was sticky with syrup, and silverware clinked against plates. The ceiling featured rough-hewn wooden beams, and the floor was ancient brick.

Hank held his mug. Across the table, Latisha sipped black coffee and ate a western omelet—no yolks. She eyed his French toast with its thick maple syrup and powdered sugar—but she didn't say anything. Cutting weight meant she must abstain from empty carbs, no matter how tasty they were.

She chewed a slice of egg white. "I got that freezer. You don't have to look anymore."

He had a tinge of guilt. He hadn't been looking, but as long as it all worked out, no big deal. "Glad to hear it."

"About my fight ... "

"Yeah?"

She lowered her fork. "I want to bet on myself."

"With how hard you train—" Hank raised his coffee, full of cream and sugar, and took a sip, "you bet on yourself every day."

"No, not the after-school special bet-on-yourself junk. I wanna gamble."

He took a bite. It's not like the bout was on pay-per-view. Also, ethically, gambling on yourself to win felt okay. But bookmakers, all the people running around the local fight-betting scene, weren't exactly on the up-and-up. Was it worth the risk? And, even if it was, who would deal with him? Sure, he could ask around—but most of them knew he was law enforcement. They didn't care that he was suspended. Even if he wanted to help, and he wasn't sure he did, he probably couldn't.

He swallowed. "You know a bookie?"

"No, but Thaddius said he does and would handle it for a price. No one will know it was me."

Hank set down his fork. Latisha needed cash—she'd made that clear. She had no one to help her, and she was sending money back home to Jamaica. But what if she lost? She was good, but nothing was guaranteed in the fight game, and Sergio was obviously banking on the blonde to win.

"If you're worried about money, I got some savings. I could loan you—"

She shook her head. "You're unemployed."

"Temporarily."

"You getting a paycheck?"

"No."

"The day job—is it restarting soon?"

"No." His mind flashed to the fugitive criminal's messed up eye and the falcon's bloody talons. "My boss is recommending dismissal."

"Exactly. I can't take your money. I'm taking the bet."

## 7.

Campus Chaos 7 took place at a local college recreation center on a steamy Saturday night. The smell from the river seeped in, and your shirt stuck to your back. Inside the venue, a black chain-link cage sat on a platform in the middle of a small basketball gym. Plastic folding tables marked VIP were in front. Behind was a ring of folding chairs and then a few rows of bleachers.

A series of curtained-off closet-sized spaces in the back of the gym served as makeshift changing rooms. In the third one, Hank pressed the rough-textured white athletic tape between Latisha's knuckles. He examined his work—he could smell the adhesive. The wrap job looked good.

He slipped on her gloves. "Keep her outside. No take-downs. No grappling. Jab. Don't let her grab you."

"Got it." She turned up the volume on her Bluetooth speaker as it played the Wu-Tang Clan song "Protect Ya Neck."

"Where's your brother?"

"Probably somewhere up to no good." She flexed her hands and smashed her fist into her palm.

"Sorry."

She shrugged. "Things come up."

"Fair enough."

The ratty velvet curtain fluttered and opened—the athletic commission's rep was there. Hank nodded. The rep came over and grabbed Latisha's gloves. He immediately signed his name on the glove-sealing tape—he didn't actually inspect the gloves. Hank could've messed with them in just about any way he'd wanted. Hopefully, the other girl's coach didn't try anything shady—there were always so many scams floating on the edges of these small-time local fights. You never knew who had some scheme running in the background—who was dishonest.

The rep left, and Hank squeezed Latisha's shoulder. "Let's get warmed up."

"Cool."

The two of them worked the punch mitts and did some light grappling defense and avoidance. Hank kept stressing the plan: no takedowns or kicks, jab the blond in the face until her will breaks, stay on the outside.

Twenty minutes later, a short guy poked his head through. "Latishia Johnson?"

"That's me."

"You ready?"

"Bet on it."

"Come out when you hear your music."

"Good to go."

The curtain dropped, and the lights dimmed.

Hank grabbed his bucket with water, ice bags, towels, cold presses, and cut-management supplies.

A moment later, Latisha's walk-out song— "Breaking the Law" by Judas Priest—started up. The music echoed off the cinderblock walls.

Hank's heart rate exploded. He looked at Latisha. Her jaw clenched, and her eyes narrowed. She shook out her arms.

He gave her a fist bump. "You got this."

"Hell yeah."

An overweight security guard led them through a short tunnel and onto a ramp to the side of the cage. The venue was half-full.

Latisha's eyes were low and she bounced on the balls of her feet.

There was a hoot, and Hank glanced over. It was Sergio. He sat at a ringside table with a large-chested woman who looked young enough to have learned about 9/11 on TikTok.

Sergio raised his glass. "Birdman."

Hank nodded.

Latisha entered the cage, and Hank went to their corner.

The lights dimmed, and "I Gotta Feeling" by The Black Eyed Peas came on.

A spotlight went to the tunnel and followed Latisha's opponent on her walk to the cage. She had a long blonde ponytail, smooth tan skin, blue eyes, ears that looked like chewed bubble gum, and a button nose. Her shoulders and arms were well-muscled.

She didn't bounce—she glided. There was no nervous energy—she was pure stillness—and she was attractive in a men's magazine cover type of way.

Sergio could make a ton of money on this fighter. She just had to win. Latisha was being set up.

Hank stood on the stool, leaning into the cage. "Latisha." She turned. "No kicks. Keep your feet planted and jab. Circle and be ready to fire uppercuts when she goes for a double. Got it?"

"Got it." Her face was low.

"Punch her in the mouth, jack up her nose, make her regret the day she was born."

"Time to set the tone."

Hank dropped a hand on her shoulder. "Let's go."

The ref went to the center and waved the fighters in. Latisha bounced and clenched her jaw. Her opponent appeared as excited as a person waiting in line at the bank.

The official raised a gloved hand. “If you want to touch fists, do it now. Nothing after the bell.”

Latish lifted her hand. The opponent walked away—ignoring Latisha’s gesture.

## 8.

The crowd appeared uninterested in a female preliminary fight—most of them were looking at their cellphones. But that didn’t matter. Latisha was ready. Hank knew it. He wasn’t here for the crowd, or for Sergio, or for money. He was here to help her.

She peeked over her shoulder. “Time to take what’s mine.”

The bell rang, time slowed, and she moved to the center of the ring.

The blonde circled right with her hips and hands low—an obvious wrestler.

Hank leaned into the fence. “Get the jab going.”

Latisha circled right and worked her left hand like a piston, taking a half-step forward with each impulse. The blonde seemed surprised by Latisha’s forward pressure. The second and fourth strikes landed flush.

On the fifth, the blonde’s head snapped back. Her chin dropped, and there was a trickle of blood flowing out of her button nose. Her eyes narrowed. She dipped right and then went for a drop-step to the left, a classic takedown entry.

Hank grasped the fence. "UPPERCUT!"

Latisha timed it perfectly, and her right hand landed. The blonde's ponytail flipped, and she landed flat on her butt. She hit an Imanari roll—a wild, spinning shoulder turn—and grasped Latisha's ankle.

Hank squeezed the chain link. "Spin! Turn! Jerk!"

Latisha did, escaped, and motioned for her opponent to stand.

Hank glanced at the crowd. Most of the cell phones were down. They were on the edge of their seats. At his table, Sergio glowered. Hank turned back to the fight.

The blonde girl slowly rose, wiped her formerly pretty nose, flicked the blood to the mat, and plodded in.

Latisha moved sideways while throwing a series of jabs—most landed. They were light—just enough to keep the other girl outside.

With each impact, her opponent seemed to slow.

Hank sat up. "Double jab! Left hook! Circle out!"

Latisha threw the jabs—the blonde got both fists up and defended. The hook came in from the side, around the defense, and landed clean. The blonde's chin jerked, and she took a knee. Latisha stepped left, grinning.

As the blonde stood, her posture was more upright. Hank realized she'd stopped thinking about takedowns or grappling. Her entire universe was Latisha's fists.

Hank's gut warmed. The plan was working.

For the next two minutes, they danced back and forth. Latisha worked her punches.

The other girl kept up her (mostly ineffective) defense while shooting half-hearted takedowns.

The bell rang, and they went to their corners.

Hank took a deep breath. Latisha had rocked the blonde with great, clean punches with satisfying pops and arcing blood. She was putting on a show. A few more fights like this and a big promotion would come calling. He glanced at Sergio. The promoter scowled, arms crossed, sipping a drink.

Hank grabbed the stool and bucket and stepped into the cage. In the other corner, the blonde's mouth was open, and her mouthpiece was out. Her chest rose and fell in deep sucking breaths. She slumped. Blood flowed in thick streams from both nostrils. There was a purple mouse over the left eye. Her cornerman fanned her with a towel, and her coach was in her ear.

Latisha sat ramrod straight on the stool. Her breathing was slow and calm.

Hank put some Vaseline on her face. "Your partner's spent. Done. Look at her. You broke her." He handed over the water bottle.

"It's all going according to plan." Latisha squinted at the other corner and took a long drink.

"Bring it home. Punch her face in. Earn that money."

"I got this."

"Keep her hands off you. No kicks. No grappling." He smacked her gloves. "It's your world. You're the main character."

She stood and winked. "Everyone else just hasn't realized it yet."

"They will."

The bell rang.

Latisha took the center of the ring and threw a body kick.

Hank grimaced. Kicks? Why would she do that? He yelled, "The plan! Stick to the plan! Calm down!"

Her opponent grabbed the leg, but it slipped out.

They circled, and Latisha kicked again.

The blonde caught it and wrapped the leg with her arms. Then, she dropped her head to Latisha's knee.

What the hell? What was Latisha doing? "Push the head! Get distance, space!"

Latisha shoved down and away and rotated her hips—her leg slipped out, and the crowd cheered.

Hank's heart rate ticked up. "Remember the plan!"

Latisha went to the center of the cage, dropped her hips, and shot a double leg takedown—immediately starting a grappling exchange.

"No!" Hank jumped on top of the stool. "Stand! Get out of there! Push back!"

Latisha drove forward.

"No!"

The other girl wrapped her right arm around the back of Latisha's neck, beat the underhook, and got her other hand on the chin—a perfect guillotine choke.

The crowd roared.

Nausea racked Hank's gut. "Guillotine defense! We worked this! Get your forehead on the mat."

Latisha's forehead came off the mat.

Hank continued. "Up on your toes!"

She dropped to her knees.

He shook the cage. "Arm over her far shoulder and pull in!"

Latisha put both arms into the other girl's stomach and pushed away.

Hank roared. "No!"

Blood flowed from the blonde's ruined nose and into her eyes. She arched her back and squeezed.

Photoflashes started from all around the arena. The crowd became noisy.

The edges of Hank's vision clouded. Time slowed, and he watched Latisha's hands. Please. The defense, we practiced it so many times, do the defense. Latisha, you know how to stop this choke.

Stop this choke.

Win this fight.

Stop this choke.

Latisha tapped her opponent's ribs.

The crowd went insane.

## 9.

In the dressing room, surrounded by the tired velvet curtains, Hank's gut tightened, and his head spun. How could this have happened? They'd trained so hard, and the defense ... Latisha knew it better than anything. The plan was working. Why would she kick? Why'd she shoot a takedown? It made no sense. All that sacrifice. She deserved to come out on top. Why did she always have to get the short end of the stick? Why couldn't she get ahead? He tried to help, and now she was beat up, had a loss on her record, and wouldn't get the win bonus.

She stood in the corner, head down, massaging her right glove.

He pointed. "You hurt your hand?"

"Yeah. I couldn't punch. I panicked and threw a kick."

He went over and gave her a hug. "I'm sorry."

"Why?"

"You lost. I'm your coach. I should've planned for this. I didn't."

"It's not your fault. Things usually work out the way they should."

Even when it didn't go her way, she still kept it all in perspective. "You have a bright future in this—if you want it. I'm proud of you."

"You shouldn't be." She held up the gloved hand. "Can you cut the tape?"

"Don't get down on yourself." He pulled out the scissors. "Whatever comes next, you'll be ready."

As Hank snipped, Sergio moseyed in alone, smirking. He wore a new watch, and his chain was different—this one looked platinum. He must've left the other necklace and Rolex at home. The pompous idiot probably had a whole collection of pointless bling. Every time Hank saw him, the accessories were different.

Latisha dropped her chin. "Nice Omega."

Sergio sneered. "You know watches?"

"A bit. You had on a Rolex Daytona the other day, right?"

"Right." He touched his wrist. "Work hard, like me, and you could own an Omega one day."

"Hopefully that day will come soon."

"Keep dreaming." Sergio took Hank's stool and sat. "Tough fight for you two."

"Yeah."

“Latisha was lighting it up,” Sergio said. “Too bad she went for that takedown.”

Hank shrugged. “Latisha had to lay off the punches. She hurt her hand.”

“Sounds like a poor tape job or a crappy game plan.”

Hank swallowed. “Or maybe your blonde just had an overly hard head.”

“She’s not ‘my blonde.’ All I wanted was to set up a good, fair fight.”

“Sure. You’re known for doing the right thing.”

Sergio reached into his pocket and produced a wad of hundreds. He peeled off one and waved it at Latisha. “A bonus.”

She took the money. “Last fight, it was five.”

“You lost. You’re lucky it’s not zero.” Sergio got up. “I’ll call you soon. Maybe we can set up another bout. I know you need cash. I want to help.”

“You already have. More than you know.”

His head tilted slightly left. He raised a hand and opened his mouth but closed it without speaking.

He left.

## 10.

At the gym, inside the office, Hank looked around. Where was Sonny Liston? He hadn’t been around since the fight. And why wasn’t Latisha answering her phone? Everyone needed to cool down after a long fight camp followed by a loss, but she’d never taken more than two days in the past. It had been double that, and she still wasn't picking up or texting him back.

He didn't want to be pushy, but maybe he should pop in on her and swing by the apartment? He checked the calendar on the desk. He had a lesson with Thaddius at three. His watch showed 1:15 pm. It was enough time.

He went to the parking lot, unlocked his Bronco, sat in the still-glittery seat, turned on "Don't Stop Believing," dropped it in gear, and drove to Latisha's apartment.

He parked and looked at the numbered spot in front of her place. Her brother's car was gone. He knocked—there was no answer. He cupped his hands and tried to look through the grimy front window, but the curtains were drawn.

A guy sat on the steps of the next entryway over, drinking a cream soda and listening to Michael Jackson on a small speaker.

Hank walked over. "You seen Latisha or her brother?"

"They left."

"Do you know when they'll be back?"

"They gone. Filled up a U-Haul."

Hank's chest tightened. "When?"

"Two days ago."

Hank's mind spun. Where'd she go? Why didn't she call? She'd needed the win bonus from the fight, and she'd kept talking about betting on herself. Damn, she didn't bet everything and lose it all? Did she?

## 11.

Hank was in the center of the mat, stretching and thinking about Latisha as Thaddius walked in in jeans and a polo shirt.

"What are you wearing?" Hank stood. "I thought we were training today."

"Nah." Thaddius held out an envelope. "Latisha paid me to give you this. Then she made me promise to tell you: open it alone."

He took the packet. "You've seen her? Where? When?"

"A few nights ago, at her place, right before the fight."

"You were close like that?"

"No, we weren't." He pointed. "I read that note, so you're about to figure it out anyway." He looked left and right. "She paid me a thousand dollars to place her bet."

Hank closed his eyes and shook his head. "And she had you bet way too much money on herself to win."

"No, fool."

"What do you mean?"

Thaddius frowned. "She bet fifteen grand on herself to lose." He dropped the package and left.

Hank blinked. To lose? The air felt sticky, and his mouth went dry. Goosebumps formed on his arms, and his back tingled with pinpricks. He grabbed the envelope, went into the office, locked the door, sliced the top off the package, and dumped the contents onto the desk.

Ten one-hundred-dollar bills fell out, along with a past-due water bill. Hank flipped the water bill over.

*Hank,*

*Sorry I couldn't tell you. This was the only way. You helped me more than I can say ... Also, Sonny's with me. You said I could keep him. I hope you don't mind. He reminds me of you.*

*Thanks for everything.*

*L*

After he read it twice, Hank pulled out a book of matches, lit the note on fire, and dropped it in the trash can. It burned until there was nothing left.

## 12.

Hank was at his home, a crumbling farmhouse built just after the Civil War. He was on the front porch, fixing a rocking chair. The paint smell filled his nostrils. There was a crunch on the driveway, and he turned. It was a sedan with dark windows.

Hank's mind flashed to Latisha. Was she okay? Did the wrong people find out she took a dive? Damn it! Thaddius ... little punk. He probably sold her out to Sergio for five bucks and a bag of ditch weed.

The car squeaked as it stopped in front of Hank. A tall, uniformed Savannah police officer stepped out of the driver's side. An older, shorter man in a rumpled suit got out of the passenger door.

The guy in the suit spoke. "It's hot as hell. Can we go inside?"

Hank waved them through the front door and let them into the kitchen. They sat around the large oak dining table.

"I'm Detective Lee Murray." The short guy shifted forward, and they shook hands. "My partner, Patrolman Charles Lidell."

"Nice to meet you both."

After a few moments of banter, including a crack about the falcon incident, the detective took out a phone, unlocked it, and slid it over. "Hit play."

Hank did. The video showed a large, one-armed, black man dragging something wrapped in a green plastic tarp. He pulled it up some steps and into a house. Twenty minutes later, the same guy left with the tarp under his arm and a duffel bag around his neck. The one-armed man had a distinct saunter.

Hank's gut tightened. Demetrius. What the hell had that idiot done? Is that why Latisha took a dive, to raise money to get her brother out of town?

He returned the phone.

The detective took it, clicked, pinched, zoomed, and gave it back.

Hank looked. The image showed the edge of the tarp. Poking out the top was the head of a woman with red hair. Her skin was ice blue.

Hank frowned. "Is that a frozen corpse?"

"We think so." The detective pulled out a pen and notepad.

"Whose body is it?"

"We're not sure. We can't find it."

What did this mean? What were they wrapped up in? Hank prayed that Latisha was okay. "Where'd you get the video?"

"From a neighbor. They live a few doors down."

"Not the homeowner? The victim?"

"No. They reported the theft. They never mentioned a body."

"What?"

"Three days ago, we responded to a robbery. The victim said he had a bunch of watches and jewelry taken, as well as a Louis Vuitton duffle bag. Also, he said his Ring cameras weren't working. As we investigated the crime, we got ahold of the neighbor's surveillance video. This happened a few days back. The victim waited to report it."

Hank leaned forward. "Why would the homeowner wait and not mention the dead body?"

"We don't know. But we figure the delay was so he could get rid of the corpse."

"He doesn't know the neighbor got footage of the redhead being dumped?"

"Apparently not. We want to know exactly what happened before we interrogate him."

"This is insane," Hank said. "If he disposed of a body, why would he bother with the police?"

"The victim said he needed a report for his insurance claim on account of the stolen items. He said his whole watch collection was gone and that it was worth a few hundred thousand, so he had to make the claim. Basically, greed."

Hank closed his eyes. It had to be Demetrius in the video. Stealing, that made sense. But why did he have a frozen body? And why did he leave it? Why did the homeowner get rid of the remains? Whatever Demetrius did, it better not blow back on Latisha.

Hank thought of his floundering career. If he got wrapped up in all this, it was over. "Do you think I'm involved?"

"No." The detective shook his head. "You have a strong alibi. This happened when you cornered that fight."

Hank's gut loosened. "Then why are you here?"

"We suspect the guy on this video is Demetrius Johnson. You trained his sister. Can you tell us where she is?"

"No." Hank took out his phone, unlocked it, and gave it to the detective. "I've called and texted her a bunch since the loss, but she hasn't responded. I swung by her place and knocked. There was no answer."

"That's too bad. Mind if I take down her number?"

"Please do." Hank scrolled to the contacts and pulled up Latisha's information.

The detective took the phone. He flipped to the second page of his notebook. "I meant to tell you Sergio White is the homeowner."

"Seriously?"

"During Latisha's bout, the thief broke in, dropped the body, and robbed Sergio blind. Only someone really in-the-know would be aware that Sergio promoted that fight, lived alone, and would be out of the house. We think Latisha concocted this plan with her brother."

"Any idea why Sergio didn't report the body?"

“I suspect the frozen redhead was left to cause Sergio a problem. He had to take care of it before calling the cops. We suspect he has had a strong, illegal connection to the decedent. The situation gave Latisha and Demetrius time to get away.”

Hank shook his head. “You’re wrong about one thing—Latisha is innocent. She was with me in front of a hundred people.”

“All those eyes. Best alibi ever.” He closed the notebook. “What a coincidence.” He stood and held out a business card. “If she calls, you’ll let me know?”

Hank took it. “Of course.”

## 13.

A few hours later, Hank lay in bed with the lights out, watching an old Micky Ward fight. His phone dinged. It was a text from a private number.

It was a picture—no words. It showed a thin, dark arm featuring an Anansi tattoo, wearing a man’s Rolex. The arm held a fruity drink with a pink umbrella. The sun was dropping, silhouetting a beach and palm trees.

Hank smiled. With a private number and no faces, it could be anyone ... No need to call the detective.

He deleted the image and shut off the phone, and everything went dark.

# Call Me Mina

# by Laura Brashear

**I took** a left hook to the jaw and savored the kaleidoscope of pain that rushed through my head.

"Shit, kid! She just missed the button. Ya gotta be more careful."

I unleashed.

"Get it, Willy!" It was my father's voice, loud and clear, like he was right up next to me. My fist met the other girl's eyebrow, and her skin split like overripe fruit. "Atta girl! Keep it up, Willy!"

He knew I hated it when he called me that, but it worked. I landed a couple of punches in her gut. When she bent forward, I connected a solid right with her chin. There was an audible crack, and she fell to the ground.

The ref, a hulking man with a gnarled beard, knelt beside the girl and asked if she was okay. He must have been satisfied with her response, because he got up, grabbed my wrist, and jerked it into the air. The room erupted in mostly clapping and cheering. There were a couple of whoops, and there were a few curses spat. My dad rushed to me and gave me a big hug, lifting me in the air and swinging me around. I focused on not vomiting.

"Way to go, kiddo! That's how we practiced." He set me back down, and I swayed. The adrenaline was wearing off. My jaw started to throb. It was going to be a bitch later.

I nodded. "Yep."

He giggled like a straight-up elementary school girl, patted my shoulder, and walked off to collect his winnings.

*Typical*, I thought. Although, I could never really figure out if he was more excited about the money or the bragging rights. Neither of which he earned.

Everyone was busy—giving money, getting money, recounting the fight. Even my opponent, a girl from one town over, had a few people around her, making sure she was okay. I was merely a thing. A racehorse. A greyhound. A cock. I was something to bet on and entertain, but after that, I was nothing.

I grabbed my duffel and walked to our truck. Dad had the keys, so I climbed into the bed and leaned back against the hot, rusted metal. The juniors at North Plains High School were reading Mary Shelley's *Frankenstein*.

I pulled out my copy, which was dog-eared at Chapter 16. I wasn't actually enrolled. Earl, my dad, forged my papers after Mom died and made me a couple of years older so I could, as he put it, "be finished with that nonsense." Nonsense, hell. From that book alone, I realized that I was my dad's own little monster.

I thumbed through the previous chapter, noting that I had highlighted Milton's *Paradise Lost*. That would be the next book I read. I hadn't heard of it, but it sounded like something that I could get into.

"Why you reading that shit?"

Some days it really took everything I had to not let him know just how much he pissed me off. "Because I want to." I closed the book, tucked it back into my bag, and sat up. "Why do you care?"

"Because you should be focusing all of your efforts on boxing." He opened his door and climbed in. I jumped out of the truck bed and did the same. He added, "That includes reading."

"Why does it matter?"

"Because word has it that women's boxing is going to get sanctioned in the U.S. soon. Then, we'll go big time."

I rolled my eyes. "Ain't nobody gonna let women box legally." Every so often, Dad would pull out the ol' *women are going to get sanctioned soon* spiel. Sometimes, I think he said it more to convince himself than me.

"Sure, they will. I'd bet—"

I switched the radio on and turned it up to drown out his bullshit. Slash was plucking the rhythmic intro for "Sweet Child O' Mine."

"You're lucky I like this song," he warned. "Watch your attitude, Willy."

"It's Mina," I mumbled. I despised him calling me that. It was just one more way to show that I could never be the son he wanted.

"What?" He gave me a side glance I knew too well.

"Nothing." I turned and stared out the window. West Texas dirt and factories. *God, I need to get out of this town.*

"We made a decent amount today, but I think if we went to a bigger city, we could make more."

I didn't answer, so he continued.

"I was thinking about Dallas or St. Louis. Maybe Chicago."

"You're nuts," I said. "There's no way we could pull any of this off in those places. And, with more money comes more chances to get busted."

"I was talking to some guys who are thinking of making the same move. They said someone told them that a lot of those places have the cops in their pockets. Besides, there are bigger fish to fry in those cities. With this 'War on Drugs' thing that the president is worried about, they're looking for crack cocaine, not some girls in unsanctioned fights."

I snorted. He was definitely hit in the head too many times in his boxing days. Idiot.

"What?"

"I don't think they'd take too kindly to illegal steroid use or illegal gambling or—"

"Why don't you just worry about throwing the punches and leave the rest to me?"

I turned back to the window. The scenery had changed to the run-down, muted colors of tract housing slapped together for nomadic oilfield workers and poor people like us. Dad maneuvered the truck onto the dried patch of grass in front of the house, as so many others in the neighborhood did on their own lawns, and killed the engine.

He grabbed my upper arm, a little too tight, and jerked me around to face him. "You had better stop this whiny shit."

I snatched my arm from his grip and got out of the truck without saying another word. I grabbed my bag from the back of the truck and went to the house. Mail poked out of the tiny black box that hung precariously next to the door. I plucked the array of envelopes out and went into the house. Dad came up behind me as I was thumbing through it.

"What's that?" He snatched a legal-sized envelope with my name printed on the front. I tried to grab it back, but it was too late. "University of Florida?" He glanced up at me, and I blushed. He held it just out of my reach and said, "You really think you're better than me?" He motioned around our house with the worn-out carpet, faded paint, and peeling wallpaper. It was clean but modest was an understatement. It was just plain sad. "You think you're better than any of this?" He chuckled. "Well, I have news for you, little girl. This ... " He spread his arms wide. "This is you and your life."

I grabbed for the letter. He slapped a big, heavy hand across my face. He connected with an area that was already injured from my fight. My vision blurred, and I dropped to the floor, but I did my best to focus on a stain on the carpet. I wouldn't acknowledge him. And I damn sure wouldn't let him see me cry. He tore the letter and rained the shredded pieces of my dream down over my head.

"Forget it. We'll be moving soon anyway." He turned and went to the kitchen. The fridge opened, bottles clanked, and the fridge shut. A pop of a beer top and a belch followed.

I reached around me, tears silently streaming down my cheeks, gathered the pieces of the letter, stood, and went to my room. The door actually locked, thanks to some modifications I made on my own. I sat on my bed and gently pieced the letter back together.

*We're pleased to welcome you to the Gator family!*

The letter went on about opportunities in the Biology department, specifically Marine Biology, but all that really stuck in my head was that first sentence. My stomach churned with excitement and anticipation. I had always wanted to be a Marine Biologist, even though I had never been to the ocean. It called to me. The letter ended by stating that there would be more information following with financial assistance materials. Of course. I had an out, but I was also stuck. I doubted they'd give me much funding. How the hell was I going to afford college? And on top of that, there was no way Dad was ever going to let me leave. I swept the pieces into the trash, flopped back, and rubbed a light finger across my jaw. Could I leave, though? Really, he was just some broke-down, has-been fighter. He couldn't find me.

*But he does have connections.* I rolled over onto my stomach. *But they aren't that great,* I reasoned. *I doubt they could reach all the way to Florida. There would be quite a few states and a lot of miles between me and them.* Could I really do it? Leave and never look back?

A knock at the door and a jiggle of the handle. "Willy, I'm sorry." I stayed silent. "Hey, don't be mad. C'mon out. Let's get dinner." He added: "Your choice."

All the wishing in the world to make him go away couldn't make it happen, so I said, "I'll be out in a minute. I need to change."

I got up, shed my fight clothes, and dressed in an old pair of jeans and a faded Blondie t-shirt. Dad was waiting in the living room. He had combed his hair and put on his own clean shirt. He pulled a handkerchief from his pocket, licked it, and ran it across my upper lip. I winced.

"You'll be all right." He folded the soiled corner into the rest of the handkerchief and stuffed it into his front pants pocket.

"I know I will."

He opened his mouth, ready to respond, but surprisingly, he let it go. With a nod, as if he'd just said the most agreeable thing, he walked to the door. I followed, wishing, like I always did, that something miraculous would happen to release me from my hell.

Dinner turned out to be Hank's BBQ Hut. His choice, not mine. It was cheap and greasy, pretty much like my dad. No wonder he liked it. We ordered and found a booth near the back. I slid into the burnt orange seat across from him and slumped against the wall.

"You gonna pout all night?" He asked.

I shrugged.

"Well, I got some news."

I picked at my cuticles.

He continued. "A couple of folks from Denver were there today."

Silence.

"They're real interested in having you come fight."

"I don't want to."

He leaned in, and I could smell days of beer drinking reeking from his pores. “I don’t give a good gotdamn what you want.” He said it low, and with a smile, just in case anyone was watching. Just Earl and his daughter sharing some joke or a story. “We’ll be heading to Colorado soon. They have a big network in Denver, and there’s lots of money to be made.”

The waitress came to our table. She was a worn-out blonde who knew Dad well. She glanced at me with a raised eyebrow, turned and winked at Dad, and then set our food down. “Call me sometime, Earl.”

“You know it, Jaylene.” He slapped her behind as she walked away.

“Disgusting,” I whispered.

“What would you know about it anyway?” Dad slathered more sauce on his brisket sandwich and took an enormous bite. I watched sauce dribble down his chin and the food turning inside his mouth like clothes in a dryer. “Eat up.”

“I’m not hungry.” I fidgeted with my straw wrapper, curling it and uncurling it.

He snagged a fry off my plate. “Eat. You need the bulk.”

“Why’s that?” I had to admit, the food did smell good, but I didn’t want to give him the satisfaction. My stomach growled in protest.

“’Cause those girls in the Denver rings are big time.”

“I don’t want to go to Denver.”

“I don’t give a damn what you want. We’re going to Denver. They’ll wash all my debt and give a decent amount extra for us to get started.”

"There wouldn't be any debt if you'd quit gambling."

He narrowed his eyes. "Careful."

"Whatever," I said and repeated, " I don't want to go." I had no idea where my sudden surge of sass and courage was coming from, but I knew I was treading on some thin ice.

"Eat."

"I'm not going, and I'm not gonna eat either."

"Fine. I'll eat yours, too." He grabbed another fry and popped it into his mouth.

Just to spite him, I pulled my plate close and spit on it, staring into his eyes the entire time. I was probably going to pay for that later, but for now, he ignored me and kept talking.

"From what I hear, you're gonna love Denver. Those mountains are something."

I swirled the straw in my sweet tea.

"Yep," he said. "They have mountains on one side and ranches on the other. All kinds of cool shit."

The rest of our meal went on like this—my dad babbling like a damn fool, and me doing anything but giving him any sort of acknowledgement.

He grew quiet on the ride home. I figured he was brewing from dinner, and I began to prepare myself for his wrath. But when we got home, he went straight to his room, and I went to mine.

The next morning, Dad woke me by jerking me out of bed by my hair.

"Time to get up, Miss Mouth. We're getting packed today." He let go of my hair, and I slumped to the threadbare carpet. I rubbed the sore place on my scalp and tried to make sense of what he was saying. The clock showed six seventeen. He kicked my thigh. I winced but didn't cry out. "Come on. Get moving. We got a lot to do and not much time. They're expecting us in a couple of days. You already have a fight."

"I told you I don't want to go," I mumbled.

"'Scuse me?"

When I didn't repeat myself, he landed another steel-toed boot against my thigh near the same spot as the first kick. This time, I cried out.

"Get your ass up and moving now."

I got to my feet. "I said I'm not going."

His backhand connected with my nose, and blood sprayed across the dancing skeleton on my pink t-shirt. I bit the inside of my cheek and tasted the metallic fluid seeping around my tongue. So many things I wanted to shout. I wanted to pummel his face until it was unrecognizable, but in reality, I knew it was stupid to even entertain those ideas.

*Shut your mouth, Mina!*

I stood completely still and stared at the floor.

"Now," he said in a softer voice, tucking a loose lock of hair behind my ear. "Get your shit gathered. I'd like to get on the road later tonight." He turned and left, closing my door behind him.

I started to cry. As much as I hated letting him win in that way, I couldn't hold back. But I only allowed myself a brief break. I grabbed a fresh set of clothes, went to the bathroom, took a quick shower, and tended to my new injuries. There were always injuries. At least there had been since Mom died. That's when he got real nasty. It's like he somehow blamed me instead of the cancer. Or maybe she stilled all the anger in his life, and when her light went out, so did his calm. When I was finished, I went back to my room and started packing.

Just like he said, we were on the road around midnight. I don't know how he was so lively, but I had a good idea he was on something. Likely speed. He chatted nonstop. I dozed, but my head kept bumping against the window, right on the place where my scalp still throbbed from the morning interactions, and I was awake again. We made it to Denver in just under six hours; the sun was coming up, and he was right: those mountains were incredible.

Dad pulled into a motel, and the best I could say about it was that all the lights in the neon sign seemed to be working—though the V in Vacancy was flickering. I waited in the truck while he went inside and got our room. He pulled into the parking spot directly in front of our door.

"Aren't you worried someone's gonna take our stuff?" I asked.

"Take whatever you're worried about. I'm not tired. I'll keep watch." He patted the gun he pulled out from under the front seat. "It's fine."

I grabbed a couple of duffel bags and followed him inside. Apparently, clean was just a suggestion for the staff at this place. Cobwebs flanked the corners of the ceiling, as did the dirt and hair in the corners of the floor. A quick glance in the bathroom revealed a ring around the tub, spatters on the mirror. The entire place smelled like a truckstop bathroom, dank and gamey. There was no way I was getting into bed or taking a shower without cleaning first. But I was too tired for any of that. I fell on the top of one of the two queen-sized beds, fully clothed, and immediately fell asleep.

When I stirred, the glowing clock near my bed said it was after four. The curtains were drawn, making the room dark. I bolted upright and searched my surroundings. Was it four in the morning? Four in the afternoon? Where was I? Nothing looked familiar. Panic gripped my chest in a vice. I fell back into the pillow.

*Deep breaths.*

Finally, I was calm enough to remember that Dad and I were in Denver. I went to the window and peeked out. Four in the afternoon. I opened the curtains a little and searched. The truck was gone. That panic started creeping up from my gut to clutch my chest again. Before it could get there, the truck pulled into the lot. Dad parked and got out with a McDonald's bag in his hand. I opened the door for him.

"Well, hello, Sleepyhead."

I took the drinks from his other hand and shut the door behind him. He set the bag on the table, pulled out a burger, and handed it to me.

"No onions?" I asked.

"No onions." He smiled. "Gotcha an orange soda like you like too."

"Thanks." I was surprisingly hungry. My hamburger was gone in three big bites. He grinned and handed me another one. I slowed down and enjoyed that one a little more.

Dad was eating his own burger. He handed me a bag of fries. I shoved several in my mouth at once and chased them with the soda.

"I met with those guys today."

It took me a minute to realize that he was referring to the people running the fights. I continued to eat.

"They want you to get started tomorrow. They have some other new girls coming in. They're hoping to get you all ranked."

*I don't want to fight anymore.* I thought it, but I couldn't bring myself to say the words.

"Whatcha think? You feeling up to kickin' some ass?"

I just kept shoving food and soda in my mouth so I didn't have to answer. He liked it when I ate because it meant I was "bulking."

"Anyway, match is on for tomorrow night around 6. They have some warehouse by the stockyards."

I nodded, threw my trash away, and went back to my bed. I pulled *Frankenstein* from my duffel bag.

"I don't know why you're always reading. Don't know what good it'll do you."

"I like learning things."

"A waste of energy. But so long as you keep fighting good, I don't care how you waste the rest of your time." He stretched out on his own bed and turned the television on to some cheesy sitcom with a recorded laugh track. His own chuckles blended right in.

I slept until a few minutes before seven the next morning. Dad was still asleep, so I wrote a quick note letting him know I was heading out for a run, or *road-work*, as he called it. I eyed the heavy bag in the corner. I guess he brought in his most important things, too.

*Nowhere to hang it, idiot.*

I grabbed the room key and headed outside into the early morning sunlight.

The air held a hint of engine grease, and a man covered in cardboard snored beneath a lamppost. I ran in the opposite direction from him and onto the frontage road. The highway was an endless stream of vehicles, but this feeder road didn't seem too bad. I made a cut into a neighborhood. Seedy houses lined the block, their patchwork lawns strewn with toys, car parts, and garbage. I paused to catch my breath, bending over with my hands on my knees when a dark blue four-door pulled up next to me. I stood upright and took a couple of steps back, nearly tripping over a two-wheeled tricycle. The window rolled down, and I turned to run in the opposite direction from the car.

"Willamina?" A man with a black pair of Ray-Bans and even blacker hair asked.

I paused and pivoted back toward the car. "Who's asking?"

He smiled a slow smile and said, "I'm a friend of Earl's. I just wanted to say that we're all looking forward to tonight."

"I don't know what you mean."

"Sure, you do." He continued to grin. My skin crawled. "The fight. Listen, your dad, he said you're a good girl. He said you listen good. So, I need to know you're going to do what he says."

"I don't—"

"Yes, you do."

I surveyed my surroundings. There didn't seem to be a lot of people out and about in this neighborhood. "Were you following me just now?"

"I just like to make sure my interests are protected." The driver chuckled, and Ray-Bans followed suit.

"I can assure you, I'm not part of your interests."

"Oh," he leaned out the window toward me. "You are." He motioned for the other guy to drive and called back out the window. "Do what your dad tells you."

I ran straight back to the motel as fast as possible. I had a stitch in my side, but I refused to stop or look back.

*Who the hell were those men, and what did he mean about doing what my dad told me? Was he threatening me?*

I made it to the room, but I was shaking so badly that I couldn't get the key to work. Dad pulled open the door and yanked me inside.

"What the hell do you think you're doing going out alone in a new city? We don't know anything about this place or the people."

I pulled away from his grip. "I can take care of myself." I went to the sink and splashed some water on my face. I finished drying it and turned to him. "Also, some of your new friends said hello."

"What do you mean?"

I noticed his face paled slightly. "Some dudes followed me on my run. They stopped to tell me that I need to follow whatever stupid plan you have."

"Yeah. We need to talk about that." He sat on his bed. I continued to stand in the bathroom doorway. "These people are big time."

"So you've told me."

"Well, they asked me for a favor, and I said yes."

"What did you do?"

He sat forward, elbows on his knees, and rubbed his hands together. My stomach cramped.

*He totally screwed you.* "What did you do?"

He lifted his head. "These guys, they know how good you are. They don't want you to come out with guns a-blazing."

"What does that mean?" I asked it, even though I caught the meaning.

"They want you to go a couple of rounds and then hit the floor. Kinda get you established as an underdog."

"Are you nuts? I'm not throwing a fight."

"We have to play by their rules. They'll set you up to lose a few, and then you can tear it up."

"Uh-uh. No way."

"Willy, you don't—"

"It's Mina," I shouted.

"You don't understand. They aren't really asking."

"Then, we go back to Texas?"

"That's not an option either."

"Why not?"

"Because you don't break deals with them."

This was completely unbelievable. On top of pimping me out to underground fighting, he had put my life in danger by teaming up with some boxing mafia. I had to get away from him and my fucked-up life.

I vowed to myself that I wouldn't throw the fight that night. I didn't have to be his monster. I could be my own creation. And dammit, the person I wanted to be wouldn't throw a fight.

I stuck to my resolve. In fact, I fought my hardest, and I still lost. I'm sure Dad was happy. I so wanted to see the look on his face when I won, but Dad was right about one thing. These girls were a lot tougher and better trained than any I'd been up against in the past. I returned to the motel with a blackening eye, a split lip, and some bruised ribs. The guys believed that I had thrown the fight. Dad did too, and he got his money. It was enough to pay for the motel for the rest of the month and then some. He was happy.

For that next month, whenever Dad left the motel, I studied. I found a local public library and began to borrow books on everything from classical literature to calculus. I wanted to be prepared for whatever was expected of me when I made it to Florida. Shortly after we had arrived in Denver, I asked the librarian for a couple of stamps. She eyed the bruises on my cheek. I knew that look; it meant folks were considering getting involved in my life. Like they wanted to call the cops or somehow intervene. I always had a response ready. I touched my face and giggled. "Got in a car accident the other day. Wasn't much, but my face still smacked into the window."

The corners of her mouth curved into a gentle smile. She handed me the stamps. "Arnica's great for that sort of stuff."

I don't know if she fully believed me or not, but I had the stamps and used them to mail my acceptance letter and financial aid information back. I would be a University of Florida Gator in the fall.

There were a couple more fights that I was expected to throw, which was bullshit since Dad said it would just be the one, but I didn't have to throw either of them. The girls were bigger than me, stronger than me, and just better all the way around. I told Dad this. He said that I had a natural ability that they didn't have, reminding me that I was his daughter, and that he was a former fighting champ. He said that I needed to train harder. So, we did. The one and only good thing I can say about that man is that he trained with me. We went to the Y twice a day. He added more weight training ... deadlifts, squats, bench presses. My extra cardio was running as soon as I woke up in the morning and jumping rope in the afternoon. If he were in the hotel room with me, I would be shadowboxing or practicing footwork. At the gym, it was heavy bags, focus mitts, and speed bags. We worked together, but I was still losing.

When Dad came to me with the needle, I was adamantly against it, but he said it was the only way to win. These guys told Dad that they were ready for me to stop throwing these fights and start winning.

"I'm a lightweight. These girls are, at minimum, middleweight. There's no way I can beat them."

He held up the syringe.

"Dad, if you're right and boxing is going to be sanctioned soon, those steroids could cause issues with us going pro."

That's when he told me that all those girls beating me were on *the juice*, and that's how they were winning.

"You're ten times the fighter they are, Willy. They just have this one thing over you." He finally wore me down, and I started using.

I had to admit I began to feel stronger and more agile. Granted, my skin was a mess with all the new acne, but it was a small price to pay for how I felt. My fights showed it. My wins and our earnings increased. Dad used the money to rent a house in a decent neighborhood. It was nicer than the one I ran through on that first day in Denver. Considerably. People in this neighborhood took care of the lawns and carried their trash to the curbs.

Dad still gambled. In fact, he found a liking for betting at the tracks. It didn't matter to me. He was giving me a small piece of the winnings, and I was stashing it away for my escape.

My last fight remains in my memory, as clear as the day it happened. I was set to fight a new girl from Omaha. She was supposed to be some hotshot. Bright sunlight streaked here and there, creating lighted bars across the darkness of the warehouse. A crowd had already gathered inside. It was July, and in spite of the reputation of being a cooler state, Colorado summers got hot. This was one of those one-hundred-degree days. The smell of sweat was heavy in the air, as was old dust. It was cloying, and I found myself struggling to breathe. The faces felt too close, and the noises too loud. My heart raced. *What's happening to me?*

I hesitated, and Dad patted my back. He nudged me forward. "You got this, Willy."

I turned to face him. "Dad, I don't feel well."

"You're just a little nervous. I've seen her fight. You can take her."

I nodded absently and let him push me into the crowd-formed ring. There she was. She was me from a few months ago. She was dancing around and rolling her head to loosen up. I closed my eyes, took a deep breath, and shook my limbs, letting the ill feelings fall from my body.

As soon as I moved toward the center, she charged me. I stepped to the right, pivoted on my left foot, and caught her cheek with a solid right cross. Someone in the crowd yelled for her to get out of that spot. Before she could, I stepped in and threw a couple of jabs below her ribs. She dropped her hands, and I landed another solid hit on her chin. She stumbled backward, and the crowd caught her. The man acting as ref, a man who looked to be in his late twenties and probably a boxer himself, went to the girl and checked her. I danced in place. The thrill of the fight coursed through my blood—it bothered me how much I liked it at the moment. I really never wanted to box, but that rush felt so damn good. I needed it as much as any drug.

The girl nodded and moved toward me with a lot less confidence. She threw a couple of timid punches. I let them connect. It felt good. It fueled me.

"Let it loose, Willy. Finish this."

"Call me Mina!" I screamed.

The girl paused and glanced at her trainer. Her moment of confusion was my opportunity. I let loose, just like Dad said. I punched and punched and punched—all instinct and muscle memory. I couldn't say where each hit landed, but when someone pulled me away, my vision cleared, and I saw what I had done. The girl was crumpled in a bloody heap in the middle of the dirt. I wasn't sure at the time if she was breathing or not. I tried to run to her. I needed to make sure she was okay, to say I was sorry, but they held me back. I realized later that I was crying. Someone handed me off to my dad and told him to get me out of there immediately. They said they'd settle up later.

We got a call later that evening telling us that the girl was in a coma. Everyone else was so impressed. I hated myself. Dad and I had talked about fights that were scheduled through the end of the month. There were three or four planned, but I was done. There would be no more. Dad left me alone for the rest of the night.

He was already awake and making breakfast when I got up the next morning. "Hey, kiddo. Hungry?"

I grabbed a cup of coffee. "Not really."

"Well, too bad. You need to get your protein." He set a plate with four slices of bacon and three eggs, over-easy, in front of me.

"I don't want to eat anything." And I really didn't.

"Will—" He corrected himself. "Willamina, you have to eat something."

I rose. "I don't have to do anything. In fact, I'm done fighting. There are plenty of other jobs out there I can do."

He snorted. "None that make the kind of money we're making with fighting."

"No," I corrected him. "The kind of money that *I'm* making. And I don't care. I can get a legit, *legal* job. Something normal." I turned to leave the room. I could tell him about school later. One blow at a time.

He moved up behind me, gripped my shoulder, and spun me around to face him. "You need your shot."

"Nope. I'm finished with that too." I jerked away from him and moved toward the front door.

"You most certainly are not."

I opened the door. "Yes, I am."

I walked out into the dry heat and descended the cement steps. I turned back to say something else, not realizing he was so close behind me. He reached out and slapped me hard across the ear. Ringing filled it, and my eyesight jiggled. I stepped back and to the side.

*Force your opponent to realign.*

Dad lurched forward off the final step, but he righted himself and grabbed for me. I moved around him. He must have realized that I was using his own defense techniques against him. He planned for my move and landed a gut punch. My breath escaped with a *whoof. Stand up and fight!*

But I couldn't. Dad was stronger than any other opponent I had taken on, and that punch stole my air. I staggered backward, wheezing.

"Had enough, girlie?"

Adrenaline moved me. I found my footing and rushed at him with my hands straight out in front of me. No technique. No focus. Pure anger and years of his abuse were my fuel. I connected and shoved him. He stumbled, tripped over his own feet, and fell back. His head connected with the corner of one of the steps. Blood began to ooze from the wound. His eyes were wide with surprise. A neighbor was screaming something, but I couldn't understand what. All I could do was stare at my dad sprawled across the walkway, his head still resting against the step.

The police came at some point. They arrested me. The neighbors were witnesses to our fight. Thankfully, that helped knock my conviction to manslaughter. I was still sent to Denver Women's Correctional Facility.

It's funny how I just wanted to escape my dad and the prison he built. I always hoped I would break free by going to college, but life has a grand sense of humor.

This new girl danced too much. She was so concerned with showing off that she wasn't ready for the solid right that I connected to her jaw. Her head twisted, and I'm pretty sure I heard a crack. She dropped to the ground. Another woman ran in and counted to ten. Then, she raised my bloodied fist in triumph. The crowd cheered quietly and then went about trading. Winners snatched their loot from the losers, and all went back to their cells. A CO peeked around the corner, saw my arm lifted and the other woman still lying on the floor, and gave me a thumbs up. I guess he bet on me. He usually did.

My winnings were placed in a neat pile on my cot when I got there. Along with some of my favorite snacks, Nutty Buddies and Doritos, there were two bottles of

Pepsi, a couple of packets of Kool-Aid, and three IOU's. Under it all was the latest book, *World of Biology*, that I had requested from the library. The cover was a beautiful image of the fractal pattern in a seashell. I rubbed my hand across it before opening the cover. A letter fell from it to the floor ... it had a gator on it.

# A Fighting Life

## by Keith Roysdon

**I remember** being nine years old when I understood how much my older brothers liked beating the hell out of each other.

I was thirteen years old when my brother killed our father.

Peter and Saul were a little older than me and had always been rough with each other and all of us sisters. The older girls gave it right back. Rachel dislocated Peter's pinky finger by twisting it after he snatched her baloney sandwich off her plate. He howled until our pop told him to shut up or he'd really have something to cry about.

One sunny afternoon, our mother looked out the window. I craned my neck to see. Saul and Peter were tussling in the front yard while the Conatsers from next door stood at the fence and watched. I didn't know some of the others who were gawking.

"The boys sure got a lot of energy today, don't they, Marie?" Mama asked me, although I knew she wasn't really asking.

Our dad was behind his newspaper. "They're just having fun." Like it wasn't as important as some story about what the Russians were up to, and I suppose it wasn't.

This was 1948, and Pops thought about the Russians a lot.

He sure paid attention when Officer Turner, the neighborhood beat cop, came to the door holding the boys by the nape of their necks and telling my folks that the roughhousing had drawn a crowd of neighbors, and they needed to knock it off. Pops usually referred to Turner as "that fucking cop." Our old man had no love for John Law, that's for damn sure, and when he saw the cop had laid hands on Peter and Saul, he stood up and opened his mouth, but Mama made him leave the living room before he got himself arrested.

I was young, but I knew enough to know that a cop at the door was always trouble. I was afraid the boys were going to be thrown into juvenile hall. My mother used that threat on them all the time.

When the cop let go of my brothers, I ran to them, tears streaming down my face, and hugged them.

"Did you see how many people were watching?" Peter whispered. He was thirteen and brawnier than Saul, who was strong and wiry for an eleven-year-old.

I thought maybe Peter was ashamed that a crowd of neighbors and passersby had stopped to watch the fracas. But no.

"There's money in this, Marie," he said, rubbing his fingertips and thumb together in a gesture even a nine year old could understand. He grinned, and I could see the raw and bloody gap where he'd lost a tooth.

Saul whispered as we watched the cop walk away. “Where’s Pops?”

“Mama sent him out,” I reassured Saul, who let out a breath.

“It’s OK, buddy,” Peter said.

Saul wasn’t the only one thinking about the welts our father raised on our backs with his thin leather belt.

Our Indiana town was still shaking off the war and burying all those sons who belatedly came home in boxes. But the factories were going around the clock, movie theaters were packed whenever we could finagle dimes for a matinee, and there was a “what the hell, let’s have fun” attitude after years of buckling down and making do.

So, yeah, I mean, the town had money to spend, and entertainment was cheap and who wouldn’t cough up some spare change to see two boys—two brothers—pummel each other for a half an hour?

Especially if one of them spit out a tooth.

“Make a muscle.” Saul grinned at me. I looked around to see if anybody was watching us where we stood in the backyard of the house we rented on the south side. No lookie-loos in the neighbors’ windows, so I flexed.

“You know I got muscles.” I said.

“Pretty good,” Peter said. “But can you fight?”

“Fight the two of you?” I shook my head.

Peter walked over, slipped his right leg behind mine and pushed me to the ground. The wind was knocked out of me but I kicked at him. He jumped back, smiling.

"If we find a girl that wants to fight, you better fight," he said. "People will pay to see girls fight, maybe more than boys."

"Why is that?" I asked, but he ignored me.

"How old are you?" Saul asked.

"Nine," I said. "You don't know how old I am? I'm your sister."

"I know how old you are. We gotta judge if you're old enough to trust you with the money. Real money."

"Jesus Christ," I muttered "Of course I am. Have I ever lost any of your nickels?"

They'd staged some fights on the playground, scrapping for change before our teachers broke it up. I'd shoved the coins deep in the pockets of my dungarees when the teacher came. Some kids—always the bullies—were happy to pay a nickel to fight Peter or Saul. My brothers always kicked their asses.

The day of that fracas in the front yard told us that kids, even kids we didn't know, would show up—and pay—to fight us, or at least watch.

We didn't want the old man to know what we were doing on the playground, but Saul had slipped up one afternoon in our living room.

"Gimme a couple of nickels," he told me. "I'm gonna go get some Bazooka Joe."

I asked if he'd bring me a piece.

"Where the hell did you get money?" our father said from the kitchen door.

I looked at Saul and he looked at me. I held my breath.

"Kid's getting good at pitchin' pennies," Peter said from the bottom of the stairs.

Our father crossed the distance to Peter and grabbed him by the arm. "Was I askin' you?" He leaned close to Peter's face. Peter shook his head.

Pops let go of Peter and held his hand out to me. I dug in my pockets and gave him the change. He turned and walked out the back door.

Saul was as scared as I was. I watched Peter. He didn't look scared. He stared after our father, fists tight by his side.

It was just a matter of time before the playground fights got us in trouble. Peter was scrappin' with a kid—Lonnie Lawson—and they got caught. Saul and I weren't right there or we would have been hauled into the principal's office too.

"Oh fuck," I said. We were under one of the trees on the schoolyard when we saw our father walk up to the front door of the school and go in.

"They found Pops instead of Mama," Saul said.

A few minutes later, we watched as our father came out pulling Peter along with him, down the sidewalk and along the street toward home.

"Let's go," I said.

"I can't go home," Saul said. His voice was small. "Pops is gonna beat Peter's ass. I don't want him to beat mine too."

I swallowed hard. Saul was right.

Yeah, we were cowards. We stayed on the playground until almost dark, putting off going home as long as we could. If this had been Normandy, we'd have huddled on the troop ship until somebody made us get out.

When we got home, supper was over and our dad was dozing in his chair in the living room. Mama was sitting on the back porch, smoking.

We found Peter up in the room he shared with Saul. He was lying on his belly. He had his shirt off and his back was crisscrossed with welts from our papa's belt.

Peter didn't look at us. He faced the wall.

"He thinks he taught me a lesson," our brother said. "He did. Not the lesson he thought, though."

We staged our first real Nickel Fight on a vacant lot. But even a small crowd of kids, when they weren't playing baseball, attracted the attention of the neighborhood nibshits. We'd only been out there an hour before some busybody sent a cop over to break things up. It wasn't Turner, the cop who'd busted up the front yard fight, and that was a good thing. If Turner had been on duty, he would have marched us home and mama would have threatened all three of us with juvie. Pops might have done worse.

As it was, it was bad enough, because the cop told everybody to get along home. With his billy club, he took a poke at a couple of the bigger kids to make sure everybody understood. The others took off and, apparently satisfied, so did the cop.

"Goddamn him," I muttered. "Chased off all our customers."

"Little sister, you cuss like a muleskinner," Peter said.

"She gets that from the Old Man," Saul said.

I gave him the finger.

Saul looked at Peter. "You ready?" Peter nodded.

Saul got behind me and Peter got in front. I looked at them like they'd come into the house smelling like a skunk.

"We gotta toughen you up," Peter said. He pushed me back toward Saul, who pushed me toward Peter. I stumbled but kept my feet under me.

When I got within arm's length of Peter, I hit him in the crotch. He went down on his knees and gasped. Saul laughed and sat down hard.

"What are you little Anderson bastards doing?" The voice came from behind me and I jumped. Saul stopped laughing.

Bobby Mullinix and two of his brothers stood a few feet away. He pointed at me.

"You," he said. "Gimme the change. I know you just made candy money."

"The fuck if I'll hand it over," I said. Saul laughed again, and by this time he and Peter were on their feet.

Larry, the youngest Mullinix brother, rushed at me. He probably thought I'd be the easiest. But I kicked him in the privates, and he bent over and sat down.

I grinned and turned to Peter and Saul, but Bobby and Wally Mullinix were already on them. Saul was on the ground with Wally on him, punching wild. I ran over and kicked the kid in the head. Saul pushed him off and sat on him.

Peter and Bobby Mullinix faced each other, and it went through my head that they must have seen pictures in the newspaper of Jersey Joe Walcott and imitated his stance. "Kill that fucker," I yelled. Saul laughed from where he sat on Wally.

Bobby Mullinix was bigger than Peter, if you can believe that anybody was bigger than my oldest brother, but while he knew the stance, he didn't know how to fight. Peter would shuffle in and throw a punch and dance back. He'd tag Bobby with a jab with his left and then bring his right down on Bobby's head and neck. Peter would dance back and Bobby, mad as hell, would follow him.

Peter put his left hand in Bobby's face, and while Bobby couldn't see, Peter jabbed his chin. Bobby's head snapped back.

"What a dope," Saul muttered.

Peter danced back. Bobby shook his head, but his eyes drifted all over the place like he couldn't see Peter.

He staggered forward and Peter put him down with a punch in the gut.

"Yay!" I barely got it out before Larry, that sneaky little bastard I'd kicked in the nuts, hit me in the jaw. It surprised me more than it hurt but, yeah, I went down.

When I could see again, I saw that Peter had laid Larry Mullinix out cold. He lay on the ground and moaned.

"You're OK, you're OK," Saul was telling me, his hand patting my back.

"Where's Bobby and Wally?" I sounded funny and I hoped Larry hadn't broken my jaw.

"Run off," Peter said. He looked down at the youngest, who was barely stirring. "Let's get him up and see if he can walk home under his own power."

"Leave the little bastard here," I said.

Peter shook his head and Saul helped him get Larry on his feet. "Let's go," Peter said to the kid.

I walked along behind them, put out that my brothers were helping the little bastard who had turned my lights out.

After the littlest Mullinix was able to walk, more or less, he started off for his house. We headed for home too.

"We couldn't leave him out there, Marie," Peter said. "He was hurt. And besides, we don't need a visit from the cops."

I guess I understood, but it still made me mad. I don't think I'd ever wanted so bad to hurt somebody.

We were out of breath, dirty and bloody. Saul whistled as we walked home.

"If you're able to whistle, you must've not got punched in the mouth," Peter said. Saul chuckled.

I stepped around in front of my brothers and they stopped.

"Tough enough for ya?" I asked.

Saul grinned. Peter ruffled my hair, which I hate, but he was just brushing leaves out before we got seen by the Old Man.

The next few months, we figured out the whole Nickel Fights racket.

Probably the most important thing we figured out is that we didn't fight on the playground or on a vacant lot anymore, where anybody could see and call the cops.

We found an open back door at the old streetcar barn and worked our asses off every day we weren't in school, moving as much stuff as we could to clear a space big enough to fight in. The city had started running buses and stopped running streetcars so they just walked away from the barn. Bums had broken into it and rats ran all over the place, but both steered clear of all our noise.

One time when we showed up to move junk and sweep up, we found two high schoolers, just a little older than Peter, on a blanket. They pulled their clothes on and took off when they saw us.

"What were they doing?" I asked.

"You're too young to know," Peter said.

"Were they screwin'?" I asked and that got Saul and even Peter laughing, and Peter never laughs.

When we got the place cleaned up, we put out the word at school about where people should go for our Nickel Fights.

"We want to get as many people here as we can," Saul said.

I jumped up and down. "I'll make some flyers."

I sat on the porch at home with sheets of paper, pencils and crayons and made some flyers for the next Saturday afternoon, telling people where to come and watch or fight. I stuck 'em up on light poles and fences.

NICKEL FIGHTS, the flyers screamed, and I drew what I hoped looked like Peter and Saul holding their fists up in Jersey Joe's fighting stance.

That Saturday, we had 50 kids show up. They each paid a dime to watch and an extra nickel if they wanted to fight Saul or Peter.

No girls showed up to fight me. While Peter was lining up—and sizing up—their opponents, one guy came up to me and Saul. He was tall and skinny and seemed older than any of the kids from the playground. I didn't know him.

"I wanna wrestle this little girl," he said. The way he looked at me—I was wearing beat-up dungarees and one of my mama's cast-off blouses—made my stomach flip.

"Get the fuck outta here," Saul told him in a low voice. The guy sidled toward the door, leaning against the wall to watch.

My pants pockets were stuffed with dimes and nickels. Five boys wanted to fight Peter and a couple wanted to fight Saul.

"You able to fight that many?" I asked Peter.

He nodded. "Line 'em up, littlest ones at the end. I'll get the biggest ones out of the way so that even if I'm runnin' out of gas before I get to them, they'll be easier than the big boys."

Peter would fight a boy, then Saul would fight one, then another for Peter, then another for Saul and so on. The first boy turned out to be Bobby Mullinix, who wanted a rematch from that day at the vacant lot. I smiled my sweetest smile at him, then turned to Peter.

"Don't be shy about kickin' 'em in the crotch," I said. "It works with them Mullinixes."

"I gotta give 'em their money's worth or they won't come back." Peter meant the crowd of boys who stood in a circle around us, not Bobby Mullinix and the other fighters, but he was probably right about both. "We gotta give 'em a real fight."

Peter and Bobby circled each other a few times and I figured out what Peter was doing: hanging back to frustrate Bobby until he made the first move.

It worked. Bobby couldn't wait any more and rushed toward Peter. My brother sidestepped the oldest Mullinix and clapped him on the back of the neck, pushing him to the dirt floor.

"C'mon, Bobby," Peter said, shuffling around while Bobby spit out a mouthful of dirt. "You gonna get up or you gonna lay there?"

Bobby pulled himself up and, like I thought he would, charged toward Peter. He veered off, though, and his brother Wally, who I hadn't noticed in the crowd, ran up and hit Peter low on his back.

"Goddamn," Saul said. "Where did he come from?"

"You OK, Peter?" I shouted over the crowd. Peter nodded in our direction and danced around the fringes of the clearing, keeping an eye on both Mullinix brothers.

Bobby nodded at Wally, and the younger brother understood: He was to charge Peter.

Saul snorted and I wondered how he found the situation as funny as I found it infuriating. "Bobby's sending Wally in to get his ass beat," he explained.

Sure enough, Peter made Wally look like a patsy. He slapped Wally in the side of the head, really ringing his bell. While Wally stood there, looking confused, Peter hooked his leg behind him and pushed him down in the dirt.

"Watch out!" I shouted as Bobby moved in on Peter. But Peter had already seen the older brother coming and sidestepped his swinging fists. Peter clasped his hands together and clubbed Bobby across the upper back.

Bobby staggered forward and fell over his younger brother.

The crowd hollered and clapped. Bobby got to his feet and looked at Peter but seemed to think better of it. He turned and walked toward the open door, pushing past the weird guy who'd said he wanted to fight me.

Wally pulled himself up and followed his brother. When he got to the door, the weirdo was gone.

After drinking some water from a canteen, Peter sat down to catch his breath. His blonde hair was plastered to his head, and he was breathing heavy.

Saul took a turn, and it was more rasslin' than fighting. The kid who challenged him got him down and tried to pin him, but Saul was able to slip out more than once.

"This guy think he's Roughhouse Jack?" Peter said, shaking his head. I wasn't sure who that was, but I figured out he must be a wrestler and not a fighter. They were circling each other.

"Pin 'em!" I shouted to Saul, who shrugged.

"Take 'em down!" Peter shouted. The crowd took it up like a chant. "TAKE HIM DOWN! TAKE HIM DOWN!"

The rasslin' kid looked at the crowd with his mouth open. That gave Saul time to rush up and tackle him like they were playing football. The wrestler lay on his back, breathing hard, and Saul held his shoulders down while the crowd counted. When they cheered, Saul jumped up and, hands over his head, ran around the ring.

A shrill whistle blasted through the old barn. I winced and covered my ears.

Inside the door, a young-looking cop I'd never seen before let the whistle fall from his mouth.

"Alright, alright, break it up!" the cop shouted. He smacked his left palm with the billy club.

"You're all trespassing!" The cop looked around the crowd. "Get outta here! Go home before I run you all down to juvenile hall!"

The crowd hurried for the door. Good thing we'd got the money up front, I thought.

Just inside the door was the weirdo.

"Did he bring the cop?" I asked the boys. Weirdo watched me, and I stared back.

"Doesn't matter now," Peter said.

The cop swaggered toward us. This wasn't Turner, the beat cop, and it wasn't the cop who had broken up our card on the vacant lot. He looked like a bully for sure, but he was young. He smiled like he'd caught us doing something. I guess he had.

The cop made the three of us sit down on the floor while he paced. He stopped in front of me. "What you got in your pockets?"

I was so scared. "Just some candy money."

The cop snorted. “Yeah, a whole lot of candy money, I bet.” He motioned for me to stand up, and he stepped toward me.

“What are you children up to?” The words came not from the cop, but from Rachel, our older sister. She stood inside the door.

She marched up to us and, before the cop could stop her, grabbed me by the arm. “What are you doing?” Rachel asked, and, with her back to the cop, stuck her tongue out at me. “Look at the three of you! If you’ve torn those clothes, you’ll go to school wearing burlap sacks.”

Rachel turned to the cop, and her voice grew as warm and sweet as honey. “Officer, I don’t know what my children have been up to, but I can assure you that I’ll teach them a lesson they’ll never forget.” She turned back to me and swatted at my backside, then at Saul, who had a faint smile, and then Peter, who tried to block our older sister’s hand. But she swatted him anyway.

“These are your children, missus?” the cop asked. Our sister nodded. “You’re awful young to be the mother of this brood,” he added. “And a beauty too.”

Rachel moved close and put a hand on his chest, near his badge. “I’m so sorry they’ve been a trouble to you, officer. Please allow me to take them home where their father and I can properly discipline them.” I swear she had turned up the family’s Scots-Irish accent and Scots-Irish bullshit.

The cop thought about it for a minute, about what he should do and what he could get away with. He leered at Rachel. “You’re married, huh?”

Rachel smiled. “Oh, officer, of course,” she said. “Don’t worry. My husband will discipline these three.”

The cop shook his head like he was clearing it, then gestured with his billy club. “Take ’em on out, missus. I’ll leave it to your discretion.”

“Thank you,” Rachel said, touching his arm lightly. She turned to us and her sweet tone dropped away. “Git! Go!”

The three of us scrambled for the door with Rachel behind us.

Outside, the weird guy watched from under a nearby tree. Rachel noticed him immediately. “Show’s over, bub,” she said, pointing at him, and he shrank back.

We were about a block toward home when Rachel pulled one of my Nickel Fights flyers out of a pocket in her skirt. “This wasn’t very bright, you know. You might as well have put up a neon sign.”

I felt stupid. She was right.

“How much did you make on this scheme?” Rachel asked. She looked from Peter to Saul. “You two might be dumb enough to fight for fun, but I know Marie is smart enough to see this as a moneymaker.”

I thought for a minute. “About 10 bucks.”

She smiled. “You owe me 20 percent. This fight and every other fight, from now on.”

I couldn’t complain. I guess I could’ve, but it wouldn’t have done any good.

Over the next year, Rachel helped us find safer places to stage Nickel Fights. We did a couple in a room at the local armory, and that worked out pretty well. But it got really good when she found us a gym to use, a real place where fighters trained and practiced.

Peter wasn't happy, though.

"What we do is scrappin', not boxing," he told Rachel as we looked the place over. "I don't want guys to think we're gonna be boxing."

The gym owner, Antonio, an old Black man with shoulders as wide as a doorway, spoke up. "Don't use the ring, then. We can move chairs back outta the way." If he thought it was odd that a recently-turned-14-year-old boy was running the show, he didn't say it.

Peter nodded, Rachel looked pleased, and Saul and I hugged.

Two times a month for six months, we ran the Nickel Fights out of Antonio's Gym. We made enough to hire an off-duty cop to work the door. Before our first fight, we described the weirdo and the Mullinix boys to him and told him to keep 'em out.

Rachel helped us get our bloody noses and swollen lips past our folks. She'd distract them so Peter and Saul could sneak up the stairs and clean up their wounds. One Saturday we thought our gooses were cooked when a kid stepped on Saul's knee. Saul hollered, loud, and we thought it was broken. Turned out it wasn't, but we kept between him and Mama and Pops while he was limping. Peter started wearing his hair so it drooped over his left ear, which was getting darker than the other.

One night after Pops came home from the glass plant, he sat down and read the paper, like always. When he started talking about an article, I thought I was gonna holler, but I kept my mouth shut.

"The cops say there's a group of kids in town staging fights," he read. "Bare-knuckle fighting. They charge other kids money to fight 'em. The cops are trying to figure out where they're holding the fights. Says they used to do it on vacant lots."

Saul and Peter looked at each other. I stared at a spot on the rug.

"You know what I think?" Pops asked. My mind flashed to the times we'd come home filthy or bloody and thought we'd hidden it from the folks.

"What I think is, fuck the cops," the Old Man said. "They're probably making the whole thing up to make it look like they're busy. All it does is make 'em look like dumbasses. What, they can't catch a bunch of kids who beat each other up?"

In a minute, I figured out how to breathe again.

In the summer while we were all three out of school, we'd stage fights at Antonio's every Saturday. Twice as many fights meant twice as much money. We made even more after we raised prices to a quarter to get in and a quarter to fight one of us.

Yeah, I was included now, and we started teaching Rachel some moves so all four of us could fight if that raked in the bucks. Rachel was pretty, though, so we didn't want her to get messed up.

We still called them Nickel Fights because Rachel said that was how we were known around town.

"People talk about these fights in the bars," she told us.

"You go to bars?" Saul asked.

"I'm old enough to go to a bar, if I want to," Rachel said, a little heatedly. Then she smiled. "Actually, I never heard anyone talk about it, but Danny has."

"Oooh, the boyfriend," Peter said. "When we gonna meet him?"

"Probably never," she shot back.

We made more money, but we had more expenses. Antonio's raised the rent they charged us. We had to pay two rent-a-cops, one for the door and one to walk the floor. It takes a lot to keep a hundred, sometimes two hundred, kids in line.

One Saturday night, after Saul's fight, a guy came to the door. I could see Marco, the cop working the door that night, let him come right in. He walked up to me where I stood, off to one side, waiting for Peter to take on a challenger.

"Can I help you?" I asked the guy.

"Name's Cicero," the man said. He wore a dark purple jacket and a purple felt Stetson.

I nodded but didn't tell him my name. "What can I do for you?"

He took a folded newspaper clipping from his jacket and showed it to me. It was another story about the cops looking into a group of kids staging fights. The newspapers loved writing about the cops being clueless.

"This is you, right?"

I'd already seen this article, the third one about the cops wanting tips and vowing to crack down on kids beating each other up for money, but I pretended to study it closely.

"Got nothin' to do with me," I said.

Cicero spread his hands and looked around the gym, which was packed. "So I guess I'm just imagining this? I'm seeing things?"

I swallowed. "Can I help you?"

Cicero smiled. "Your oldest brother. Peter. My boss has a job offer for him."

"He's not here," I said, and barely had the words out before Peter strode out into the ring for his latest bout. Cicero laughed.

"I'll wait," he said, and sat down and watched the fight.

After the fights, I watched a tall blonde sitting, legs crossed, on one of the few chairs we hadn't put away. She watched as Peter and Cicero talked at a table near the locker room.

Saul made a face. "That's Annie."

"Who?"

"The girlfriend."

"Peter has a girlfriend?"

Saul rubbed his eyes. "Yeah. She's why that gangster is here."

I held up my hands. "Stop. That guy with the hat is a ... gangster?" Saul nodded. "And what does Peter's girlfriend have to do with a gangster?"

"Cicero works for her father. She's the reason he's here. Peter said he told Annie about what we do—"

"He isn't supposed to tell anyone!" I said.

"—and she said her dad wanted to offer Peter a job."

Before I could ask what kind of job, I was distracted by the sight of Peter and Cicero standing up and shaking hands, which Cicero turned into a hug when he pulled Peter in.

The girlfriend—Annie—clapped her hands and skipped over to them. She melted into Peter's side.

Cicero and the girl left and Peter, a towel still around his neck, came over. He studied the floor of the gym as he walked up.

"That looked like ... something," Saul said.

Peter let out a long breath. "Cicero asked me to come work for them."

"Doing what?" I snapped.

"Fighting. Maybe some security sometimes. Keep Annie out of trouble."

My face was hot.

"So you're just gonna ... leave us, huh? End of the Nickel Fights. End of the Anderson family."

"Dammit, Marie, we knew we couldn't keep doing this forever. Besides, you don't even like this all that much."

I poked my finger hard in Peter's chest. "Don't tell me what I like and don't like, goddammit," I said. "You don't know what I like and don't like."

"It's not the end of the Nickel Fights," Saul said. "It's not the end of the Anderson family."

Peter nodded. "He's right, it's not."

"Don't talk to me," I said, and turned away. "I'll count the till and make sure you two and Rachel get your shares. I already paid Antonio and the rent-a-cops." I got the metal strongbox out of the desk and walked toward the door.

Peter and Saul called after me, but I didn't stop.

I was thirteen when my mama died and my brother killed the Old Man.

Mama had been getting skinnier and skinnier and ate every aspirin in the medicine cabinet. It never made her headaches better, though.

The Old Man stopped reading the newspaper and they piled up on the porch. He'd always been a drinker, but the more time Mama spent curled up in bed the more time he spent curled up in the bottom of the Old Forester bottle.

Saul and I sat on her bed and cried the night she passed. Rachel sat in the chair in the corner, her face wet.

"She's in heaven now," she said.

"No such thing," Papa said from the bedroom doorway.

Saul, fifteen and still skinny but looking almost grown, got up off the bed and pushed the Old Man away from the door. "Get out," he said. "Get the fuck out."

Before Saul closed the door, we could hear Pops fall back onto the coffee table.

Rachel drew Saul close and held him while he cried. She reached out toward me, and I leaned into them.

"I'll try to call the girls," Rachel said. Our two oldest sisters had moved back down to Tennessee, to the little town we all came from. “Do y'all know how to get hold of Peter?”

I nodded. I was pretty sure I could find him. He'd moved in with Annie a few months ago. He'd come over to see our mama once and got into an argument with the Old Man. He hadn't come back.

“OK,” Rachel said. “Find him and tell him to come home.

She touched Mama's cheek. “Open the door, Saul, and let the Old Man come in to see her.”

But Pops was gone. The coffee table was smashed from where he fell on it, and the front door was standing open.

I went to the apartment where Peter and Annie lived, but nobody came to the door. One night a few weeks ago I ran into Peter and he told me Annie's father was taking them on a trip, like a trip on a boat.

“You lookin' for your brother?”

I jumped and turned. Cicero, this night wearing a dark red velvet jacket and red hat, was standing in the driveway. “You do claim him as your brother this time, right?” He smiled a tight little smile.

“Our mama died,” I said, and all of a sudden I was crying.

Cicero's jaw fell. “I'm sorry, kid.” He didn't move. If he'd tried to hug me, I'd have hit him. I figure he understood that.

“They're gonna be gone for two more weeks,” he said quietly.

I wiped my face with my sleeves. My breath shuddered as I walked past him toward the street.

"You want me to tell him?" he asked from behind me.

I nodded, but I wasn't sure if he could see it in the dark.

It was 37 days before the welfare office woman showed up at school. The principal called me into his office out of history class. Her hair was pulled back tight and she wore glasses. I'll always remember how she fiddled with her pen.

I tried to sink into the chair. I knew what she wanted. She'd shown up at the door one day when I was the only one home. The older girls had blown into town and blown right out again after Mama's service. Saul was busing tables at Orv's, a little diner. Rachel had gone to work as an office girl for an attorney downtown. I was going to school and trying to keep my head down.

The Old Man never came back. Rachel and Saul made just enough to cover the rent on the place. When I wasn't in school, I slept on the couch. I kept Mama's bedroom door closed.

That day the welfare woman knocked, I pushed the curtain to one side and peeked out. She had a bunch of papers in her hands. I carefully put the curtain back in place. I sat on the floor.

But she caught up with me at school. She laid it all out: Our mama was dead, Pops had left town, and a judge had said that me, Saul and Peter had to go into what she called "the system."

"What does that mean?" I croaked out.

"You'll probably go into a foster home. Because your brothers are still juveniles but too old to begin foster care, they'll probably go to the children's home."

Juvie, I thought. Mama had always threatened the boys with it. Now they were gonna go.

"As a matter of fact, your brother"—she looked down at her notes—"Saul is already being processed."

"What?"

"Your brother got picked up by the police early this morning. He was ... fighting. For money."

I thought of the nights Saul had come home late and ran upstairs. He was hiding black eyes and bloody noses from me. He always had money to give to Rachel to help with the rent.

I hadn't wanted to think he was fighting, but he brought home more money than he could make at the little restaurant. So I kept my mouth shut.

Somebody knocked at the principal's door and he opened it.

Rachel.

I ran to her and hugged her. She looked at the welfare woman like she already knew what was going on.

"I have a lawyer, and he's ready to go to court so I can be appointed Marie's legal guardian," she said. "Can you release her to me until we go to court?"

The welfare office woman looked Rachel in the eye. She sighed.

"Are you going to stay put, here in Middletown?"

"Yes, yes," Rachel said.

The woman shuffled through her papers. "I'll give you until the first of the month. Then I'll send deputies."

"Thank you," Rachel said, eyes wet. I buried my face in her dress.

"What about Saul?" my sister asked.

"He's in the system," the woman said. "It'll be up to the judge." She straightened her papers and shook hands with the principal and Rachel. She looked at me. "No more Nickel Fights." I watched her, my jaw tight, as she left.

Saul looked bad. He sat on one side of the courtroom and managed a smile, but I could tell he was hurting. Maybe worse than he hurt after the roughest fights.

"He's not eating what they're feeding him at the children's home," Rachel whispered as we waited our turn before the judge. "Danny's been talking with the superintendent of the home. It's like Saul has given up."

Danny. Rachel's boyfriend. Her boss. The lawyer.

A couple of minutes later, Danny came into the courtroom. He stopped and squeezed Rachel's shoulder before he walked up to the court clerk and handed her some papers.

Another man, another lawyer I guess, walked in and gave the clerk papers. He gave copies to Danny, who looked at them and over at us.

"What? What is it?" I whispered to Rachel, who shrugged.

Danny sat down at the table in front of us. Rachel tapped him on the shoulder with a questioning expression. Danny shook his head and motioned for us to stand up as the judge entered.

The judge asked Danny his name and who he was representing. He replied that he was representing me and Saul and was asking for custody of us to be awarded to Rachel.

When the judge indicated it was time for the other attorney to speak, he said his name and that he was representing Joseph Anderson, who was seeking custody of Saul and me.

Joseph Anderson. The Old Man. Our father.

Danny and the other attorney argued back and forth for a few minutes, and I didn't understand most of it, not because it was complicated but because my head was in a fog. How could the Old Man get custody of us when he'd walked out on us?

Why did he even want us?

The attorneys talked again. Danny seemed upset. The other attorney called our father's name.

Most of the people in the courtroom weren't paying attention. They were here for their own cases. They didn't care.

But I stood up, and Rachel stood up, and Saul stood up to watch as the Old Man walked in and stood before a chair next to the judge. He put his hand on a Bible and repeated some words.

The Old Man's attorney asked him questions, and our father said he'd been gone for weeks because after our mother died, he hitched a ride south and worked loading and unloading boats in Wilmington, North Carolina. He swore he didn't know what had happened, didn't know that Saul was in juvie and that I might go to live with a foster family, or he would have hired a lawyer sooner.

He cried, can you believe it?

His attorney asked that the judge rule right away. "Summary judgment." I'll never forget those words and what they meant.

Danny argued that Joseph Anderson wasn't a fit parent, that Rachel would be better for us.

The judge opened his mouth, and I thought everything was over.

"No," a voice came from the back of the courtroom.

Peter.

The judge asked who he was and why he had any legal standing in the case, and Peter explained as he walked forward that he was brother to the Anderson siblings, and he thought Rachel should get custody of all of us.

"Me included," Peter said. "I won't be 18 for another month,"

As Peter stood before the judge, he unbuttoned his shirt. Everyone in the courtroom stopped whispering and watched Peter.

Peter dropped his shirt on the floor and turned to show his back to the judge.

He faced the judge and everyone could see the red puckering scars that crisscrossed his back.

"Joe Anderson did this," Peter said, crying. "He's never been a good father. He shouldn't have custody of any of us. He did this before and he'll do it again." He looked from Saul to me. "He'll do it to my brother and sister. All he wants is control, to be the boss.

"Please, your honor," Peter added.

A growl came from the Old Man. He got up from his chair and strode toward Peter. Rachel and I stood up. Danny put his arm across us, blocking us.

Peter didn't fight. He didn't defend himself. He didn't stop the Old Man from slapping him, from striking him, from punching him. He didn't flinch at our father's blows or the stream of curses that came from his mouth.

The bailiff grabbed our father's arm and pulled him away from Peter.

That's when the Old Man, who had been raging the whole time, collapsed to the courtroom floor.

The judge ordered the bailiff to go get help. He came back in a minute with a lady in a starched nurse's uniform who checked his pulse and listened to his chest and checked for breath under his nose.

"I'm so sorry," the nurse said. "He's had a heart attack. There's nothing I can do." The bailiff had, by this time, left and come back with a doctor, who checked the Old Man and said the same thing.

Peter handed the doctor his shirt to cover our father's face.

Peter, who never raised his fist to the Old Man, despite the whippings and the beatings.

Peter, who won his last fight by not fighting.

Peter and Annie had packed their shiny Ford so full of

their stuff that there was barely room for them and the baby. On their way out of town, they stopped by the house.

Danny and Rachel were drinking cold High Lifes on the porch. Rachel got up and hugged Peter so tight I thought he was gonna pop.

"You look natural like that," Annie told Saul. He was holding the baby. They'd named her for our mother.

"You really gotta go?" I asked. Peter nodded. "We're gonna stop in Seven Angels and see the girls, but Annie's pop's got a job for me in Atlanta. He's already got a house lined up."

I shook my head. What kind of job, I wondered. "Just be careful, OK?" Peter ruffled my hair and I pushed his hand away.

"Hey," a voice came from the end of the driveway.

It was the weirdo.

"I wanna fight the girl," he said.

Saul handed the baby to Annie and started forward, but I stopped him.

"I still know how to do this, goddamn it," I said.

Peter leaned toward me and whispered, loud enough for everyone to hear.

"You know, punchin' 'em in the nuts usually works."

I turned to the weirdo and smiled.

# The Grit

## by Meredith R. Lyons

**A trickle** of blood and sweat stung my eye. Annoying to get cut in the eyebrow, but this fight was nearly done. Banshee was overconfident. Enjoyable to pick apart.

At five foot six I was probably the smallest Grit fighter at this level. But I'd made a career of taking down larger opponents. That's why they called me the Scorpion.

I blinked. Shook my head. As if I were blinded, frantic.

It was all Banshee needed. She shifted her weight, lifting a knee, and I seized the opportunity. When she drove that knee back and extended her cross in a superman punch, I twisted, elbow ready, sliding to the inside of her arm and clocking her straight in the face.

She went down like a ton of bricks.

And didn't get up.

I backed into a neutral corner, bouncing on my toes to stay warm and loose, but I knew it was over before the ref called it. An earth-shattering roar went up from the crowd. I waited for Banshee's corner to scrape her off the canvas before striding to center, but I couldn't hold back my grin, split lip and all.

Tristan let out a loud whoop from my corner. My eyes flicked in his direction, catching his grin as he added his applause to the din. I knew my brother was fit to burst, but he had to maintain some neutrality. The ref lifted my hand, and what sounded like all of New Orleans exploded anew.

The announcer's voice echoed through the loudspeakers: "Your Scorpion, champion of the South, maintains her undefeated title! The final bout of Twenty-Forty-Five's Grit tournament will take place one week from tonight, right here in Crescent City!" The crowd went feral. Drinks were hurled into the air, money was tossed into the ring, and I could barely make out the spectators pounding and embracing each other in the ringside seats.

Tristan held the ropes open for me, and the ref swept the pile of cash toward us. Groceries tonight. After tucking the bills into a pocket, Tristan yanked my grappling gloves free so that I could sign some autographs, pose for pictures, and collect a few bucks on the way out. The tips after these fights often sustained our family between bouts.

Once in the locker room, Tristan sank into the ancient velvet parlor chair and let a groan slip free.

"I'll be quick," I said, trying to keep the concern from my voice.

Tristan flashed me a crooked grin, dark eyes sparkling beneath unruly black hair. He'd been running his fingers through it all night and now it stuck out at every angle. "Take your time, champion."

I pushed out a smile and darted into the bathroom.

With every win, my locker room got nicer, and this one sported mirrors on every wall, making it impossible to ignore my reflection. As I stripped down, I couldn't help cataloguing my injuries. Split eyebrow and lower lip. Clawed torso. With only a week to heal, keeping the abrasions clean would be important. I ducked into the shower.

My brother taught me everything I knew about fighting. He was the best in the Grit until five years ago, when some psychopath called Sabertooth went after him with his reinforced mechanical jaw. The Grit Commission sent him to their doctors, but there wasn't much they could do. Now, it was all Tristan could do to disguise his limp. Even standing in the corner while I fought took a toll on him.

I scrubbed the sweat from my hair first, then soaped down the rest of my body. This hadn't been a bad fight, injury-wise. Lots of cuts and bruises, but nothing broken.

I bit back a hiss as soap ran down my body and collided with the claw marks on my ribs.

Banshee was famous for her long nails.

Which is why I'd made sure to break as many as I could.

Once I was dressed in baggy jeans and a clean oversized t-shirt, I took another glance in the mirror. Dark brown eyes stared back at me from beneath choppy black hair. The split bisected my lower lip. I'd have to work hard not to chew at it. No black eyes this time, fortunately. The claw marks on my neck weren't bad. I backed up to take in my entire reflection.

Up top, no one would guess I was the Scorpion. I didn't even look old enough to be allowed in the ring. All I was, outside the Grit, was a skinny kid with a duffle bag.

Tristan and I swung by the store on the way home. As usual, I grabbed most of what we needed while he moved slower, leaning on the cart to save his leg. Which is how I missed the bottle of cheap champagne until checkout.

"What's that?" My eyebrows nudged together.

He bumped me with a shoulder. "Relax. My treat. Tonight's special."

I made a show of sighing and rolling my eyes, but secretly, Tristan's pride warmed me like the sun rising in my chest. He so easily could have been resentful or bitter after his career ended. Instead, he threw everything behind me.

The brightly lit alley behind our apartment was deserted when we arrived. Before Tristan even finished unlocking the gate, we could hear the tumult of eight-year-old feet thundering down three stories of wooden stairs, making more noise than should be possible for someone under sixty pounds.

"Nyxa, slow down, or you'll split your head open," Tristan called over his shoulder as he shut the gate behind me.

An inarticulate squeal preceded her as she rounded the last stairwell. In an impressive display of vocal stamina, she held the sound for the duration of her descent, long brown hair flying behind her like a cape until she crashed into me.

"My God, the lungs on you, child." I couldn't hug her back since my arms were braceleted with laden grocery bags, but I grinned down at her.

"Nyxa!" Tristan pulled two bags from my left elbow. "What did I tell you about grabbing people right after a fight?"

She instantly released me. "I'm sorry."

I handed her a bag. "It's okay, Bub, you can help me with wound care later as penance."

Tristan offered her another bag. "How many can you carry?"

"I think ... three." He handed her two more, and she immediately turned and sprinted up the stairs with an enviable amount of pep.

I shifted the remaining bags and started after her.

We climbed three stories in silence, partially to save our breath, but also to avoid waking any neighbors that Nyxa hadn't already disturbed.

Nyxa had left our back door open, spilling light onto the balcony.

"Let me take these." Tristan grabbed half of my bags and squeezed ahead of me. A smile tugged at the corners of my lips as he dug the bottle out. "Let's get this on ice! Our girl is one fight away from Grit Champion!"

My smile stretched into a full grin as I edged my way into our tiny kitchen, stuffed with cheering family. Groceries were passed around amid general chaos; my mother exclaimed over the claw marks, Nyxa nearly got stepped on, Tristan tried to make it to the fridge, my father hollered to keep it down, and thirteen-year-old Felix scared a yelp out of me by appearing from beneath the table for a hug.

Finally I was shoved toward the bathroom to soak in epsom salts while dinner was prepped. I grabbed clothes from the dresser I shared with Nyxa, unable to hold back a grin as a cork popped in the other room. My smile faded when I saw the pile of mail on the scuffed entryway table.

And the corner of red poking out.

I pinched it with a finger and pulled it out from beneath the bills and credit card offers.

Notice of Possible Indenture.

A hand plucked the card from my fingers and replaced it with a tube of antibacterial ointment.

"Aoife, you're not supposed to be poking around tonight." My mother hid the red card and pushed me into the bathroom.

"When did they come? What are we behind on?" I let her shove me over the threshold and close the door behind us. I dropped my clean clothes onto the toilet as my mother ran water for my bath and poured in a generous quantity of epsom salts.

"You washed these out?" She lifted my shirt to examine the scratches on my torso. "Good. Go on, before it gets cold."

"What are we behind on?"

She ignored me, her dark eyes shadowed as she grabbed a bottle of shampoo.

I waved her off. "I've already done my hair, Ma. Answer me, dammit!"

She smacked the top of my head. "Language!"

I folded my arms and stared at her.

Her shoulders slumped. She set the shampoo on the sink. "They came by earlier. Fortunately your father convinced them to wait until after your championship."

My throat tightened. "Who do they want?" Medical companies no longer sent bills to collections. People were given the option to pay it off immediately in cash by selling or borrowing whatever they could, or signing up for indentured servitude in one of the factories or farms owned by the corporation they were indebted to. My father had been in an accident on the way home from work years ago. We hadn't been able to dig our way out from under those bills before Ma had complications after Nyxa's birth. We'd been inching closer and closer to indenture for most of my life.

"Tristan volunteered, but they won't take him."

I squeezed my eyes shut, clenching my teeth until my jaw twinged.

"Better if he keeps managing you anyway," she continued. "I can go, and Felix can start working."

"Tristan and I are doing this so that Felix and Nyxa can stay in school and get to college, Ma!"

"Aoife, you worry about the next fight." She nudged me toward the tub, turning to go. "Soak for twenty minutes at least." She closed the door behind her, shutting out the sounds of my family's laughter.

My chest ached.

I should be used to this. My fights were all that stood between my family and the edge. Even with Felix working at the corner store after school.

Thirty minutes later, I pasted a smile on my face while my family split Tristan's bottle of champagne and tossed back food. I reached for the coffee mug that Felix offered, but my father snatched it.

"The winner deserves a clear glass so she can see the bubbles." He pushed the mug back into Felix's hands. "You take that one. Give your sister the tall cup."

I raised an eyebrow. "Felix is having champagne now?"

I dropped to the sofa beside Tristan; one thumb flew over his phone, a short glass in one hand. "He's thirteen, he can handle it." He didn't glance up from his phone.

"I can't be the *only* one not having any celebration in my cup!" Nxya protested.

I patted the sofa. "Sit next to me, Bub. You can have a taste of mine." I hadn't had a drink since the tournament started, and there was no way I was finishing this entire glass.

"Tell us about the fight," Felix called out as he shoved a desk chair into the main room, his mug of champagne balanced on the seat.

I let Tristan do most of the blow by blow, jumping in to color the story with things I noticed about my opponent or her corner. As I spoke, Tristan glanced at his phone, and the wrinkle between his eyebrows deepened.

Before I could ask who he was talking to, little fingers at my wrist pulled my attention to Nyxa tilting my glass toward her lips. I switched it to my other hand to avoid an accident. "Okay, sneaky, just ask. Here, small sip, like this, okay?" I took a dainty sip before passing the glass to my sister.

Cheeks flushed, Nyxa fit the glass between her grinning lips. She sipped, then passed it back, smacking appreciatively.

"Well?" One corner of my mouth slid upward.

"I thought I would taste the bubbles more."

"Tristan, any news about the final?" My father was nearly finished with his glass. He and my mother fixed their eyes on my brother's shaggy head, still bent over his phone. My chest tightened.

"They're doing this last one a little differently." Tristan tapped decisively.

I straightened. "Different how?"

"The match will be the same, boxing ring, anything goes." Tristan set his phone aside. "And Shadow Wolf doesn't have any weird fangs or claws or anything. He fights pretty clean, like you, Aoife."

I nodded and took a larger taste of champagne. Unlike traditional cage matches, the rules for the Grit allowed anything. The fights were still mixed martial arts in a standard boxing ring, but with added spice. If you had a signature dirty move, you were encouraged to bring it into play. I only fought dirty if the fight went to the ground, but I tried to make sure that didn't happen.

"They're doing a documentary-style thing between now and the fight. They're sending over stuff for you to sign and we'll start in the morning." He took his first sip of champagne.

"What am I signing?"

"A release saying that you'll allow all of your training and interactions with Shadow Wolf to be filmed. And the family needs to sign releases for getting-to-know-you footage and stuff. They'll be editing as they go so that a new show streams each night."

My spine stiffened. Tristan knew how private I was. "That means we can't review anything first."

"They're paying." Tristan's eyes never left mine as he flashed his phone screen.

My mouth dried out. I plucked the phone from his fingers and scanned the sentences above and below the number. This would help. This might even give my family enough wiggle room to figure something out if I lost. Especially if I couldn't fight again afterward.

I handed the phone back. "When does this start? When do we get the papers?"

A sharp buzz announced someone downstairs. Tristan pushed to his feet. "Right now."

Tristan and I woke early the next morning, after the entire family signed forms that we only had time to take a cursory glance through the night before. I would have no privacy until the fight was over. Neither would my family, but money was money. My mother had bustled about cleaning the house, mug of champagne in hand. Basically, we'd given permission to be interviewed anywhere at any time before the fight.

Nyxa and I shared the bedroom in the back, by the stairs, while Tristan and Felix had the one in front, facing the street. Our parents slept on a fold-out couch in the living room. Our plan had been to quietly slip out, but Ma shuffled from the kitchen in her ancient robe, passing us two thermoses. "Here, already fixed." She smiled then and grabbed Dad's big toe. "Get up, Daniel," she whisper-yelled. "We can make the bed and sleep in the kids' rooms in case the camera people come by early."

My lips thinned, but Tristan elbowed me. "Thanks, Ma," he whispered.

I forced a grin and brandished my thermos, grabbing my gear and exiting quietly behind my brother.

We went through the front door this time, and didn't speak until we were on the street. The air was humid, the sidewalks still damp with last night's rain. The sun hadn't even risen, and the concrete was steaming.

I flipped my thermos open with a pop and took a gulp. "Ugh, this is yours."

We switched silently. Tristan drank his coffee black. He took several long swallows, then let out a long, "Ah-hhhhh."

I rolled my eyes, then broke the seal on my thermos and was pleased to find plenty of cinnamon and milk. "What's happening this morning?"

"Just some very light training." I noticed a slight hardening in Tristan's jaw. "This should be a rest day, but they want some footage, so we'll wrap your hands and you'll walk the treadmill for a bit. I may ask you to shadow box if they need something more, but I told them you need recovery time. After that, you're getting a massage, which they're paying for."

My eyes flicked up. "Who's massaging me?"

Tristan shrugged. "I said I needed your muscles worked on, and they said they would hire someone. It's in the contract that they can't show any ... parts."

My shoulders curled inward. "I just don't know how I'm supposed to be able to relax while someone is filming my massage."

"Do your best. It's money," Tristan muttered.

I blew out a breath, then took solace in warm coffee.

"Do you want me to stay in the room with you?"

I nearly choked. "What?"

Tristan's cheeks flushed. "If it would make you more comfortable, I'll sit in the room while you get mass—"

"God, no. If I'm going to relax, the last thing I need is my brother in the room while I'm naked under a towel or some shit." I snorted. I'd never had a real massage before. "Just ... be near the door in case I scream or something?"

He chuckled and shifted his bag to his opposite shoulder. His limp was barely noticeable this morning. "You'll be meeting Shadow Wolf before your massage, so —"

"He's here already?" Out-of-towners didn't usually arrive until a day or two before the fight.

"That was part of the deal, and I guess this documentary thing was his team's idea." Tristan rolled his eyes. "They're going to get some footage for intros this morning."

I tilted my neck from side to side to release the tension pulling there as this new reality sunk in. I felt like everything was pressing in on me. I didn't have much, but I could always come home and let the mask drop. Melt back into my most basic form around my family. I didn't have to pretend injuries didn't hurt, pretend I wasn't tired ...

*Didn't you?*

I took another gulp of coffee and turned the question over. I blurred things for my family out of love. Yes, things hurt, yes, I was tired, but it was for them, so I muscled through without complaining.

This is just a different kind of muscling through.

I lifted my chin, ignoring the tightness in my chest. "I think I can handle that."

One block from the gym, I noticed a dude leaning against the building. When he saw us, he tossed his cigarette and waved to someone out of sight before disappearing. I elbowed Tristan.

"Camera crew," was all he said.

Sure enough, when we turned the corner, two cameras had us in their sights. I tensed, fingers tight around my bag.

"Just walk normally," Tristan murmured.

He held the door open for me, which I pretended was normal.

Once inside, things proceeded pretty much like Tristan said. While I changed into workout gear, two men filmed the empty gym. It was difficult not to stare while they lit a completely inert heavy bag and shot it from different angles. I nearly tripped on the treadmill.

A woman, who introduced herself as Sherlia, asked Tristan if he could show her around the back. The gym had been cleared for the morning's shooting. He bumped my incline to eight before leaving with her. Asshole.

I smoothed a wrinkle in my prettiest red handwraps. My mother bought them when Tristan told her he was going to train me himself. She'd gone to the gym with him and got them at a discount. To lock in the color, she soaked them in vinegar overnight. My red wraps were just as bright now as they were five years ago.

Camera ready.

The incline was finally making me sweat. I dabbed at it with my wraps, part of me wondering if I should leave it for film aesthetics. I dismissed that idea; there was more where that came from.

A commotion at the door snagged my attention in time to see a cameraman backing over the threshold, focused on a hooded figure in a silk robe.

Shadow Wolf.

I let my gaze linger long enough to clock his height and weight before looking away and throwing a few straight punches as I walked to look more impressive. The Grit didn't have weight and gender categories. If you were the best, you fought the best.

I clocked Shadow Wolf at six-foot-one. Maybe six-two. He would have reach and weight on me, but that was nothing new. I'd never been able to eat enough to bulk up. Tristan and I focused on weight shift—making every pound count—and speed so that I could move in and out quickly. Getting inside of a taller person's guard was second nature.

I shadowboxed until the last of Shadow Wolf's camera crew disappeared inside the men's locker room, then made an executive decision and stopped the belt. I fought yesterday. I still had open wounds. I didn't know where the hell my trainer was, but I was done walking.

I left the cardio equipment and dropped gracelessly to the mats, extending my legs and leaning forward to grab my toes. My hamstrings protested, but I lengthened my breaths and held until the muscles started to relax. I maintained the stretch until Tristan sidled up to me. "They want to get footage of you meeting Shadow Wolf before you go in for your rub down."

I exhaled my irritation without lifting my head. "Are we skipping the solo shots then?"

He shrugged. "I'll check. I don't want you to do anything after your massage. If they want to film you hitting something, they'll have to get it now. Be right back."

I continued with my stretches, forcing slow, deep breaths. This pageantry was going to get old quick, but I reminded myself of the money and forced my shoulders away from my ears.

My head snapped up at the sound of approaching footsteps. Tristan, flanked by two cameramen. I pushed to my feet.

"They just want some shots of you stretching," Tristan said when he reached me. "I'll help with a couple and then you can do some on your own."

I nodded stiffly as the cameramen introduced themselves. Saul and Wes.

Saul offered a warm smile. "Just pretend like we aren't here. Talk like you normally would. Don't look directly into the camera. Other than that, you can't mess up."

The first few minutes were stilted. I couldn't help being hyper focused on the cameras in my periphery. Tristan also seemed stiff and formal until he noticed my arms locking up. He grabbed my shoulders and jostled me. "Relax! Damn."

A genuine chuckle tumbled from between my lips as I pushed him off. "Well, then be more relaxing, asshole."

After that, things felt more natural. Tristan and I joked and bickered as usual until the cameramen said they had what they needed.

Wes left to alert Shadow Wolf's team while Saul looked me over. "May I?" He didn't wait for an answer, tousling my sweaty hair. He tilted his head, then flipped it a different way, plucking strands around my face as if he could place each hair individually. "I just don't know what mood we're going to strike yet," he muttered, and I wondered if he was talking to me or just musing to himself. "Then again, fierce and sexy is never the wrong answer."

I bit back a laugh, but couldn't help shooting a look at Tristan, who just shrugged as if to say, "Whatever works." At least they weren't putting makeup on me.

At that moment, Wes returned with Sherlia, who clutched an enormous tackle box. "We don't know what angle we'll be working yet, Sher, so keep it natural, but maybe give her a boost."

Sherlia nodded her glossy red head decisively, set her case down on a nearby bench, and flipped it open to reveal an array of pressed makeup and brushes. I sucked in an audible breath. I must have made some kind of face, because Tristan grabbed my elbow.

He leaned in close. "You need a better poker face, stat. Have you ever been paid to do something so incredibly easy before? No. You haven't. I don't care if they want you to wear a clown nose, chill out and let it happen."

I clenched my jaw and tugged my elbow free, but cooperated while Sherlia fanned soft brushes over my face, using more makeup than I thought possible to achieve a 'natural' look. She decided to leave my split lip for 'authenticity' but gave me a salve to use on it to help speed the healing.

I vibrated with nerves, eager to get away from the cameras. My chest hollowed when I realized I didn't know when that would be.

Finally, I was deemed just the right amount of "authentic" and "attractive."

"We just want to get a feel of the energy between you and Shadow Wolf, so do what you would for any other fight," Wes instructed while Sherlia spritzed water over my face and hair. He had me positioned just outside the locker room door, setting me up to meet my opponent.

I forced a smile. This was already so far beyond "any other fight."

"You'll walk in, he'll turn around. Shake hands and introduce yourselves. Justine Everly is in the room. She'll ask you both some questions, and we'll go from there. Good?"

"Justine Everly, the social media lady?" My eyes flicked from Wes to Tristan. I must have missed that in the mounds of paperwork we skimmed last night. The human interest stories Justine Everly highlighted on her channels got world-wide attention.

"That's right! Millions of her followers will be meeting you tonight." Wes smiled toothily before waving Saul into the room ahead of us.

Saul paused at the door with a pen poised over an index card. "Sweetie, how do you pronounce your name again? Justine wants to get it right."

I nodded. "Just drop the first two letters. Eee-fah."

He scribbled something on the index card, then glanced at Wes.

"We're good to go. Start rolling once you're in." Wes pulled Tristan into position slightly behind me and to my left. "You're her brother right? Maybe put one hand on her shoulder. No, the other ... yes, perfect, you can drop it once she goes to shake his hand."

Sherlia flicked her fingers through my hair one more time, then gave Wes a nod and backed away. He hoisted a camera onto his shoulder. "Aoife, count to five, then open the door." He stepped behind us.

My face burned. I shut my eyes as I fought the embarrassed grin trying to break free. This entire circus was absurd. *You're already small. You don't want Shadow Wolf seeing you as a giggling idiot.*

That sobered me up. Tristan's hand was stiff on my shoulder as we stepped through the door. Justine stood facing me, curly dark hair a glossy cloud around her shoulders, a bright smile on her pretty face. Saul was just behind her, the camera aimed at me. I pasted on my fight face, lifted my chin, and approached the robed figure on the opposite side of the room.

Shadow Wolf turned, dropped his hood, and my heart stopped.

Tristan's hand tightened painfully. I froze, fighting the impulse to back into my brother's arms.

Keegan Flynn's blue eyes brightened when he saw me. "Hey, Aoife," he said softly.

"*You're* Shadow Wolf?" Tristan's voice was an octave too low.

*Breathe,* I told myself, sucking in air and blinking hard.

But no matter how many times I opened my eyes, Keegan was still standing there, staring at me as if he hadn't disappeared a year ago, leaving my heart in shreds.

Keegan's gaze flicked to Tristan. "Hey, Tris." He stepped toward me, extending his hand. "Aoife—"

Tristan threw me behind him. "Don't touch her."

The energy in the room shifted. The joy and eagerness pulsing from the crew surrounded us like fireworks. Justine stepped forward. "You two know each other?"

In an instant, I hardened. Shoved down the hurt and shock and stepped around my brother. "No." I struggled to pull my fighter's mask back in place and grabbed Keegan's outstretched hand, pumping once. "Nice to meet you. Good luck out there." I let go and turned away, but Keegan held on.

"Aoife—"

I jerked my hand out of his grip, but refused to yield a step."*You* can call me Scorpion." A small, mean part of me reveled in the hurt that flashed behind his eyes. Collected it. Put it in a little box to gloat over later. Meanwhile, old fissures cracked anew, fracturing my heart. I faced Justine. "You had some questions?"

She grinned and cleared her throat, her gaze hungry.

Keegan brushed his fingers down my arm and goosebumps instantly stippled my skin. "Aoife, please ... "

Tristan tugged me backward, his hands clasped protectively on my shoulders. "If you touch her again outside the ring, I will beat your face in myself."

I refused to look at Keegan, keeping my eyes on Justine, my face cold and bored. I hoped only Tristan could tell I was trembling.

"Obviously the two of you have a history?" She extended her microphone to me.

"I don't know him," I said.

"I'm in love with her," Keegan proclaimed, as if daring me to argue. "We were together for four years." I felt the warmth from his body as he stepped closer to me. "Aoife, I didn't want to leave like that. I had no choice."

"I don't care." I kept my eyes on the influencer, hoping my face didn't betray anything as my heart continued to shatter. "Next question?"

She grinned. A shark scenting blood. Around us, Saul and Wes jostled for fresh angles. This must be their dream come true. Or had they known about this? My lungs froze. Had they intentionally set me up, knowing my history with Keegan?

I wanted to kill everyone in the room.

Aside from Tristan, whose hands were burning hot on my shoulders.

"Aoife, you obviously had no idea of Shadow Wolf's true identity." She flashed her hazel eyes at Keegan. "But the story seems different for you, Keegan. Did you know Scorpion's identity before you accepted this match?"

I heard Keegan's long exhale, his gaze burned into the side of my face, but I kept my eyes forward, my entire body rigid.

"I knew who she was," Keegan said. "I wanted to see her. I miss you, Aoife."

Those four words snapped something inside me, and I jerked toward him. "And you didn't think to fucking pick up a phone? Write a goddamn letter?" Rage and heartbreak threatened to choke me, and I swallowed hard. A year. An entire year with no word.

"You changed your number." Emotion tightened Keegan's stupid, handsome face. "Your family moved. When I was finally in a place to contact you, no one would—"

"So nice that you 'got to a place' where you could stroll back into her life." Tristan's words dripped sarcasm. His hands still dug into my shoulder, as if Keegan was going to rip me away from him.

Justine had her footing again. "Tristan, you obviously witnessed your sister's relationship with Keegan. Why is it so important to you that she stays away from him? Will you let her fight?"

"She's going to fight." Tristan's voice was steel. "And he's not going to mess with her mind before the fight, either."

Keegan's head snapped toward Tristan. "I'm not trying to—"

"Don't give me that bullshit!" Tristan stepped around me to lean into Keegan's face. "You're going to pretend that you coming back and spinning this whole lovesick sob story isn't you trying to mess with her? You think it'll make her go easy on you? Think again, asshole."

Keegan's jaw twitched as he looked away from Tristan and moved toward me, but Tristan put a hand on his chest and glared at the cameras. "We're done here. Any questions you have for Scorpion, you can ask after her massage. Let's go, Aoife."

Tristan dropped his arm around my shoulders, steering us toward the door, but Keegan grabbed my hand. "Aoife, that's not what I'm trying to do. Can we please talk somewhere?"

I'd barely glanced at him before Tristan spun and smashed Keegan's nose with an overhand right.

I let the warm water from the gym's dodgy showers beat down on my skin. If nothing else, the water pressure here was great. In the adjoining room, Tristan's still elevated voice echoed through the women's locker room as he iced his hand and participated in an on-camera debrief. Most of which boiled down to, "I warned him twice not to touch her." Occasionally peppered with, "Aoife should be resting after her fight yesterday, not dealing with head games from the opposite side."

I shut my eyes, pressed my palms to the slick tile, and leaned into the water. This was one place the cameras weren't allowed to follow me, and I needed to get my head on straight.

Keegan.

Keegan Flynn was Shadow Wolf.

My last memory of him was watching the sun set while we walked in Crescent City Park. "I love you, Aoife," he'd said. "I know things are hard right now, for both our families, but I want to find a way to make this work."

I'd pulled away from him, wrapped my hands around the metal railing of the gate and gazed out over the river. Was he suggesting we move in together? Both of our family units were on the brink. If we moved out ...

My back warmed as Keegan came up behind me, placing one hand on either side of mine. He leaned in. "We don't have to stop helping our families," he breathed into my ear. "I just ... want to find a way for us to start building our own life."

He'd disappeared the next day. His family's apartment emptied. Rented within the week. His phone disconnected. His job was as clueless as we were.

If I hadn't had to work to keep my family afloat, I would have spent the following months in bed. As it was, I was a ghost, barely eating, coasting through days like an automaton. But we needed money from the fights. I'd been forced to step up.

Keegan showing up here ripped open not only the wounds I'd sustained when he disappeared, but threatened to bring back that ghost of a person I'd been after he left.

I shut off the water.

Keegan Flynn was already dead to me. No reason I couldn't kill him again.

I stepped into the locker room, wrapped in a fluffy red robe—my Scorpion color—supplied by the show. Even though I was fully covered—the robe reached my knees—I felt weirdly exposed. Since I was going straight to my massage, I wore only bottom underwear beneath.

Tristan straddled a bench between the lockers, his back to me, a camera aimed at him, and Justine chatting him up. One shoulder rested casually against a locker, but her eyes were sharp. I pulled my lower lip between my teeth. I didn't know much about the entertainment business, but I knew these people would use anything they filmed.

I cleared my throat, and Tristan whipped around. When his dark eyes fell on me, the concern shining there tugged at wounds I'd been trying to stitch shut. He stood swiftly, hauling me into a hug.

"Fuck him. Just ... fuck him for doing this. How are you doing?"

The camera had silently followed, and I realized that Tristan had been chatting with Justine for so long he *had* forgotten they were there. I, however, had not.

I returned his hug, did my best to smile serenely, then pushed away to look him in the eye, fully aware that the cameras were catching every move. "I'm fine, Tris, honestly." I pushed the corners of my mouth a little higher. "He's not the person I knew, no matter what he says. I got this." Sharp grief slipped between my ribs like a knife, but I kept smiling.

Tristan cupped my chin—the second knuckle on his right hand was split—his eyes scanning every inch of my face as if searching for physical injuries. More likely he was checking for signs of tears. But I'd cried over Keegan enough when he disappeared.

"Okay." My brother stepped back. "You ready for your rub down?"

I nodded, trying to read the room without looking directly into the cameras. Was he in trouble for punching Keegan? It didn't seem like it. Maybe it depended on whether Keegan's side decided to press charges. Or how badly his nose was broken. I rolled my shoulders back and down. If no one was saying anything, maybe I didn't have to worry about it.

I tapped Tristan's right hand. "Did you break anything?"

"Nah." He flexed his fingers. "Maybe his septum. Although it looks like that's happened once or twice since he left."

I'd noticed that too. A little bump high on the bridge of Keegan's nose that hadn't been there before. But more importantly, it seemed Tristan wasn't in trouble for now. Probably because he made good television.

I let them guide me to a repurposed office in the back. They'd draped all of the walls in curtains, and the only furniture was a massage table and chair. There was barely enough space left to move around the massage table.

"Cozy," I remarked, fingers clenched around the thick collar of my robe. Saul and his camera trailed me. A petite woman stepped out from behind the curtain, her dark hair slicked back into a bun. She reached for my hand with both of hers.

"I'm Mina. I'll be taking care of you today. Any specific requests?" She cupped my right hand between hers as if it were a bird.

"I have some scratches, so maybe be careful around those."

She nodded, large blue eyes locked on mine, waiting for more.

I ran my tongue over my teeth. I didn't want to give away any potential weak spots in case Keegan watched this later. "I guess my shoulders are always a little knotted. I'm sure there's some other tight spots. I had a fight yesterday."

She nodded again, patting my hand. "I'll just step out while you get undressed. You can hang your robe there and just slip under the covers face down." With a squeeze, she released me and slipped away. Saul ducked out also, thank God.

I stepped quickly out of my robe, hung it, then wiggled between the sheets. There was a warmer on the table. A sigh slipped from me, my muscles already loosening. Maybe I could take a nap. I dropped my face into the cushioned opening and shut my eyes.

Mina's voice floated in. "All set?"

"Mm hmm."

The telltale woosh of a curtain being pushed back had me lifting my head in time to see the other half of the room revealed. My stomach dropped as my eyes darted around. Wes's camera joined Saul's. Sherlia leapt into action, placing a light on my side of the room.

A second light illuminated another massage table. With Keegan on it.

"No." I started to sit up, remembered I was topless, and froze.

"You're going to have to get used to being in the same room as me." Keegan's nose was swollen, but it didn't look like it was broken. Although dark bruises were forming beneath his eyes. Guilt coated my stomach. I ignored it.

"This is not just being in a room with you," I hissed, turtling into the sheets. "This is ... this is ... "

"Intimate?" His eyes glinted with amusement. He actually thought this shit was funny?

*This whole setup was probably his idea*, I thought, rage scraping against my sternum. Wes shifted his camera's position, and I remembered that all of this was being filmed. I shoved my face back into the cushion and closed my eyes.

"Aoife, it wasn't my decision to leave you."

I wished I could close my ears. Mina placed her hands on my back. "Three deep breaths," she murmured. I obeyed, trying to forget the cameras, the lights, and Keegan. I was under no obligation to give these people anything other than a good fight. I didn't have to rip open my heart on camera.

"Aoife—"

"I'm trying to relax," I snapped. "Unlike anyone else in this room, I had an actual fight yesterday, and I have another fight to win later this week."

He sighed, but mercifully shut up. The cameramen were probably disappointed.

I tried to will my muscles to relax, every cell in my body achingly aware of Keegan's presence just a few feet away.

No cameras followed us home. Thankfully, our family wasn't around when we got there, although the house was cleaner than I'd ever seen it. I peeked into the room I shared with Nyxa.

"Wow, Ma must have been on the warpath. Nyxa even put away her pony diorama." The floor beneath our window normally hosted an ever-changing scene of model horses in a fenced in pasture. Sometimes with other dolls incorporated. The area was now bare, the ponies and accompanying plastic fencing resting in their shoebox on the bookshelf.

"Yeah, Felix's comic books are stacked in the corner. You can actually see the floor between our beds." Tristan popped his head around the doorframe. "I'm going to head down to the shop to catch Ma and let her know about Keegan."

I pinched the bridge of my nose, trying to remember what day of the week it was. "Kids at school?"

"Yeah, but they're both due at the store once they get off. Felix is stocking this afternoon and Ma's keeping Nyxa until one of us can collect her."

So Ma could fill them in.

"Do you mind if I stay here and take a nap?" I asked, wincing at how small my voice sounded. Now that the cameras were gone, my walls were crumbling. I wanted nothing more than to curl up in my own little space and lick my wounds.

Tristan stepped into the room, pulling me into a gentle hug. "Are you okay? You want to talk?"

"No, give Ma a heads up." I shut my eyes, squeezing him back. I didn't say that I was okay. I wasn't. "Maybe text dad too, in case he's able to check his phone during a break or something." I sighed. There would be no reaching our father. As a janitor at a high security government building, he made the most of any of us—aside from me when I won a fight—but there was no communicating with him while he was at work.

Tristan didn't push. He let me go and backed toward the door. "Call if you need anything? I'll pick up something good for lunch. But if your door's closed when I get home I won't wake you up."

As soon as Tristan left, I crawled into bed and curled up facing the wall. I thought for sure the tears would come, but my eyes remained dry. I breathed around the jagged edges of my heart and eventually drifted off.

The rest of the day was mercifully uneventful. Tristan and our mom managed to alert everyone to Keegan's dramatic reappearance, sparing me the discomfort of their emotions on top of mine. Keegan had been a fixture at our place. It was accepted that the two of us were together, so he was treated like family. I'd been hit the hardest when he disappeared, but no one was unaffected.

Although Ma badgered everyone to keep the place clean, just in case, no cameramen broke down our door. I should have been grateful for the reprieve, but I was wired, waiting for the other shoe to drop. Maybe they were filming Keegan's family first.

My stomach swooped. Were the twins with him, or had they stayed on the east coast? Assuming that's where they had run off to. After his father died, every cent Keegan earned went to help his mother and younger siblings. Their family had been just as close to the edge as ours. Guilt nudged at me for not asking about them, but he had completely blindsided me. Of course I wasn't going to make small talk.

We ate dinner in the living room in front of the family laptop, which had been moved from the office for the dubious honor of streaming the first episode of *Gearing Up For The Grit*. Although the last thing I wanted to see was my face on camera, I begrudgingly agreed that the show could contain valuable intel. Keegan's team would undoubtedly watch, and I should also be aware of what they revealed about me. And the family was excited that I was sharing a screen with Justine Everly, so I kept my squeamishness to myself.

It started pretty generically, with Justine outlining The Grit's history over footage obviously edited in advance, her voice often overlaying footage of our past fights. I had to admit, they made me look pretty badass.

When they transitioned to the spots they'd filmed earlier, I almost choked on my falafel.

They'd taken the footage of me stretching and zoomed in close. Slowing things down and cutting the shots in a way that was ... sexy.

I smacked a hand over Felix's eyes. "This is inappropriate!"

"Don't be so dramatic." My *mother* waved a dismissive hand at me without taking her eyes from the screen. "You look nice."

Felix squirmed away from my hand, and I covered my own eyes. "Just tell me when this part is over."

A bitter, "There he is," from Felix had me dropping my hands. They'd done the same thing with Keegan, zooming in for close shots with dramatic lighting and slow motion. My eyes flicked to my little brother. Arms crossed tightly over his chest, spine ramrod straight, glaring at the screen from behind his black-framed glasses. He had loved Keegan. When he'd first gone missing, Felix had been the one continually saying, "He'll get in touch with us, Aoife, I know he will, and he'll explain it all."

After three months, he'd stopped.

"*Hey, Aoife …* "

My gaze snapped back to the screen in time to see the camera pan to me, frozen in shock. Embarrassment slithered through my stomach as I pushed my plate away and pulled my legs up onto the couch. Every emotion ran clearly across my face for the world to see.

"You need to eat." Tristan reached over Felix and pushed the plate back toward me just as on-screen Tristan told Keegan not to touch me.

Face burning, I focused on my plate. Nyxa leaned against me. "He looks so sad," she whispered. And in spite of myself, I looked.

While I was standing behind Tristan, trying to get a grip on myself, the camera did a slow zoom on Keegan. And Nyxa was right, he was devastated.

But was he really? Or was this just some fancy camera work?

"It doesn't matter if he's sad. Aoife's going to kick his ass," Felix bit out, still rigid.

I mechanically pushed food into my mouth. Chewing although it tasted like sand. Forcing myself to swallow through an increasingly tight throat.

Everyone gasped when Tristan punched Keegan. "Yeah!" Felix unclenched long enough to high-five him. "He deserved it."

I reached for my glass of water and gulped down half of it, my chest tight. Nyxa was still pressed to my side, whether for her own comfort or to offer me support, I wasn't sure. My mother shushed everyone with a flap of her hands as the camera cut to Keegan. His corner—two professional-looking men in tight black shirts—tended to his nose. It wasn't broken, but it streamed blood.

Justine was with him. "Do you think you'll press charges? Tristan Brennan is not a competitor."

"I'm not pressing charges," Keegan said as clearly as he could with his head tilted back and a bloody towel covering half his face.

My father grunted, the first reaction he'd shown. He set his cleaned plate to the side, his eyes finding Tristan's. "Don't hit him again."

Tristan dipped his chin once. We were silent for several moments. If Keegan pressed charges, it would go badly for us. At the very least, I would lose my corner.

The stream wiped to Tristan defending himself in the locker room while he iced his hand. It cut to Keegan, sitting alone with an ice pack on his face, then switched to a close shot with Justine off-camera asking, "So Aoife was your girlfriend?"

Keegan dropped the ice to the bench beside him. "She was more than just my girlfriend." He swallowed, throat working, but didn't say anything else.

"But you knew she would be here," Justine prompted. "What did you think was going to happen, Keegan?"

Keegan slowly unwrapped his hands, shrugged. "I don't know, I just ... I didn't think it would be like this."

"Like what?"

His dark lashes flicked up as the camera zoomed in. "I didn't think I'd still be so in love with her."

My mother actually gasped.

The video cut to the massage room, and my insides shriveled. I hadn't even told Tristan what happened. My face slowly warmed as an image of me and Mina filled the screen. Mina's serene face gazed up at me as I told her my shoulders were tight. I hadn't realized how big my eyes were, how tightly my hand clutched the robe's fluffy lapels. I looked terrified.

"Do you get to keep that robe, Aoife?" Nyxa practically shrieked.

My mother pointed at Mina. "I bet it was nice to get a real massage."

I shrank further in on myself when the camera cut to the curtain sweeping back. From Keegan's perspective, On-Screen Aoife lifted her head, eyes going wide. The camera cut to a view of the entire room. The entire family shrieked or gasped.

"You didn't tell me they pulled that shit!" Tristan half-stood from his spot, throwing his napkin to the table. I wrapped my arms around my legs and pressed my face into my knees. My entire body flushed hot. They played the entirety of our exchange from the tables. I glanced up once after my final volley to see they had cut to Keegan's reaction again.

Once again, his eyes darkened with pain. My heart twisted just as anger burned hot. How dare he? Was he just playing all this up for the cameras?

It was clear they were milking the former-love-interest angle for all it was worth. When the credits rolled, I collected the three nearest plates and strode to the kitchen. But our apartment was far from large, and even with the water running, I could hear the conversation from the main room.

"I can't believe he's doing this after breaking her heart." Felix. I'd never heard my earnest little brother with so much rage in his voice.

"There's more to this story." My father. "No matter what they put on that screen, no one really knows what that boy has been through in the past year."

"Well, it really doesn't matter." Tristan. "Aoife's gonna kick his ass."

Tapping at my window jolted me from a dead sleep.

I flipped to my feet, yanking my knife from between the mattress and box spring before my eyes landed on the figure crouched on our back steps. Even with his hood pulled up, I recognized Keegan. How the hell had he found me?

Making no effort to conceal the knife, I thumbed open the locks and slid the window open two inches. "Go away," I whispered, glancing toward Nyxa's still sleeping form.

"Aoife, can we have one conversation without cameras in our faces?" Keegan whispered, his long fingers curling over the edge of the window frame.

I sighed. I squeezed my eyes shut, lowering the knife and feeling every ache in my exhausted body.

"Keeeegaaaaaan!" Nyxa squeaked in the loudest whisper ever. Before I could say anything, she hopped out of bed, straightened her large sleep shirt and shoved the window all the way open.

"Hey, Bub," Keegan whispered, and my heart lurched. I'd forgotten that Nyxa allowed Keegan to use her family nickname. Then he was climbing through the window.

"What do you think you're doing?" I rasped.

But Nyxa's arms were around his neck as soon as he crouched to the floor. He hugged her back and I sighed, stuffing my knife back into its hiding place. I plopped to a seat on the floor.

"How are Bridget and Connor?" Nyxa asked. My stomach dipped.

Keegan smiled. "They're good. We live in New York now, and they stayed up there with our mom. I'll tell them you asked about them. They miss you."

Nyxa settled to the rug, folding her legs beneath her as if guys climbed through our window regularly. "Why didn't you tell us you went to New York?"

Keegan's eyes swept to mine, holding for a heartbeat. "I couldn't tell you. Our family got black-flagged for indenture. There was no putting it off."

In spite of everything, fear curled up my spine. Being red-carded was bad, but once you were black-flagged that meant no room for negotiations. Get your affairs in order and your one bag packed because someone was coming to collect you in twenty-four hours.

"Who did they flag?" I asked. A chill rolled over me that had nothing to do with the open window.

"Me and my mom. The twins would have been put in the system."

My throat tightened. "We would have taken them."

He snorted. "You know they wouldn't have given them to you even if you applied. Your family was only one step further from the edge than us."

I dropped my eyes, that red card swimming through my mind.

"We got lucky; a great-uncle from my dad's side finally found Mom and said he'd help, but we had to leave fast. We left that night with bus tickets and one bag apiece. We had to ditch our phones and everything."

This all made sense. It answered every question that had been rolling around in my mind for the past year. Except for why he had never reached out. And why reappear now? Why this way? I tried to restack my little bricks, but the walls around my heart were crumbling.

"I'm glad you're all okay," I muttered. "But Nyxa and I need our sleep, and lurking outside bedroom windows is creepy. If we keep whispering we'll wake someone else." That last part was true. Nyxa whispered about as quietly as a rooster.

I flinched when Keegan slid a hand to my cheek. When had he moved so close? "Aoife, for the love of God, please give me ten minutes." His thumb brushed my cheekbone.

I pulled away, heart pounding. "I don't know what you think ten minutes is going to change."

Nyxa sighed dramatically, swiping the back of her hand across her forehead before she stood. "I'll pretend to have a nightmare and go crawl in with Ma and Dad."

"You don't need to leave, Nyxa." I wrapped my fingers around her hand.

She squeezed back. "You need to talk or whatever." She pulled away and threw her arms around Keegan, her lips moving by his ear. His face went still, and although she had been whispering loud enough to wake the dead before, I couldn't make out her words. When she leaned away, he pushed out a small smile that didn't meet his eyes. She patted him on the shoulder and strolled toward the door.

As soon as she'd shut it behind her, I turned to Keegan. "What did she say to you?"

He ignored my question. "It took six months to get our file cleared." His blue eyes were bright. "Even with my uncle—who I'd never met before, by the way—paying everything off, we had to stay off the grid until it was resolved. I wanted to talk to you, Aoife. I missed you so fucking much." He put his hand over mine where I had it pressed into the rug. "And New York is cold as hell and everyone is brusque and in a hurry."

I just stared at his hand. Covering mine completely. "So your family is okay."

His thumb brushed along my wrist. "Yeah, the twins are—"

"So you can forfeit." I finally looked him in the eye. "Your family has help. Mine just got red-carded."

His jaw tightened when I dropped that news. "Isn't the money from the behind the scenes stuff helping with that?"

"Why do you think I'm doing it?" I answered flatly, a slow burning anger growing behind my ribcage. "Do you think I enjoy getting ambushed by my ex on camera? That personal shit is being broadcast to the entire country for funsies?" I moved closer, hissing inches from his face.

"If I could have told you before I would—"

"You found me just fine tonight. I'm calling bullshit. In fact, I'm calling bullshit on this whole thing. Get out." I stood so quickly, gray spots flooded my vision for an instant.

It gave Keegan the second he needed to get in front of me and wrap his hands around my arms. "*Listen* to me," he pushed out through clenched teeth. "I can't forfeit because my uncle put this show together."

That stunned me into stillness.

"It was part of the whole deal." His words tumbled out in a hurried whisper. "He would take us in and clear our debts, but my mother had to agree to a conservatorship. Basically he makes the decisions for our family until the twins are fully independent. So, if he pays for college for them, it will be after they graduate and have their own jobs. Right now they're both in boarding school. My mother is taking coding classes. She's struggling, but she's doing her best. Since I was already a fighter, he threw me into this. Got me the best trainers and said I was going to make it to the finals and give

Justine a good show. He's one of her sponsors. I have to see this all the way to the end." He swallowed.

My brow crinkled. "Did you tell him about me?"

He shook his head. "I knew Scorpion was you but ... I wouldn't have put it past them to rig some of your fights to make sure we didn't face off." His throat worked. "I didn't want you to lose that way. And selfishly, I wanted to see you. After everything was clear, I was allowed to get online again. I checked my accounts. I got all those emails you sent me. And I did try to write back, even though ... "

I had blocked him. My last email had been an emotional mess. With no word for months, I was never going to forgive him. So I spewed everything I felt for several pages, then blocked him on absolutely everything.

I pulled in a shaky breath.

"I wanted to see that you were doing okay now. That your family was good." His hands swept down my arms until his fingers found mine. My skin tingled, but I didn't pull away. He brought my hands together, cupping them in one of his and playing with my fingers, following the movement with his eyes. "Thought maybe I'd see who your new boyfriend was."

Something sharp twinged near my heart.

Keegan shrugged. "Figured I'd hate him a bit, but ... hopefully he'd be ... " He cleared his throat. "Treating you nice or whatever. And I could move on, too."

But there was no new boyfriend. My family was still on the brink. And I was not okay.

He moved closer, his sigh ruffling my hair. "Then you walked into the locker room and ... God, I'm sorry, Aoife."

My eyes were burning. My muscles locked up with the effort of holding back tears. "What did your uncle say after the episode today?"

He huffed a laugh, but there was no humor behind it. "He fucking loves it. Says it's all over social media, people are eating it up." His tone went bitter. "Told me to keep it up, but under no circumstances was I to throw the fight and let you win."

I stared at him, willing him to look at me, but he continued watching our hands. "What did you say?"

His eyes finally found mine, a cutting sadness lurking there. "I told him you would hate me forever if I let you win."

My lips curled. "True."

He tried to slide his fingers under my chin. I pulled away, but didn't step back. Cautiously, he guided my hands to his shoulders, then dropped his hands to my waist. I tensed.

Keegan dropped his forehead against mine. "I've replayed it in my mind a thousand times, Aoife. I've imagined grabbing you in the middle of the night and telling you we had to go. Sending you a coded letter. Once I almost mailed you a postcard. Just a blank postcard from New York. But my uncle found it before I could get a stamp."

My breath was hitching, my fingers curled into the fabric of his shirt. Soft. Expensive. But he still smelled the same.

His lips inched closer to mine as he whispered, "I never stopped loving you, Aoife."

A creak and a grunt from the hall. "Let's get you back in your own bed, Bub."

I shoved Keegan toward the window as Nyxa wailed, giving us a warning. Keegan scrambled over the sill as the first tear cut a path down my cheek. I reached up to slam it shut, but Keegan caught a glimpse of my face and shoved a hand against the bottom rail to hold it open.

I knelt in front of it, trying to wrench his hand away, another tear following the first. They were coming faster now.

Keegan curled his other hand around the nape of my neck. "I love you. No matter what happens."

"Don't do this to me," I wheezed, throat burning, face breaking as my walls finally cracked. "I have to kick your ass in a few days."

"I'll love you even if you kick my ass," he said while Nyxa's fake tantrum grew louder, spurring my own tears on.

"My heart can't take this, Keegan. I can't let myself care again and then—"

A flash of light from the alley caught our attention.

A camera crew.

They must have followed him here. Who knew how much they'd caught. I shoved Keegan away and slammed the window as he fled.

Tristan and I got back to training in the morning. No sparring until I healed a bit more, but mitt drills and bag work were a go. I wrapped my hands and grabbed my sixteen ounce gloves. Tristan had me wear heavier gloves on these days, both to condition my arms and protect my hands. We were well into a drill, a camera floating around us, by the time Keegan arrived with his team. My skin prickled when he paused at the edge of the mats, watching. But when I didn't look back, he moved on.

Later, when Keegan tried to approach during a break, Tristan waved him off, his expression hard as granite. The back of my neck burned, but I kept my head down, knowing that if I met his eyes, he'd see right through me.

That night, they aired our balcony scene. Justine had brought in another influencer, famous for reading lips, to translate what we said, and she was infuriatingly accurate. They caught everything: my tears, Keegan's professions of love, his fleeing. They twisted the knife by splicing in footage of me studiously ignoring him during training.

To my surprise, Keegan reiterated his family's escape story during an on-camera interview. I wondered what the Debt Enforcement Initiative would think of that.

Over the next few days, Tristan pushed me harder than ever and managed to keep Keegan away from me. Still, every evening a fresh horror rolled out on the stream. To my family's utter mortification, they'd managed to interview Nyxa at school, and she had happily complied. Upon angrily rifling through our copies of the paperwork, my father was mortified to see that they had agreed to this.

"Aoife cried and cried when Keegan disappeared," she supplied, eyes wide, little fingers wrapped around the straps of her backpack. "He was like part of the family. They were for sure going to get married and then he was gone. She couldn't find him anywhere and she stopped eating and got really skinny and it was so sad."

She concluded the interview by informing Justine that our family had been red-carded. "No one thinks I know." She rolled her eyes. "But that's why Aoife has to win. Too bad it has to be against Keegan. It's very sad, don't you think?"

Our parents cursed themselves for not reading more carefully, but Tristan reminded them in a hollow voice that we had been ambushed in the middle of the night with more fine print than we could possibly have gone through in the time they were pressuring us to sign.

Public attention only ratcheted up. There were memes. Opinion articles. Requests for interviews poured in. But the show had exclusivity, so we could only do the ones they oversaw. Tristan demanded very specific parameters, but I hated every second of it. Tristan told them not to ask me about Keegan, but they all tried anyway.

Keegan didn't try to come by the apartment again.

The day before the fight, I was strung so tight I didn't think a thousand massages would have loosened my shoulders.

The final pre-fight episode was a two-hour special. I almost didn't watch it, but there was no way I could sit in my room while the rest of my family clustered around the laptop.

This one started with a recap, a few clips of our fights, a reminder of how brutal The Grit was, and then our unexpected personal history. My face when I saw Keegan for the first time. Tristan punching him. My tears on the balcony, complete with subtitles. Even Nyxa got a clip. "It's very sad, don't you think?"

Justine shifted to how the story had captured national attention, flashed a few of the memes, and then some protest footage I hadn't seen before. "What's that?"

"People have been protesting the indenture system," Dad said quietly.

I blinked, then refocused on the screen. Justine's team had collected street interviews.

A grizzled old man in a raincoat confronted the camera. "Look how young those kids are. That little girl is ruining her body fighting—literally fighting—for her family's freedom. Because they had to go to the doctor and got behind? What is this?"

"We're just all hoping they get together." A redhead in her twenties stood with a group of friends outside a movie theatre. "They're obviously in love. They deserve a happy ending!"

"*We* deserve their happy ending!" one of her friends screeched.

My heart stopped when Felix's face filled the screen, the tag beneath him giving his name and our relationship. The collective familial groan was deafening. Cries of, "Couldn't you have tried to run away, sweetheart?" "When was this?" "I want to strangle these people!" died down quickly as Felix started speaking in that older-than-thirteen way of his.

"I really hated Keegan when he first showed up. He didn't have to ambush my sister like that. No one else saw how messed up she was when he left. I even wondered if he was dead after a while. Because he would never leave Aoife like that if he could get to her. Or at least, that's what I thought."

The microphone tilted toward Justine off-camera. "And what do you think now? Do you still hate Keegan?"

Felix took a breath, glanced at the microphone, then blinked owlishly. "Now I hate the people in charge of the Debt Enforcement Initiative. And everyone who's in charge of this entire system. My sister doesn't have any good choices right now. Keegan doesn't have any good choices. They have to get in the ring and hurt each other. They have to hurt someone they love because there's nothing else they can do."

Everyone was quiet for a moment while the screen cut back and forth between footage of me and Keegan training. I glanced at my little brother, sitting straight-backed beside me.

"I'm sorry," Felix said, not sounding sorry. "I couldn't just say nothing."

Tristan put an arm around his shoulders, pulling him into a hug.

The studio sent a giant SUV to pick us up the evening of the fight. Ma, Felix, and Nyxa got ringside seats—although I didn't like my younger siblings sitting front row to the carnage—and since Tristan was allowed a second, our father was the obvious choice. The corner's second had to remain silent; only Tristan could give me instruction, although they could confer with each other discreetly during the fight.

We stepped from the car with duffles full of shiny new clothes and spotless gear, courtesy of the show. I hugged Ma, Nyxa, and Felix goodbye, throat tight and heart hammering.

Even in the locker rooms, the crowd was deafening.

I pulled my robe out of the bag and shook it out. It was dark red, trimmed with black. The body of a scorpion rested on my spine with the tail winding down the left side and up the right, effectively making up the entire train.

My father and brother pulled jackets from their own bags, each displaying the same scorpion. "At least the gear is nice." Tristan checked his watch. "Alright, we gotta get out there."

Dad put a hand on my elbow. "No matter what happens tonight, I am so very proud of you." He dipped his chin toward Tristan. "Both of you."

My eyes stung, but my lips trembled upward. "Thanks."

Tristan wrapped his hand around the door handle and lifted his eyebrows. I took a breath, shakily tucking all the soft pieces of myself away. When I nodded, Tristan pulled open the door, and the cameras were on us.

The roar of the crowd hit me like a physical blow. I barely heard my entrance music as we marched toward the ring. Everything else faded away. I knew my family was seated somewhere close by, but I didn't look for them as I climbed through the ropes.

Keegan and his team were already there. Our eyes met, and my heart lurched. Tristan tapped me. "Let's avoid your typical openers for the first couple rounds. Keegan has always been tough to knock out, so let's make points a priority up front." He rinsed my mouthguard and shoved it in place. "This is why we've been training for stamina."

I nodded. Grit fights were officially fourteen rounds, but most never made it beyond six. I already knew this one would go longer.

Every muscle in my body tightened. My chest buzzed with nerves as I stepped toward the center of the ring. My eyes flicked to Keegan's gray irises as we faced each other. Something devastating flashed there before his gaze shuttered. We touched gloves and slid into fighting stances. I dropped my eyes to his chest and waited for the bell.

Keegan struck first. I slipped his jab and was inside his guard in an instant. Two quick body shots and I danced away, aiming a roundhouse at his hamstring en route, which he dodged.

The rest of the round continued that way as we felt each other out. Keegan landed a few strikes, but I thought I might be ahead. I trotted back to Tristan at the bell.

"Way to control the round," he said, giving me a squirt from the water bottle. "You've proven you can get inside his guard, so he'll be watching for that this time around. Let's get your feet more involved, see if you can weaken his lead leg."

I technically picked Keegan apart for two more rounds, but the crowd was getting impatient. Even the ones holding posters with our names sitting inside a giant heart wanted a show. Although my goal had been to control the rounds, Keegan hadn't exposed any glaring weaknesses. I had a feeling that both of us were still holding back.

I glanced at his corner between the fourth and fifth rounds to see a man in a suit yelling at Keegan. Technically, only his corner should be talking to him, so this guy must've been important. Probably the infamous uncle.

Tristan saw it too. "I don't think we're going to get away with the same shit this next round." He swiped my face with a towel. "Keegan knows you don't like the ground, so he'll probably try to take you down. I think it's time for the big guns. After the last four rounds, he won't expect it."

Sure enough, Keegan surged forward at the bell, going for a takedown. I shifted my weight, lifted my knee, then smashed my heel into his chin. The front kick to the face was one of my favorite openers, which is why I waited to pull it out. Keegan was difficult to rock, but his right hand dropped a few inches as he stepped back to regroup. I chased him with a spinning backfist, landing a left hook immediately afterward. Keegan yanked his right hand up to block, and I sank my right shin into his unguarded stomach.

The noise from the crowd swelled. Instead of backing off as I had done in previous rounds, I continued to press, breaking up punches with kicks.

Finally, Keegan managed to circle out, knocking my jab to the side and coming over my left with a hard cross, effectively breaking my blitz. Our eyes met, a flash of pain flickering behind his gaze before he slammed his elbow into my face.

I had no choice but to back away. My ears rang. A coppery tang washed over my tongue.

Keegan didn't wait, but drove his shoulder into my stomach, propelling me into the ground.

I twisted, driving my elbow between his ribs, making space before he could throw his full weight on top of me. I managed to get my knee between us, but Keegan's forearms bracketed my neck, going for a choke. I thrust my hand between his arm and my neck.

He dropped his head and shifted his weight, pushing a small sound from my throat directly into his ear. He froze, hesitating for half a second.

I took advantage, yanking my arm from beneath him and jamming a knuckle into the space just behind his ear. Where the head goes, the body follows.

When he unbalanced, I shoved with my knee then rolled away, springing to my feet just as the bell rang.

Tristan swiped at my face with a towel, and it came away bright red. He swapped it for the tin of petroleum jelly Dad held and slathered my left eyebrow with it. "You're going to have a shiner, but hopefully we can keep it from bleeding into your eye. Keep your left guarded. We cannot let him open this up again. I want elbows to his body this round. Knees into his IT band. Get in, hit hard, get out."

The next several rounds were messy. The crowd was getting the show they wanted, but some viewers—possibly the ones who were only here for our "romance"—occasionally broke into chants of "stop the fight."

The officials ignored them. Nothing short of a knockout was stopping this fight.

In the tenth round, I managed to drive a knee into Keegan's face. His nose had ballooned to the point that breathing had to be uncomfortable. Keegan favored his left side where I'd been driving elbows into his ribs whenever I got in close.

I paid for it, though. Keegan hammered away at the cut on my left eyebrow, successfully opening it up again. My eye was so swollen, I could barely see out of it. He no longer let me inside without dropping an elbow or an overhand somewhere before I danced away. And his blows were landing more frequently.

When the bell rang on the twelfth round, I practically fell onto the stool that Tristan shoved under the ropes. "We're gonna cut to let the blood out or you won't be able to see, okay?"

I dipped my chin once, shutting my good eye as Tristan jumped into the ring. He crouched in front of me. A flash of steel, then a sting beneath my eyebrow. Blood ran hot down my face, chased by Tristan's damp towel. Then a sting as my father smeared jelly over the new wound. "Just two more rounds. This is probably going to decision, which we knew was a possibility. I think you're ahead on points already, so I just want you to hang in there. Don't take any more damage, okay? Stay at kicking range and don't let him take you down."

Standing up from the stool had me panting. My vision stuttered. I couldn't take any more hard head hits. My bell was already rung.

Keegan didn't seem to be faring much better. He was now favoring his left leg in addition to his side. He even switched stances, putting his right foot forward. The bell sounded. My calves protested as I bounced to the balls of my feet, faking energy I did not possess.

Keegan threw a few sluggish jabs, but I didn't take the bait, staying outside of his range and biding my time. My skeleton felt like lead. My muscles dragged but I parried his next strike, forcing my limbs to shoot in just close enough to land a sidekick to his lead leg. He switched his stance, and I realized too late that he had been faking the leg weakness. I avoided the full hit, but he still caught me with his jab. My eyes stung as blood from my reopened wound splashed into them.

The world tilted again. I stumbled away, throwing straight punches to keep Keegan off me while I shook off the hit. He knocked my jab down and tried to come over the top of my guard, but I brought up my front kick in time to catch him in the chest. My weight shift was too far back, and instead of throwing him into the ropes, the kick had both of us staggering away from each other.

Our clashes became sloppier. Keegan may have been faking the severity of his leg injury, but he was clearly still in pain. He tried a couple of messy takedowns. I barely slipped out of them, but it cost me points.

My head swam, nausea beginning to set in. I counted the seconds until the end of the round. Just a little bit longer.

With just moments left until the bell, Keegan came at me with a spinning side kick. I wasn't fast enough to step back and threw up my forearms to block.

The sharp snap of my left arm breaking echoed throughout the stadium.

Empathetic shouts from the crowd drowned out my pained cry. Keegan's eyes widened as the bell rang. "Aoife ... "

I stumbled away from him, gingerly cradling my arm to my chest as I plopped onto the stool in my corner. Tristan jumped in front of me, pulled out my mouthguard. "One more round, just hang in there." His brows were knotted, face lined with tension.

"Tris, you have to wrap my arm," I gasped. It was already swelling. I fought to keep from writhing as pain lit up my nerves.

"If we wrap it, he'll know it's broken and—"

"He knows it's fucking broken!" I shouted, agony tearing my words. "He felt it snap. The entire crowd heard it. It's one more round, Tris, just wrap it, please!"

My father was already tapping him on the arm with an extra hand wrap. One of my pretty red ones. Tristan snatched it out of his hand. "Okay, give me your arm." He shoved my mouthguard back in place, and I clamped my teeth down on it as my brother wound the fabric around my swelling forearm. Tears sprang to my eyes, and I sucked in deep breaths.

Too soon, the bell clanged for the final round. I staggered forward, eyes locked on Keegan. He didn't look much better than I felt. His left eye was swelling, and his injured leg moved stiffly.

I switched stances, keeping my left arm back. The energy from the crowd was odd, cheers and applause cresting in waves with cries of "stop the fight!" peppered throughout. From somewhere on my right, Nyxa shrieked, "Hang on, Aoife!" I resisted the urge to glance toward her.

Keegan threw a few probing jabs, his eyes no longer shuttered. It made it so much more difficult to read the emotion he no longer had the energy to hide. Clenching my teeth, I knocked his arm to the side with a crescent kick and followed up with a right to his sore ribs, drawing a grunt from him and driving a pang into my gut. His eyes found mine and my vision blurred. I must have swayed because the crowd gasped. When I refocused, concern darkened Keegan's good eye.

But he had no choice; he came at me again. This time faking a knee, but he was so spent he couldn't control his tells. I slipped his follow-up cross, falling into my standard fighting stance automatically before switching to southpaw again.

I tucked my broken arm to my chest, not daring to use it. Although my legs felt like anchors, I managed a three-kick combo and landed another solid hit to Keegan's injured leg, pulling a cry from him. The sound slid into my heart like a knife.

*God, I'm sorry.*

He rallied and started using his reach, throwing long straight punches continually. He didn't seem inclined to kick, but he staggered after me as best he could. He knew I couldn't risk going inside his guard now. Not with seconds left on the clock and a broken arm.

But I had to do something. My arms were mostly useless, but my legs still worked. I used my right hand to parry, taking shot after shot at his lower body. The noise of the crowd crescendoed as the ten-second warning sounded.

Mid-kick, I felt the ropes touch my back. *No!*

In spite of the pain, I switched back to my conventional stance and knocked his next cross aside with my broken arm, agony shooting through every nerve, before coming in with an overhand right, landing a glancing blow on his nose. Teeth clenched against nausea, I threw everything into a spinning hook kick. I could barely see anymore, but felt my heel connect.

Keegan's arms dropped and his face went slack. The ref leapt between us just as the final bell clanged. Keegan dropped to his knees, bringing one hand up to grip the ropes in a valiant effort to avoid collapsing.

"Keegan ... " I started toward him, but the ref pushed me toward my own corner.

That was all it took. No sooner had I spotted Tristan, already climbing between the ropes, than the world tilted. The canvas came up to meet me with alarming speed.

An annoying beeping pulled me into consciousness. My head felt twice its usual size. I ached everywhere, but the pain felt far away. Drugs. Hospital. I blinked, taking in my surroundings. Tubes, machines, and bleached white everything. A small television mounted high on the wall quietly played a news segment.

My head dropped to the side. Felix was seated in a chair to my left, nose in a book. He glanced up when I moved, a tiny smile curling his mouth. He glanced at his page number—the nutball didn't use bookmarks, just memorized page numbers—then closed the book and turned to me.

"It's after eleven p.m. on the same day of the fight. You have a fractured radius. And a concussion, but you're going to be fine. I picked out the color for your cast. Everyone has been taking turns sitting with you since visiting hours are technically over, so only one person is allowed at a time. We've convinced them I'm seventeen." He smiled like a Cheshire Cat.

"What happened?" I croaked, my voice creaking like an octogenarian smoker.

"A double knockout." Felix pushed his glasses up the bridge of his nose. "Keegan hit the canvas seconds before you did. But since the fight was technically over, it went to the judges. It was close, but you won by split decision."

I lifted my left arm. A cast with red wrapping covered it from knuckles to elbow. "NYXA LOVES YOU" had been scrawled across it in black marker.

"Where did they take Keegan?" My stomach turned as I asked. Was he already on the way back to New York? Was he going to disappear again?

Felix stood, set his book on the chair, and marched to the curtain dividing the room. He pushed it out of the way, revealing another bed containing a very battered, very still man.

Felix peered down at Keegan, tilting his head, then shrugged and crossed to me. "You look pretty bad, but not quite as bad as he does. He has a concussion also, severe bruising on his left leg, and a cracked rib."

"Why isn't anyone with him?" I couldn't tear my eyes away from Keegan's motionless form.

Felix shrugged. "His team is off the clock." He glanced up at me. "Ma told them to put him in your room so we could watch out for both of you."

My throat tightened. "Has he—" My voice cracked and I cleared my throat.

"He hasn't woken up yet. Are you thirsty? You can have ice chips, but that's about it. I just have to ask at the nurse's station." He was already moving toward the door. "Be right back."

I let my eyes fall shut, exhausted. For a few minutes, I just listened to the soft beeping of the machinery. At least the Grit Commission would be covering the bill.

"Aoife?"

One of Keegan's eyes was now open and focused on me, the other still swollen shut.

I attempted a smile. "You'll be happy to know that I won. But by split decision. Apparently we passed out seconds apart after the bell rang."

He groaned and made to push himself upright.

"I wouldn't do that if I were you. Felix says you have a cracked rib."

He grimaced and lowered himself back down. "But you're all the way over there."

My lips curved upward, which was a little painful. "Maybe we can ask them to move us closer together."

"I'd really like that. I don't want to go back to New York right away, Aoife. Not unless you come with me."

His open eye was shining. "Now that this is over, do you think ... maybe ... "

I swallowed, the back of my throat burning. "I think, maybe."

"I was correct in getting two cups," Felix announced, heading to Keegan. "Since you have two working arms, you can hold your own. I'll help Aoife if she needs it."

"Thanks, Felix." Keegan took his ice chips. "I missed you a lot. So did Connor and Bridget."

"Of course you did. I'm delightful." Felix held a cup out to me, the pinking of his ears the only indication that Keegan's words affected him.

I dropped a few ice chips into my mouth. *God I never knew ice chips could taste or feel so good.* Felix glanced toward the TV, then tucked the cup into the crook of my elbow just above my cast.

"We should watch this." He grabbed the remote control and turned up the volume. A vocal crowd of people marched across the screen carrying signs.

"What is it?" Keegan asked around a mouthful of ice.

"Protests," Felix said, dropping the remote to my blankets and grabbing my cup. "Your show raised awareness about the indenture system. People are angry. They want the laws to change." He smiled and shook the ice chips at me. "You started something good. For a lot of people."

I popped a few chips into my mouth, focusing on the news anchor.

" ... two fighters are currently hospitalized, but both are expected to make full recoveries." A photo of Keegan and me from over a year ago flashed on the screen. We were grinning and holding up our high school diplomas. "The one question everyone keeps asking—well, aside from *will they get back together*—is if they'll be involved in the MSFA organization."

"They want us involved?" I reached for more ice.

"What is MSFA?" Keegan asked.

Felix nodded. "Medical Stability For All. They want you to speak at rallies and stuff. I guess the group has been operating for a while, but your story has given it much more visibility. It would be good for momentum to have you both on board. Justine's followers are apparently donating a lot."

I glanced toward Keegan, raising my eyebrows. Which hurt.

He gave a lopsided smile. "What do you think?"

I winked. Not painful. "It might be nice to do a different kind of fighting for a change."

# Bourbon Brawl

## by Ashley Erwin

**Gutterball Gary** gripped that rope like it were a bucking bronco, like he's six sheets to the wind on a double dawg dare, and one of his buddies had just slammed down a hundo, sparking out, "That there weren't no way in fried hell he's gonna be able to hold that barrel up there for more than six flat."

He were going on five after five, except it weren't no dare. That bona fide bastard were holding steady-Chevy ten-feet high direct overtop Rusty Reynolds planning a drop—any second now—of that 53-gallon barrel. And just to put some optics on that right quick, that's five hundred pounds of booze spelled out with a capital B. That'll slam down on a fella and kill him dead 'fore the thing even goes to pop its cherry. And once that juice does start to spill, once 'em staves, which is what they call 'em individual portions of wood bent up and fitted inside 'em two metal rings (right proper sort of business that is) that wood was going splinter in long, sharp shards that, if you're lucky and already dead, won't do nothing but gouge the hell outta your body. But let's say that fella Rusty Reynolds somehow or another gets that jack rabbit pep in his step to go on and shake tail a little, moving out of the fire zone so to speak, and don't get his ass crushed to smithereens. Well, 'em splinters are gonna be a whole other problem ain't they? And to complicate things, cause we's in the complicating part of it, right in the meat, ya know, right there in that waft of bourbon piston shifting alive, that thick-rick notion charging warm nuzzle squeeze on your innards as to the fair dereliction exposed, we're gonna need to boot-scoot-and-boogie on out of here tout suite for a Quick Rick Rewind to earlier.

And it might be of note that the precarious occasion of Rusty Reynolds, standing as he were in the middle of Rickhouse 5, amongst all 'em barrels of booze aging ...

"Hold on a second, we got a clarity issue, here."

(A rickhouse is a tall, long building akin to a warehouse, that depending on personal preference of the distillery, will or will not have windows, meaning glass, or bars pot-marking the face and sides of it, and it'll range give or take quarter of a football field, maybe sometimes longer. And inside that behemoth of wood or metal or brick, there will sit anywhere from 10,000 to 60,000 barrels of aging bourbon just waiting for the primed time to be picked and sipped.)

"Better? Good."

... were caused by what Gutterball Gary'd refer to as a "slack-jawed-boy."

Now, it's going to be a hard one to maneuver so keep calm and tugalug along.

The "slack-jawed-boy" had less to do with the physicality of John-Boy's face than it did with 'em loose spurting lips that'd go 90 miles a minute if given the right amount of fuel, AKA bourbon, and well if he weren't in the middle of spelling something right Gawd awful on the back patio of Tate's in Nulu ... Nulu, meaning "New Louisville," as Gutterball Gary was coming in direct off the clock for a quick pick-me-up before the long head home.

And it were known that of all the crater-faced companions that John-Boy ran around with, the one that Gutterball Gary could not and would not stand, was none other than Beaufort Biggen, aka Bitty-Beau. And if you got any inclination as to where this story's going to go, then you know for gawddamned sure that it were none other than Bitty-Beau that John-Boy were talking and telling his story to.

"Well Pete come off that tractor with a shit-kicking grin about the size of fucking Texas wanting nothing else than to send that pork-fat-boy right into next week for what he did to his brother, Bobby. And by Gawd, if Bobby weren't standing there on the sidelines egging the whole gawddamned thing on. Pulled his John Deere shirt off and had that loose belly just'a flapping in the wind out there with all 'em cars whizzing by. And that damned road were so fucking skinny that tractor done stuck out like a sore fucking thumb, it did, forcing all 'em blue hairs on the way to Sunday School to pull 'em Oldsmobiles right 'round it and go to clog up the damned thoroughfare to the point that it had cadenced out to the long line of cars waiting in some bugle horn fury that the whole lot of 'em were going to be late for Pastor Green's sermon. And that simply wasn't going to cut it for little Miss Hattie Vaughn, who took it upon herself to ram that size 4 foot down on the gas pedal and start driving against traffic with a threat to hell that she'd take the lot of them if they prevented her move."

Now, far be it from me to keep you from a good story, but there's another little spit of clarifying that might could lend itself pertinent at this very juncture, if ya catch my drift. Not only was John-Boy a known attitudinal embellisher, which kicked into gear right around the time that fourth beer and third bourbon hit, but he was also a bad drunk, one that had been banned from near about every establishment in the entirety of Jefferson County and was in fact only allowed on the back patio of Tate's because Tate was his cousin and, well, John-Boy there weren't so much a paying customer as he was the forced attrition of Tate's aunt's bad taste in men. And as doubtful as it may be to hear, Tate simply and firmly believed that there was no amount of barring John-Boy from the bar that was going to actually keep him out 'cause sure enough every time he did, the long show of poor-scuffling-boy through that narrow alleyway and down the street only lasted for a good swift thirty before he was back with a fresh pulled frosty out the cooler in his truck and a flask full of nothing good.

It would then go without saying that this next response was not therefore unjustly timed. "Hold your horses, John-Boy, we all know what you're trying to do here and it simply ain't going to work this time. You fess up and tell the truth, you hear."

To which, after taking a very long sip, John-Boy began anew with a heartfelt, "Ya got me there, sure enough did."

See, the thing of it were, everyone in town knew the truth 'cause not only did it make the Sunday Gazette, but it also made the local news, and there was no way on this green earth that anyone was ever going to get it out of their heads the image of little Miss Hattie Vaughn standing on the side of the road flashing her undergarments while Bobby, the one who was actually driving the car, to charge down that road going faster than a bullet and damn near kill that little old woman if it weren't for Gutterball Gary scouting for his escaped-from-the-home-aunt and pulling her out of harm's way.

And Bobby, having a very strong relationship with the mayor of the town, having been a long-standing member to the Private Horse Society that met every Thursday evening for the last thirty years, that very same club that garnered legacy tighter to the chest than a pair of aces on the river, did in fact not spend a lick of time in the holding cell before he was publicly careened out the door by said mayor and walked dubiously down the front steps of the government building with nothing more than a polite pat on the back and the ushering of what sentiments hearsay recollected as, "Maybe take it easy on the sauce for a while," of which he most certainly did not. Because not two days later in an act of spite and perhaps retribution to the fact that he took one helluva whack on the noggin once Gutterball Gary got his Aunt to safe keeping, which were in the hands of his childhood best friend Frank Freddie, forever known since the age of five as Fast Frank Freddie, did Bobby ram his dually truck into Gutterball Gary's mailbox and ruin his wife's pink petunias planted close therein.

It could then come as quite the understandable scenario that when Gutterball Gary walked further into Tate's and saw the regalia playing out, hearing that same dumb story that'd took three left turns at true and never did find its way back, that he were persnickety pissed and weighing as it were the main objectives of his ill temper, Rusty Reynolds laughing until his beer near shooting out his nose, Bitty-Beau with the knee slap of the century as he worked through a side stitch of a giggle, and John-Boy there still clapping flap in the wind with even more falsehoods, that he did what any man set to suppressed rage would do. He bee-lined it for the bar and said, "Tommy ... " (Tommy, Tate's half-brother who just so happened to be folded back into the family once their prospective parents found a rekindling of feelings after a shared karaoke delight of Reba's "Fancy on loop") " ... it's going to be one of those nights."

In the South as I'm sure it might very well stand in similar measure in other more gregarious settings, "one of those nights," sits in the synonymous holding that things are about to get fucked. It's been said and sometimes believed that the Northerners more versed towards drinking until passing out drunk with the occasional stealing of public property, that of a road sign with innuendo, the ever-daunting drive-through rager of cheeseburger showdown, or the allusive and somewhat troubling capacity for the dreaded visit to an ex. But in the South, and this was true without fail, when there was the grand annunciation of "It's going to be one of those nights," you can bet your bottom dollar that means one thing and one thing only: there's going to be a fight, and

Gawd willing it might very well be as Tommy replied, "one for the books," to which the undertow'd inference that it might very well teeter into that most rarest of realms, "A barn burner," which were exactly what Gutterball Gary's lifted eyebrows spoke to.

The further solidification of cement drop came by way of Fast Frank Freddie's cellular device positioning with haste underneath the table with the ever-discreet lowered down glow of the grand call-to-arms cavalcade text to the goodest of boy's group:

Tate's. Five. FREDDO for Gutterball.

The bat signal of FREDDO had been used since grade school only under the most dire of circumstances, the grand recollection of when Jerry Two-Ton got his front teeth knocked out by Reginald Dalton, the unnatural alignment of cascading stars on the failed attempt of Marion Billy-Bob Anders to win over the hand of Gloria Eden, a most unfortunate tangling that resulted in he getting pulled from the girl's nicely-but-never-asked-for-borrowed-father's-car by the nape of his neck and a battered and broken arm, and then the never-to-be-forgotten rumble of Conner McDaniels and his three cousins, which resulted in the unlucky breaking of five arms and two shins. But of all the instances used since, never in the history of its utterance had it been sent on behalf of Gutterball Gary. And so, when those three close friends saw that most daunting of PING come through, every single one of 'em who now made their living as Ricker Riders for the McDaniels Distillery dropped what they were doing in a flurry of truck exhaust.

"Quick question, and pardon the intrusion, but what the hell's a Ricker Rider?"

(In the land of Bourbon, there are two secret keepers amongst the lot, the Master Blender and the Ricker Riders, both of whom are integral to the outcome of the juice. See, it's the Ricker Riders' job to take the vats of big daddy booze off the truck and tuck it in for a nice long nighty-night inside the Rickhouse, and of course it's the Master Blender's prophecy to ensure what's laid down is later good. One in direct accordance with the other and both in symbiosis together.)

"Gotcha. But why Ricker Rider? Why the name?"

(Well, in the McDaniels Distillery, the rickhouses are still beholden to the days of yore, with small 4 X 4 elevator platforms that the Ricker Riders load barrels up and on, and then pulley system to the floor of preferred maturation. It should be noted that not just yesterday, all five of the lot, that of Gutterball Gary, Fast Frank Freddie, Jerry Two-Ton, Marion Billy-Bob Anders, and Conner McDaniels had just laid the last of Row 6 Column 9 in Rickhouse 5 yesterday.)

There hadn't been a fight in the McDaniels Rickhouse since '92, the dreaded Langley Boys versus the eldest McDaniels, a five-on-five full throttle bash and brawl that'd landed all ten of them in the ICU for the better half of a week and out of work for another six months after. It was a frowned-upon figment that when uttered in polite society quickly followed by a whipped hush in hopes the event to never be revisited again, but in the secrecy of midnight, once the whiskey set to flow and the charge of kindness settled from the day, the legend persisted, that long yarn extending from the past a blaze of glory with that most coveted of golden carrots, and it was this very sentiment that propelled Gutterball Gary to leave his station at Tate's bar and mosey up to the table of ne'er-do-wells with a singular force of attrition holstered in his gut ... *settle this once and for all* ... and hollered out for all the crowd to hear: "Challenge!"

There were two things custom dictated soon as those words bare fell on the floor: first one to haul ass to the meet-up-point, chose the terms, and second, bets started soon as the point called out, which were banshee'd from the back of the bar by none other than Tate himself, declaring, "Bar's closed!"

And buddy if you think you've ever seen spit-fire-fast before, I got news for you, ya sure as shit have not, 'cause 'fore there was even a chance for movement to start crawling forward, 'fore John-Boy was gifted with a full hard look from his beer and bourbon post, that dribble of wet spilling down his front, 'fore that spiked fire boiling cauldrons in his chest getting the jet engines of feet to respond and get going, 'fore Bitty-Beau clocked up to that fair strong 11 on good ole Gary there with 'em meat grinders of his ready for pound and fist, there came a growling roar from the street where ...

Outside. Green fog choked lampposts, oxygen clamoring to the floor, Ford Bigfoot Cruisers and hunting lights blind the front of Tate's. Mean, fury rumbling carriers of hell, their engines roared, their grills taking inches on the line, their mouths grumbling for bones and burials, fangs painted across the metal hoods hungry for the next fresh kill, lumbered forward some unnatural beasts bent for savagery. From beds and bars and burdens, they'd appeared in the night, the human juggernaut snaking through the countryside in American made steel with one mission, one tranced induction into the ether, one guiding trajectory, one imperial doomed decision, to cause havoc and mayhem and leave nothing in the rubble.

Gutterball Gary tore from the bar yipping at the heels of a fight, Fast Frank Freddie gripping tight to his left, the fallout of John-Boy, Bitty-Beau, and the just-from-the-shitter Bobby carrying tow at their backs, all of 'em bum-rushing towards vehicles, all of 'em ripping and ready for what were to come next, for the outcome of years and years of bad blood spilling on the ground, for the senseless and stupid reprisals stacked over decades, the shoulder checks at gas stations, the under-the-breath-insults, the continued narration of that stupid gawddamned story that everyone knew not to be true. And as John-Boy fought after his phone, hitting buttons faster than a pit viper, calling in his own crew, the terrorizers in trucks, the lot of Marion Billy-Bob Anders, Jerry Two-Ton, and Conner McDaniels were already peeling out and burning rubber with Gutterball Gary and Fast Frank Freddie riding cow-tip in the back hailing down the Halls of Valhalla through the night.

Oh, there was going to be a fight alright, and it was happening at Rickhouse 5. A repeat of history, a tonality of doom brought down by five-on-five and Gutterball Gary was hellbent on being the victor and the whole of Tate's bar followed with.

Fast and loud they pulled up to the coal black building looming in the McDaniels' field leviathan large, all five of Gutterball's team propelled from their trucks Chimera strong, cutting the giant padlock off the Rickhouse door, shuffling past walls of barrels and booze, they poured inside the room, the summer's bellow of a corridor trapping the heat near the ground, and they began preparing for the fury to come, lighting lanterns, grabbing rope, ripping metal, positioning in corners throughout, readying themselves for what would come for their victims. Gutterball Gary and Fast Frank Freddie took the first posts, anchored on the two rickers closest to the entrance, their heavy boulder buster hands pulling the levers up 'til they was both 10-feet high as Marion Billy-Bob Anders and Jerry Two-Ton began hauling barrels to the dump room, unloading the juice three at a time with the smash of wood into the other, while Conner McDaniels readying piston point in the center on a two-by-four running the quadrant of where booze would spill when the time came.

Outside, Tate collected cash, the bar patrons who'd followed numbering in the thirties placing their bets, 6-to-1 odds. Who would fall first, who would land knuckle last, who would be the victor and by what measurement would it be held? Flasks and beers yanked from coolers, knives untucked and checked in boot sleeves and belt holsters in case the rage spilled out, in case water was needed on the fire. Sheriff Lenard couldn't be trusted, but his first Deputy, Don Mathers was tipped the McDaniels would be lit, and he having enough due diligence about him did the next honest thing a man could in such instances and phoned up Fire Marshall Jimmy Hues who would have his boys on standby as well. And it seemed despite the late hour and the working school night and the only-in-the-know nature of the fight, the entire town seemed primed for the waking for as if called forth by some grand silent telephone looming from house to house, the word began to spread in warm golden glows as lights clicked on in sequential effect and the crowd grew.

"For those of you mangy lot who ain't versed in what's about to go down, who've found their way here by sheer luck of following the crowd, who might better've kept his ass glued in the seat of my bar and waited it out, cause the lock-in were guaranteed to be free." Tate stood on a cinderblock handing out the business to folks when the horde came rolling in, when the tires jerked and wrenched near every spot of green that field held, and when that brood of hard pressed foul wrecked boot to dirt, Tate went into it once more: "This will be the first of three. Three rounds, three chances of five-on-five, of run-with-the-devil dances, it'll begin soon as that lot ... " all heads turned for the zoom, zeroing in on John-Boy, Bitty-Beau, Reginald Dalton, Bobby, and Rusty Reynolds. " ... soon as they cross this threshold, the event begins. Bets close in five."

A flurry of action moved through the crowd, wadded up green folding from pockets, sourced from purses, pulled from bras and socks as each one rushed Tate for the final bell as Rusty Reynolds and his crew huddled up for the run of show, which portended like this ...

Having newly found himself in the fold of the present company, Reginald Dalton was not all that well-versed in the historical malfeasance of his-versus-them inside the Rickhouse, but he did know better than to start getting squirrely with questions in a pressure cooker and allowed himself the quiet rectitude of what he'd always referred to as *little mouth* while Rusty talked in their makeshift football huddle.

"In the shit, boys, that's where we are, smack dab in the middle of it and the only way we're getting out is clawing right the fuck through it. So, here's how it's gonna go: John-Boy, you and Bobby gonna take two-on-two with Marion Billy-Bob Anders and Jerry Two-Ton. Bitty-Beau, you keep yourself glued to Conner McDaniels while Reginald Dalton and me'll clamor on Gutterball Gary and Fast Frank Freddie, ya hear me?"

Probably important to give some contextualization that getting glued to Conner McDaniels weren't so much a task as it were a handicap 'cause Bitty-Beau had himself a leg shorter than the other by quite a bit and when standing went for proper lean onto his orthopedic shoes, which were a good six inches thicker on the bad'n then it was on the good, and though he would not give one utterance nor heed to the limp it caused, it was prescriptive in its natured giving, that, Conner too, despite his presenting, had his own set of shortcomings which came by way of a shallowed heart and small bird-like chest, which will be a note of contention in the soon-to-come.

"Now, when we bust through there," Rusty pointed behind him to the Rickhouse doors, "you find your man and stick to 'em like pigs to shit. Rules of engagement are simple: don't get too mangled you can't make it to the Dump Room when any and all left standing will go head-to-head simultaneously. Fists, feet, arms, and legs are fine, heads'll do in a pinch, and for all things high and mighty don't be the ones to grab assets first. Let them set the course cause we's on their ground, but in the event they do, and buddy by Gawd you better believe it'll happen, you grab the meanest around and you give her hell, boys. This'n here's gonna be one for the books, the one that replaces '92 from the rafters, the ones the kids whisper on when they's at truck tie-ups and the beers are a'flowing. Don't go disappointing."

They broke up like it's two minutes left in the 4th under Friday Night Lights and took to a slow walk to the doors, Tate towing close behind to garner constitutions. "First of three, Gents, horn'll honk on the two, you'll get a quick 30-second breather, and then it's back to it. All those left standing by the second will move to the Dump Room Final, all against all. Winner's determined by the team with the most left standing. Clean as it gets. And this goes without saying but let me make this very clear, if you are packing, and Rusty, I'm fucking talking to you, you walk on back to that truck of yours and put it in the glove."

Rusty's offense cut through his chest as he daintily pressed his hand there with a, "Clean as it's gonna get, Tate."

It would later get told, many years down the line, that had Rusty actually been packing, the night may not have landed on such bad wrong, but in the tradition of

Rickhouse fighting, specifically that which broadens the bench to a full set of five. Truth be told there weren't ever going to be a right in how the night landed, no matter how inclined the men were to turning it otherwise, and as Tate left their circle to disappear behind those doors delivering much the same to Gutterball Gary's crew, the pit of him started that internal alarm that this might very well be the end of brawls once and for all.

They charged running full speed. Jet fuel in their veins. Rage in their hearts. The gut full totality of their beings churning bourbon spew as their feet peeled gravel from the floor and the masses on watch were barely able to move aside as they pushed through them. John-Boy was the first through the door, the first of five, Bobby tied to his side by that invisible thread hunting for Marion Billy-Bob Anders and Jerry Two-Ton, hate pooling them together on the razor's edge of frenzy as they tunneled underneath Gutterball and Fast Frank Freddie. Barrels stacked ten rows high on either side of 'em as they went after the scent, as the booze clogged the air spitting sting and red in their eyes with a high-octane pinch, their fingers beginning to swell with the itch of hit that'd started crawling on their skin soon as their feet touched board.

Heats what they were supposed to do, the lot of 'em going in two-by-two, but didn't a one of 'em stick to that plan. Squeezed down that corridor amongst the hot and sweat already forming drip on their brows as Bitty-Beau yelled out from behind 'em, "There," he pointed, "they's in the dump room, the bastards."

And called to cue, 'em boys followed their consiglieri's finger towards the end of that hall where Conner McDaniel stepped from a mountain of booze and was hurriedly yanking a rope from hell itself or so it appeared. Pulled from under the wood planks at their feet and running the entire vertical link, the sad saps with already too much gun in their speed and nowhere near a slowdown, were forced to watch as Conner hollered out all buckshot and brew, "Welcome to the brawl, you dumb motherfuckers!"

Now, whatever 'em boys had prepared for, whatever they thought they were running into quickly turned asunder and crumbled to the floor as they watched that rope lift and yank from the length of the walkway between where Conner stood and where their feet were quickly gaining ground to, and the aide they thought the other might bring in the comfort of arms dissipated faster than overproof hitting the floor, spilling out a worse case of double-Dutch fucked than even their sorry minds could fathom, for that rope did finally come a-calling that distance between 'em, triggering those crusty-ass boards to divide and break into large crags, and just like horses without a reined-up pull, they both fell on that other side, feet plunging through.

And do you know what two full-grown men sound like when their ankles break, when 200 pounds of meat comes crashing down a passageway no bigger than two cans of beer, or better yet: can you fathom the shock and awe spreading cross 'em boy's face when their legs betrayed 'em smashing knees into baby arm splinters—well buddy, it ain't a yip that comes falling out when bodies drop. Or clock this one back in the tinker for one quick second, take 'em two now swollen and red on the floor, blood leaking out 'fore they'd even got a chance to get a lick in, and throw onto the fire flame the sheer and utter wash of stupidity that were rock climbing over them as Jerry Two-Ton and Marion Billy-Bob Anders, the very lot they were set to guard and charge come rolling 'round the corner with a booby-trap all their own, the subtle and slow pull of the tiniest piece of wood, but one that were mighty as a pen, getting pulled from between two ominous barrels of booze, and loosening that grand fiend of 500 large to come rolling down the tracks on the two stuck-in-the-muck lads. More guttural than screech what they sounded as that barrel charted close with the full green light of GO and Bitty-Beau, not being near the friend those sad saps might've thought, high jumped the lot of 'em, landing by God's graces on his one good leg and hobbled down after Conner McDaniels.

Concurrently, back at the entrance where Gutterball Gary and Fast Frank Freddie still held course, Reginald Dalton and Rusty Reynolds began wolf-tracking through the door. Eyes full twitch and snout pointed direct, they stalked their prey with beats pounding the doors of their chest. Gutterball motioned to Frank, his fingers holding the five, as Reginald and Rusty inched closer 'til just under foot, he layered it out, "You dumb sumbitch," and both of 'em dropped, their hands loosening grip on the pulley, their mouths spread Jack Nicholson grin, and just as those rickers were set to crash dummy land overtop Rusty and Reginald, both Gutterball and Frank stopped 'em short, slamming only their heads and smashing 'em barrels down with the drop.

And do you want to know what 250 pounds of steel and wood feels like when it smashes against skin—it breaks the capillaries instantly and on sight, bruising that white into a brandished array of purples and greens. Odd how fast it happens, how fast the cheek starts to disintegrate, how fast the body starts to break down, emulsifying almost at the drop of a pulley. Imagine the instantaneous rupture, the collapsing of particles, the kaleidoscope of colors that forms by the mere dropping of two fellers on an elevator shaft. Imagine the horror of the mind trying to reconcile the injury, the absolute and utter devastation and glee of the ones who put the fuckers there, and the sudden realization that so much more harm was yet to come, as the boots jumped off the shaft and came crunching near their broke and brittle faces.

They woke with a thunderclap, the summer storm cracking heat lightning across the sky, holding back tears that'd soon come. What part of 'em believed the night to go different had transitioned to train-off-the-tracks real swift like as John-Boy and Bobby took in the full grimace of their hanging-by-a-thread ankles, but the mirrored horror of Rusty and Reginald peeling back layers of skin on their face were the sure-fire-shit-supreme of the evening at the end of Round 1, and truth be told, the lot of 'em weren't looking fit for the wear compared to Gutterball and his crew who stood unscathed and unruly. Only saving grace for 'em boys that come were by the way Bitty-Beau standing madder than hell as Tate began laying out the rules for Round 2.

It were decided after the dreaded calamity of '74 and the much disputed winner between the Barons and the Wallaces, that at the cessation of each round, the score needed announced and corroborated by a second to avoid the cluster of Blood and Bath that concussed that evening so long ago. And tradition had bore it necessary in the last twenty to confide an element of writing for further solidification and documenting, and so it was that Tate made his mark after sharing the news, that "Indubitably, round one goes to Gutterball's team."

"Now, 'fore we get caught up in the steam on round two, we need alignment that both teams, ready and willing to continue on in melee." Tate gave a gander to Rusty, who, understanding the assignment, was already in the pursuit of structure reprieve as he ripped the very same board that'd sent him to his current state and started wrapping his ankle to it.

"Agreed."

And satisfied, Tate carried over to Gutterball Gary for the same and with the sudden ding of the bell, it were full-tilt-boogie-time again with Bitty-Beau seeking retribution and revenge, monkey-clamoring after Conner who barrel dove right for that bad leg of his and clear clipped that boy like a rock on a windshield. On him like burnt-on diner bacon grease Conner was, pulling that poor bastard down so's his legs clanked over top Bitty-Beau's shoulder and then went for the ill-reputed and not often used playground slap. Where all anyone could see once they swallowed down that sound of puny screams skidding out were the flutter of hands moving back and forth across that boy's face and weren't a none of 'em immune to the humiliation going so's that Bitty-Beau's companion, Bobby, feeling that disgraced lump of embarrassed crippling up his center, couldn't stand it no longer and army crawled over to his compatriot and started elbow pummeling into the back of Conner's knee.

And boy oh boy didn't that kickstart the bloody aspersions spewing out 'em feller's mouths with *you fucking fuck* being the choicest phrase landing out of Gutterball as he plowed into Rusty Reynolds, who were trying a breakaway for a rip-n-deal with a whiskey thief on the wall, and very soon thereafter misjudging his lunge and finding the bare boot of a heel ice-breaking his shin bone in two, or the reigning champion of *cocksucker* grinding fist after fist into Jerry Two-Ton by John-Boy there, both of 'em heavy in the exchange of niceties, but the curdled ubiquity of *motherfucker* shoveling sledgehammers on every inch of skin it touched was the overall crowning starlight of the evening. And as with many occasions when the fists start'a flailing and the red starts'a flowing, what inevitably captured the hearts of all those busy with the entertain was the only thing that mattered, the cacophonous and intoxicating redolence of skin crashing into skin. The euphoric rise of tension that breathes in the muscles, that spurns a man forward with yet another hit, and as Tate dipped his big bouncer boulders in between the mess with a, "That ends round two," the dawgs were reluctant for calm, still biting at each other, still full swing. And it weren't until Tate, bearing no other choice after he took a haymaker to the chest, pulled out that ruler of disputes, that silencer of teams, and popped off that Colt he always carried by his side.

Of all the environs in the world to go firing a gun, one of the worst fucking places was in a Rickhouse surrounded by totems and pillars of booze, booze that for the majority of argument's sake is leaded at a start proof of 124.8 in the McDaniels household, and one that if given even the remotest of opportune chances at dance and spark would've lit up the entirety of that place with a Big Time Fucking *BOOM*.

There are some that would argue this was the perxact moment of discord and disarray that shifted the evening, and to Tate's credit it were said that he was just following through, corralling the masses, preventing further calamity from ensue, but Gutterball Gary would utter later buttressed in between the carnality of liquid to lips and nothing left to lose, "Between me, you, and lamppost, he just didn't take too kindly to getting hit's all. Bastard just didn't know how to read the room." And so, the finality of the evening and round three, having no annunciation of winner moving through, took a rather mimetic point of view and it went down a little bit like this in double-time cue inside the Dump Room.

(Now, what is of particular import here and something most certainly worth mentioning is not all Rickhouses hold a dump room. In fact, the archaic and aforementioned volatility of aging spirits would solicit not the most friendly of aesthetics to start haphazardly dumping copious amounts of extremely flammable liquid into what is best described as troughs forming a horseshoe around a large and for all intents and purposes stage centered in the middle. You might very well recall as the men first entered the current engagement that Jerry Two-Ton and Marion Billy-Bob Anders were seen rolling three barrels at a time to this very same spot and perhaps with further laser-eyed-view the image of Conner McDaniels working a large beam that ran the quadrant of the dump room might come front of mind. What wasn't mentioned previously, however, and something mischievously tricky indeed, was that the board he was holding piston point on rose. As in to ascend, like Christ on a Cross. The mechanism's progeny, a first of its kind in the state of Kentucky and one that rare few carry since, but in its heyday of operation, it worked much like a meat rail system in a butcher's factory. A true measure of ingenuity for the McDaniels when first introduced and an opportunity to appease the labor shortage of the Great War and the women who were then working the line.

Customarily during that time the creation of a new industry, gunpowder, replaced most all production of bourbon, and the McDaniels grand empire was of no exception, thus a relevant but teeny-weeny tidbit that no one from the evening except Conner was taking into consideration—the little bulbs of Great War leftover prickling the synapses in hidden spots along the top of that very same board looming six feet high above the bourbon bath. And because of this, a yarn of complicated men dealing with complicated things, it should be noted that amongst all the items in Conner McDaniel's pockets right now, the pair of matches burned the brightest. And it is at this time, the narrator might suggest popping in the quiet and friendly little tune to accompany your reading pleasure (...The Prodigy's "Firestarter").

Soon as the gun went off, Reginald Dalton and Fast Frank Freddie were on Tate, hands grabbing after wrist and fist, elbows crashing into clavicles as their feet climbed up on knees and legs to knock that metal down. And some behemoth fiend of liberty, Tate stood weathering the blows, countering their jabs and thrusts as he desperately tried to shake the boys off. And what an odd thing it were to watch the teams turn nuclear, to join hands side-by-side, to reroute the computer, so to speak, even if only briefly, even if it were just long enough for Gutterball Gary to get a leg up on Marion Billy-Bob Anders who was in the barebone bottoms of the heap gnawing on Tate's ankle for a release. But sure enough it didn't take Gutterball Gary to be right proper fed up with bullshit, and once he got his big thick thunderclap forearm round Tate's neck, he took that boy for a straight drop on the ground and a Rikki-Tikki-time-out of a sleeper hold.

The onlookers who had now made their way to tribal up 'round the fighting didn't take too kindly to their MC getting knocked off the block like that, and one of 'em feeling inclined and right properly impaired decided that the best course of action would be the chucking of a beer bottle into the mix. In fact, this fine and kind sir felt so impassioned that he regaled the allegiance of his neighbors beside, enlisting their similar plan of attack, and far be it from me to deny the utter chaos of what raining beer bottles and an angry mob will do to a situation. However, one would wonder certainly that this rather stern cause of action, should perhaps not be repeated and yet with such zeal and fervor to that arched beer flow, that eruption of like-minded pals took it upon themselves to continue the hurling and whirling of devastation destroying these men as they gripped and ripped and slipped in the now sloshing booze geysering up from the troughs as Bitty-Beau was repeatedly attempting to drown Conner McDaniels was something of a *fait accompli.* Or just five inches from McDaniels's flailing legs, the sublimity of Fast Frank Freddie's face as he continued picking up and dropping Cena-attitude-adjustment-style John Boy's little ass, but what took the cake, the real rabble rouser of the group was when Tate finally woke up from his little cat nap and that twisted motherfucker right there, the holder of the peace, the Grand Bambino of Bourbon Brawl Town chose violence, and he started laying into the closest body near, which just so happened to be Gutterball Gary.

Tate grabbed hold of that beam up above and viper-coiled his boots to his chest then sent 'em flying out electric-city-gritty on Gutterball Gary, slamming that man square up with his size 14 shit kickers and sent him a high-flying over that crowd 'til he splatted into the bottom row of barrels on Row 3, Column 6 and broke a good 100-year-old piece of wood from its resting that went to unloosen a Gawd Almighty fuck of bourbon barrels. And that hooch went to rolling so gawddamned fast off that row that it took to rough and tumble on the set up next to it and weren't no time before collapse were a problem. But Gutterball Gary didn't come there to start no shit without finishing it, and right directly after he landed in that pool of bourbon and got his bearings about him, he came off that ground with a highfalutin showtime kick that knocked every single tooth out of the front row of Tate's mouth. Straight bulldozed 'em Red Wing boots through that fella so's that all 'em rambunctious lots of look'sees standing 'bout ready-Chevy with their next beer to chunk took a backseat in silence. All of 'em, that is except for Bitty-Beau-Bitch, who'd squirmed his way just far enough to see 'em leftover remnants of his fallen comrades and the ripe red ruby cherry just'a waiting for him to pick from the past. And before you could hardly blink an eye, that dumb motherfucker took out a smoke and Zippo lighter and flung that flame mile high towards that long-forgotten gunpowder.

When the dust'd settled and somehow-or-another, by a miracle no one was equipped to explain, every single body in there left unscathed other than 'em boys who'd originally started the fight, and as the story'd go despite subtle deviations, the technical and agreed upon narrative was that Bitty-Beau had felt so ashamed of his behavior that he'd took to the woods, hightailing it right out of town. Even Tate, replete with his dentures, would spell the yarn true from behind his bar, and weren't a one of 'em in town who'd go to refute it. Not John-Boy, Bobby, Marion Billy-Bob Anders, Reginald Dalton, nor Rusty Rutherford, even though every single one of 'em, including the crowd that stayed on despite the initial shock and awe of that flame traveling heavenly and every sphincter in that room gripping tighter than hell at the *BOOM* that was about to come, the white dove visage of the most unlikeliest of Saint-sorts arched through the abyss of looming doom, and in perfect football spiral interception knocked that lighter closed and out, and lo and behold by the mightiest of momentous moves, it was the paltry saving grace of a Mich Ultra can that saved the day from ruin.

Bitty-Beau on the other hand got the ever-living shit beat out of him until his face caved in and all ten and both teams of men walked that fucker out three clicks to the west of Rickhouse 5 and dumped his body in the cement foundation of Rickhouse 7 to be poured mañana. And 'cause there is a very special bond that occurs when ya get the shit kicked outta you that necessitates the full raucous bacchanalian sweep that is getting drunker than a cooper's cat and blacking out in a field or a lawn, 'em boys proceeded to drink clear cross to that other side, where the insults turned to "Buddy, you's fucked up, but I fucks with you," and if you've seen or experienced the grand revelation that is Southern boy blackout, then you too know what occasion we speak of. You know that the morning would come with fresh-from-the-oven biscuits, and poured over the halves gravy, and eggs more orange than yellow filling their plates, and perhaps if you've spent more time than not in the South, you know as well, that somewhere in the back of one of their trucks would be a ripped-from-the-street sign plucked in a hurried rush, and just maybe, if you are lucky enough to have spent a summer in the state of Kentucky as the temperature never dips below bathwater warm despite the time of night, that when those boys walked into Wild Eggs to stuff their bellies and get back on the clock that they did so with a fire in their hearts that spelled, “Now, that was one helluva a good fight.”

# The Cleaner

# by Jason Allison

**Blood's tough** to get out of concrete. It looks smooth when you're standing, but up close it's lined with tiny grooves and tracks. Porous is the word. Soaks liquid right up. Cue the bleach.

I dump half a bucket of the stuff onto a stubborn patch. Half water, half industrial-grade solvent. I use the mix to peel rust off the machinery. The stink makes my skull burn behind my eyes. I should be wearing a mask.

"Joey, you done dicking around yet?"

"Two minutes."

"What'd you say?"

I hold up a pair of gloved fingers. People say they can't hear me. That I'm quiet. I don't know. I keep on scrubbing with my other hand.

Footfalls get louder, Ernesto coming my way. His boots cut into my sightline. I ignore his approach. My eyes are watering. A tear drips into the bleachy, bloody mess. It mixes in and vanishes.

"Stubbs got his ass smoked tonight. You see Vasin catch him with that elbow?" With a thumb Ernesto sparks his flint wheel and lights himself up. "I wonder how many times his nose's been broken."

"He hurt bad?"

"That's him you're mopping up, so ... "

I toss the brush into the bucket. The foamy water turns an ugly reddish-gray.

"You got plans tonight?"

I look at him.

"What? You must do *something* after fight nights."

He ashes onto the concrete. I keep looking at him. I'm forty-six. I live alone. I work Facility Maintenance—a fancy title for mop-pusher—at Heickelstein Steel in the South Bronx, on the industrial side of the Bruckner. I'm also on probation. So no, I don't do anything after fight nights.

Ernesto rubs a small scar on his chin. He does this a lot, a nervous twitch.

I set my hands on my thighs. The concrete looks better. Not perfect, but passable. I line up the two buckets and push myself upright. It takes effort. The years have not passed easy. I haven't let them.

"What do you need?"

"It's not me," Ernesto says, checking his watch. "The man wants to see you."

I look at him again. Ernesto shrugs.

With an ancient broom—the wide, heavy kind—I guide the mess toward the drain. Heickelstein's went up in the thirties. Used to be a lot of factories in the area: radios, tool and die companies, vacuum cleaners, pianos, and caskets. Time has shuttered most. It's also caused Hickelstein's floor gradings to shift. The blood's got to go. I help it along.

"He say what about?" I fall in next to Ernesto and we start walking.

"All I know's it's Stubbs related." He gestures with his cigarette to his face. A movement I can't unpack.

We walk. On either side of us stand these blocks of machinery. Massive and complicated, darkened now by shadow. During the day the factory produces steel used in "industrial applications." Two nights a month the football field-sized loading dock hosts no-rules fight nights. I clean up after both.

Mister Bobby started hosting the brawls after catching a UFC event in Vegas. He likes feeling like a mogul, I guess. I questioned his decision-making; Mister Bobby's no thug and I worried the fights'd draw a crowd he doesn't know how to handle. So far, though, we've done alright. No shootings. Turns out there're a lot of people in this city who want to stand close to men—and women—battering each other senseless.

"There he is."

"Mister Bobby," I say.

The man's office hangs from the rafters, at the end of a long set of grated steps. Picture windows frame the factory floor below, the empty floor where Stubbs had lost big an hour ago. Mister Bobby comes from behind his desk; it's wider than my apartment. He shakes my hand, which embarrasses me. Mister Bobby's a decent guy, and I'm a felon. I don't deserve his warmth.

"How're you feeling, Joey? Good? The knees holding up? I got a thing with my back when I twist wrong. Hurts like a mother. But I don't need to tell you that. We all got problems, right?"

Mister Bobby's a decade younger than me and drives a black-on-black Range Rover tagged with Connecticut plates. Runs a business that employs 94 full-time workers. His problems are not my problems.

"Ernesto said you needed to see me."

Mister Bobby's expression dims. I worry he's ending the fights—the envelopes I get for after-match cleanups pay the insurance on my Toyota.

"You still driving that Honda?" he asks as heads back to his desk.

"It's a Matrix. A Toyota."

"What's that?" He shuts a metal cash box. The night's gate take and busted bets.

"Yeah," I say, louder. "I got it."

Mister Bobby slides the cash box into the safe. Locks and spins the dial. He's too trusting, I want to tell him. Mister Bobby maintains no security. Ernesto's a trusted dayshift straight earning some bi-weekly extra. As far as I know, there's not a gun in the building.

"I need a favor." Mister Bobby slides the box into a safe that'd gone unused for years—no business deals in cash anymore. He spins the dial and tugs on the handle before turning back to me. "Stubbs took a hell of a beating tonight. You see the match?" I shake my head, but he's thumbing his phone. "Not nearly as fast as he used to be. Losing that hand speed. That's Ray talking, not me. Anyway, I'm wondering if you can do me a favor. I'll throw you an extra bill."

"He needs a ride home?"

Mister Bobby hesitates. "Walk with me."

The blood pours from his head. I look at Ernesto. He

shrugs, again.

"You with me, Stubbs?" Mister Bobby bends low, sets a hand on his shoulder. "Fucking Vasin."

We're in the workers' combination locker/break room. Stubbs is sitting on the lunch table. His bare feet dangle off the concrete. Stubbs is a lightweight, I think. I don't know the classifications. He's ripped, but he's small.

"Head wounds bleed, Mister Bobby." Ray's laying into Stubbs's skull with a tube of liquid wound closer. Krazy Glue for the octagon set.

"I'll be okay," Stubbs says, his slurring words coming out sideways. He sounds broken.

"No." Mister Bobby sets his hands on his hips. "He's got to go to the hospital."

We all look at him. I'm no fighter, but I'd told Ernesto we'd need a doctor sooner or later.

"Mister Bobby," Ray says, "how's it gonna look?"

"ER doctors have to call the cops," Ernesto says.

"That true?" Mister Bobby asks me.

In this crew, the three years I did for Rob Two make me an expert. "I think they're supposed to."

Ray pinches Stubbs's split skull skin tight. Mister Bobby winces.

"We need someone in-house," Ernesto says.

"I'm working on that," Mister Bobby says, rougher than usual.

Behind him, Ernesto and I trade another look.

"I'm fine," Stubbs mumbles. He gets off the table and immediately goes down. Like a puppet whose strings got snipped. Ray's on him quick, and I help. We hoist Stubbs up by his armpits. He's heavier than he looks and still sweaty and probably stinks, but the solvents have killed my sense of smell.

We reset Stubbs on the table, and Mister Bobby gestures for Ernesto and me to join him by the door.

"You've dealt with the cops. You know what to say. Get him changed and throw him in your Ford. Drive him to Lincoln. Come up with a story. You, uh ... got jumped on the way to your car. Something like that. He can't die in my shop. Dad'll freak."

After his third heart attack Mister Bobby's father retired to Naples. Mister Bobby shows us pictures of the lemon tree in his old man's backyard.

"I'll take care of it," I say.

"You're a good man, Joey."

I'm not, but I nod anyway.

"You'll lock up?" he says as he grabs his coat.

"Course."

Mister Bobby walks out. On the table Stubbs is leaning *way* back. His blood has pooled under his feet. I wonder why Ray can't babysit Stubbs. I wonder what my P.O. would think of this scene. The answers don't come.

"How much you think he's got in that safe?"

The question makes me stop chewing. Before tonight, me and Stubbs had never spent a minute alone. We're stuffed into my Matrix, a Crave Case of White Castles on the dash. Stubbs digs into the bag between his feet. Rubs some anti-bacterial gel onto his hands.

I've parked way out in the Point, almost on the water. The morning lights the Bronx gently. The trucks from the food market and waste companies are parked and quiet. On Sundays this city can approach serenity.

"I figure twenty grand, easy," he says.

Stubbs downs entire sliders in a bite. He's got Play-Doh ears and a car wreck face. I keep glancing at his bandages, hoping the staples underneath hold. The doctors and nurses at Lincoln didn't care who'd attacked Stubbs, didn't comment on a scarred face that suggested the man could handle himself. No notifications were made. The waiting room was full. Next customer, please.

"I don't know."

"Alright, maybe I'm wrong. Maybe twenty's high. But it's a lot, right? It's got to be. The fans're paying, what? A hundred a head just to walk in? That's before they lay any cash on the card."

And before the overpriced beer and liquor Mister Bobby sells from the makeshift bar. If the Forty-First Precinct cared at all about police work, Heickelstein would be padlocked. Luckily the cops around here have other concerns. Or maybe none at all.

"I don't think about those things."

"How can you not?" I stare at my murder burger, and Stubbs goes on. "We all know your story. You recognize a score when you see it. Mister Bobby's just begging to get hit."

I'm not hungry, but I finish another slider. My stomach hates me. Stubbs shakes his head and looks away. A marked NYPD car slow rolls out of the abandoned warehouse at my nine o'clock. The driver fists a yawn. I wonder how many hours they slept.

"Who's we?" I say, still eyeing the cops.

"Huh?"

"You said we know your story."

Stubbs pulls a grease-stained napkin across his mouth. The slurring, concussed version of him's gone. Maybe it's a fighter thing, recovering quick like that. I've been hit a few times. I did not snap back.

"He's got no security. Bobby's sitting on a pile of dirty cash and knows fuck all about protecting it. He's ripe." Stubbs pauses. "And you got the key to the castle."

He's right; on my belt hangs a keyring like a school janitor. I also know the alarm codes.

"I like my job."

That wasn't true, but it's all I deserved. And my pay stubs satisfied Miss Perkins down at the probation office. I fire the Toyota up. The odometer's sat in six-digit territory for years. I sleep alone in a basement studio in Throggs Neck. I've spent years in concrete cells in upstate prisons. Spoken to family through glass. I see Miss Perkins once a month. I'm old enough to know opportunities like Stubbs's are mirages. But some angles can't be ignored.

"I figure it's more like thirty-five," I say as I shift into reverse. "Forty on a good night."

Stubbs's elbow-mashed face breaks into a wide grin. He starts smacking my dash.

"I knew it! Holy shit!"

As I pull off, I wonder what just happened. I didn't have to tell Stubbs about the money. I could've let it go. I remind myself there's a big gap between talking and doing. Prisons and graveyards are filled with men who've tried bridging it.

The Toyota chugs down Oakpoint Avenue. Its engine won't last much longer.

On Sundays I visit my sister. Standing invitation, but I take her up on it rarely. Steph's husband drives long haul for UPS, and she's a teacher. They got a small house in Dobbs Ferry—semi-detached, driveway but no garage. It's nothing special. But their small successes remind me of my failures.

"Not for nothing, Joey, but you look like shit."

I'm exhausted; I've nicked my fingers three times with the potato peeler.

"You still working that overtime?" she asks.

"Sometimes." I toss another naked spud into the bowl.

"You know ... "

"Don't," I say. She wants to offer me the attic. "I'm fine where I am."

"I'm just saying, it's nearly finished. You and Victor could drywall the rest. Make it homey."

"Homey?"

"The kids'd love to have you around." In the living room, Steph's sons are playing *Grand Theft Auto*. They barely noticed me when I walked in.

"It's a hassle to get your probation office changed."

"But people do. Right?"

Steph sets down the paring knife. She's younger than me by eight years. Teaches Special Ed and wants the best for everyone she knows. It's a sickness in her, the desire to help. I'm not afflicted.

"When's Vic getting back?" I ask.

She taps her phone with a knuckle. "Figure twenty minutes." I go back to peeling. Steph can't stop herself. "You spoken to mom lately?"

"She texted me the other day. You teach her how to do that?"

"It's not exactly splitting the atom. What'd she say?"

Steph slices silently through the potatoes. This is our mother's recipe we're making. The years fall away and I remember tasting it in the old apartment, Mom holding mayonnaised potatoes out on a wooden spoon, the hit of pepper, her free hand protecting the floor from stains, the cleanup. Stubbs's blood muscles into the scene. Flowing like a river toward the rusty grate.

"Joey, you with me or what?"

I shake myself out. "Um, she just asked how I'm doing, if I'm eating right. Standard mom questions."

"She worries about you."

For a time neither of us speak. Digitized gunshots rock the living room. Victor walks in, reusable grocery bags dangling from his hands. The kind thoughtful people use. We sit down to eat. Victor asks about the factory. I ask about his route. After dinner Steph serves ice cream. Victor's got a chair he settles into. He reminds me of Dad in a way, wincing as he sits. Some pain in his back or legs that'll never get better. They want me to stay and watch a movie. I drive back to the Bronx.

I push my broom, wipe pubes out of urinals. Scrub the shower room tile. That Friday, Ernesto steps to me. I'm out by the loading dock. Union men are lowering a slab of purpose-cut steel onto a flatbed tractor trailer. It looks like half an arch. Or maybe a swan's neck. They wear helmets and coordinate movements over radios clipped to their vests. I've got a roll of trash bags stuffed in my back pocket.

"I'm hearing the next one's gonna be big," he says.

I say nothing.

"Stubbs talk to you? After the hospital?"

"Don't be stupid, Ernesto. You got a good gig."

"I'm moving to Florida," he says at a whisper. "Construction's blowing up down there. Highway overpasses, on ramps, off ramps. The industry's printing money right now."

I say nothing. Again.

"There's no law says you gotta stay in New York, right? You can get your shit transferred."

I kick at a wad of gum that's melded to the floor. How many times have I told the guys? I pull a scraper from my pocket and start prying it up.

"I'm gone at the end of the month. One way or another. But it'd help to have a little startup cash. The man won't even miss it."

I wrap the gum in a paper towel and pocket it. "I don't know about Stubbs. All the shots he's taken. But you're smarter than this. You ever been arrested?"

His turn to say nothing.

"Exactly. You want to move, move. I'm on probation. Whatever you're planning, leave me out of it."

"What's he gonna report you for? Robbing his illegal fight club?"

The swan's neck has settled onto the flatbed. Workmen strap it down with chain binders. They carry ratchets as big as my arm. Their gloves aren't covered in piss. They don't carry ancient gum in their pants.

"The man's figuring he'll have sixty-K in the till."

Something smashes onto the floor. Ernesto yells at a worker and drops down off the loading dock.

I wonder what the weather's like in Orlando.

When they knock on my door, I know they're committed.

"You gonna let us in, or what?"

I scratch my jaw. I step aside.

"All we need's to make a copy of your keys," Stubbs says.

"The gate, the dock door, Mister Bobby's office," Ernesto says.

I sit on my twin bed and point at the folding chairs leaning against a wall. You know, for guests.

"There's other guys who have those keys."

"Yeah," Stubbs says, smiling. He's missing a molar. "But they ain't been to Green Haven."

"That's why you should listen to me and forget this. How old're you?"

"Twenty-seven," Stubbs says.

I almost pull a double take. I'd had him for his late thirties.

"You're young, yet. Don't throw your future away. You got plenty of time to land a big fight in a real arena. The UFC, like they show on TV."

He shakes his head and looks at his hands. His knuckles are scabbed over and his fingers don't line up.

"I'm taking off-the-books matches in a goddamned factory. You think I got a shot at the octagon? They lemme spar with the real fighters. Get their sweat going. That's it. I've hit my ceiling." He points at the staples in his head, looks at me square. "I got a cousin out west. Part owner in a marijuana operation. The legal kind. I can get in on it, provided I bring something to the table."

On the ceiling there's a water stain that's gone from beige to brown to black to mold. It's inhuman, living below ground.

"Mister Bobby's not a bad guy," I say, for reasons that escape me.

"You check out Stubbs's head?" Ernesto asks.

"He stepped into that fight. No one forced him into it."

"That's true," Ernesto says, "but Mister Bobby doesn't pay what he oughta."

"You happy with your take home?" Stubbs asks as he scopes my cell-sized pad, the filthy casement window cut high into the wall.

"I get paid for what I do."

"But if you did this," Ernesto says, "you'd get paid for what you're worth."

"No, I'd get paid for the chance I'm taking. And I measure that in years, not money."

"Like he's even gonna report this," Stubbs says. He gets up and moves like he wants to start pacing, but the confines don't allow for that and he sits back down. "He's soft, Joey. Born into his spot. He's not holding the fights for the cash, he's got plenty of that. He does it 'cause he wants to be a part of something."

"Don't we all?"

Stubbs just stares at me.

"A third," Ernesto says. "And all you gotta do is copy your keys."

I find myself doing math. Twenty-thousand dollars, if Ernesto's estimate's to be believed. The numbers in my head worry me. This is how the slide starts, the entertaining of fantasies. Stubbs opens his mouth like he's starting in on the hard sell, but Ernesto stays him with a hand.

"Why do you do this to yourself?" Ernesto says. "This place, this life. You know I asked Sanjay about you? He said he offered you an apprentice spot back in December, but you shot him down. I know guys'd kill to get their card. Not you, though. Ex-con mopping floors passes up a chance not many felons get. I can't help but wonder why."

I try to wait them out. Turns out Stubbs and Ernesto are more patient than I'd thought.

"Libby Drouillard," I finally say.

Ernesto and Stubbs trade a look.

"When we came outta the store there was a cop car a block off. Just dumb, cosmic luck. The wheelman took off through an intersection. There was an accident behind us, and this woman died. The wreck didn't kill her, turns out she had this heart condition even she didn't know about. A genetic defect. That's the only thing kept the DA from charging us with felony murder. We didn't kill Libby, but I think about her every day. If she didn't get in that wreck, maybe she'd've seen a doctor. Some routine checkup would've shown she had something wrong. All the ways it could've gone different. She was only thirty-four."

"So you doing this is, what," Stubbs says. "You punishing yourself?"

"Penance," Ernesto says.

Outside a garbage truck rolls down the narrow street. The casement window shudders.

"We didn't kill her," I say to my dry, cracked hands. All I hear's the labored sounds of my own breathing.

"You didn't rat," Stubbs says. "*That's* why Mister Bobby trusts you."

"You think there's some kinda code. Trust me, there isn't. Someone always talks. Usually it's the smart one."

"Then why didn't you flip?" Ernesto says.

"Cause I think maybe I'm stupid."

Miss Jenkins sits small behind a desk piled with paper. I wonder how she works here, this dim, oppressive office. Walls painted puke green. The phones always ringing, hallways lined with criminals. Like me.

Miss Jenkins reaches for something, then freezes, like she'd forgotten what she was doing. She shakes her head and mumbles something as she spins to her ancient computer.

"Pay stubs."

I hand them over. Miss Jenkins barely looks at them, hands them back. I'm a box to be checked. A professional obligation.

"Any issues at work?"

I shake my head.

"Police contact?"

"None."

"Have you used any illegal drugs?" A sigh accompanies every question.

"I just gave you my urine."

"There's tests and there's questions. You know how this goes."

I nod and hold up a hand. "No drugs."

"Are you engaged in any illegal activities?"

I'm the broom for an unlicensed fight club frequented by felons and thugs. Untaxed and unauthorized. Cash for booze, no ABC license. The nightly wager take runs into five-figure territory.

"No," I say.

She chugs from a giant iced Dunkin' as she scribbles notes in a folder containing my life. It's so thin.

"If I ... " I begin.

Miss Jenkins looks at me over her readers.

"If I wanted to get my probation transferred to another jurisdiction. Like Westchester. Or maybe Florida. What's the procedure for that?" I pause, then add, "I might have a job waiting for me down south."

She cocks her head and blinks. Like she'd forgotten something and I'd just reminded her.

"Didn't I tell you about this?"

"I never asked before."

"I think you're on the list."

She pulls a paper from a stack, way down at the bottom. Like a magician whipping a tablecloth from under the plates and glasses.

"I'm pretty sure you qualify," she says.

"For what?"

"Early discharge." Her eyes scroll left to right as she reads the sheet in her hand.

"From probation?"

"Goddamn you ask a lotta questions. We sure as shit not talking about the army." She hands me the paper. "Right there, third paragraph. I didn't mention this to you?"

I shake my head. The section she directed me to mentions budgetary concerns, probationer conduct, whole-person considerations, societal reentry, and—again—budgetary concerns.

"The state's spending too much eyeballing small-timers like you. Based on Albany's guidelines, you eligible for discharge from post-release supervision. You sure I didn't tell you about this?"

"I'm sure."

"Losing my goddamned mind." She lays a hand out. "Gimme that. It's eyes-only, probationers ain't supposed to read it."

I hand her the memo. She slaps a sticky note on it that says "33B DISCHARGE." I feel a stirring in me, recognize it as hope. The sensation terrifies me. Hope pushes the weak and the stupid to do things they shouldn't. Better to go without.

"What's this mean?"

"It means," Miss Jenkins says as she slips the memo in my folder, "you can start thinking seriously about your next chapter. All I need's my boss to sign off on the discharge form. Which she will right quick, 'cause we don't have the personnel to handle the roster we got. The state running outta money's a godsend."

"Is there, like, a judge involved, or something?"

Miss Jenkins waves my question away. "I'll call when the papers are signed. You'll just have to come down for your discharge certificate." She looks at me. "Everyone else I told this to's reacted a bit more ... enthusiastically. You gonna miss me or something?"

"Just surprised is all."

I get up. It takes effort. I feel a weight on me. I'd used my probationer status as a shield with Stubbs and Ernesto; *I can't, I'm on post-release supervision.* Miss Jenkins thinks she's set me free. She has no idea.

The stench of sweat hits me as soon as I walk in the gym. Even my damaged nose smells it. I stand just inside the door, unsure where to go. I don't exercise, never been in a martial arts studio. A long-legged kid kicks a cushion held by a man twice his age. His shin thumps heavy into the foam, over and over. I could measure time by his consistency. To my right, a girl in cornrows throws punches at a heavy bag. The chain connecting it to a crossbeam rattles. Her fists quickly blur. I wouldn't last a minute.

Stubbs is jumping rope way in the back, on a spread of blue mats tucked against the cinderblock wall. With my hands tucked into my jacket pockets, I make my way over. Fighters side-eye me as I pass. I don't belong here, and we all know it.

Everybody on the mats is barefoot. Me and my boots stay off to the side. Stubbs's rope cuts the air like a whip. He hops on one foot, then the other, then both. Feet shoot out, then back in. Like he's dancing. If he's a second-rate fighter, I can't imagine squaring off against the pros.

Stubbs clocks me and motions toward a fire door propped open by a brick. When he joins me in the alley, he's wearing Nike slides and a ratty zip-up.

"Is me coming here a problem?" I don't have his cell number and wouldn't use it anyway. Cops use call logs to prove conspiracies. That I know this—and considered it—concerns me.

"Nah. Fighters respect privacy." He spits into the gutter. It's tinged pink. With a finger and thumb he reaches into his mouth and tests a tooth.

"You okay?"

"Javon goes a little too hard sometimes. Ray's been on him to let up."

I nod like I know what that means.

"You looking to get a workout in," Stubbs says, "or's you here about something else?"

I squint into the sunlight. I could've spoken to Ernesto. He's level-headed and pragmatic—excluding the job he wants to pull. But I needed to gauge Stubbs. He's the youngest of the three. That makes him unpredictable.

*The three*. In my mind we've become a crew.

"What's your plan?"

Stubbs's bent nose and flattened features pop. He steps close to me. His hands are still wrapped from the sparring session.

"All we need from you's the keys and the code. Me and Ernesto'll slip into his office, empty his safe. We'll lock up and reset the alarm. We play it right, we'll be halfway to Colorado before he comes in Monday."

"What about the video?"

"Nice try. You know he cuts that off on fight nights."

I don't say anything.

"You wanna scrub toilets the rest of your life? Cause I'm done with this shit. I got this ringing in my ears, never goes away. I been hit so many times, and for what? My last legit fight was two years ago. I'm just not good enough, Joey." The admission nearly breaks him. "That's the truth. I been training since I was in junior high, and I'm already on the back end. Never headlined a card. Farthest fighting's taken me was to some auditorium up in Plymouth. I wanna teach, though. Maybe I can find a kid's better than me, make him into what I'm not."

Why'd Miss Jenkins tell me about the early discharge?

"How're you gonna get into the safe?"

"Ernesto's got the combo."

I look at him. Stubbs's face lists on one side, like it's melting slow.

"Mister Bobby keeps the digits on a Post-It in his desk. I don't think he ever used it before he started hosting fights. Why would he? How many businesses deal in cash these days?"

A fighter in his teens pops out of the fire door. Me and Stubbs go quiet until he's off the block.

"This's the perfect plan. He's not part of this world."

Like Stubbs or Ernesto are.

"You know how many guys in prison thought they had the perfect plan?"

Stubbs counts off his wrapped, twisted fingers. "No guns. No tying people up. No home invasion bullshit. We're talking in and out fast, nobody gets hurt."

His broken body reminds me that's rarely true.

I'm mopping Mister Bobby's office when a woman walks in. Long jacket, collar popped. She pauses at the door, like she's not sure she's in the right place.

"Help you?" I ask.

"I'm looking for Bobby." She's young and speaks with an accent. Not uncommon in New York. Russian or Ukrainian, I think. "I have a two o'clock."

"They had an issue on the floor. He'll be right back."

I drag the mop across the vinyl. She moves to a dry spot. Her shoes look expensive. She's the only woman in the building but stands with her shoulders back and chest out. She puts off relaxed confidence. I finish up and run into Ernesto on the stairs.

"There's a woman in Mister Bobby's office."

He checks his watch. "She's early."

"Who is she?"

"Elena. She's our new doctor."

"Where'd he find her?" I ask.

"That kid, Vasin? He hooked them up."

Vasin's the one who sent Stubbs to the ER. His chest is covered in what I know to be prison ink. Up in Mister Bobby's office, the windows frame Elena's backlit silhouette. She lights a smoke. The flame makes her face glow for a second. Then it's out.

Miss Jenkins leaves a voicemail on my phone. My post-release discharge has been approved. She'll call me in a few days to pick up my certificate. New York State has no legal hold on me. I can travel freely. Even move, if I want to.

I find Ernesto on the floor. The cutting and molding machines make a terrible noise. Our ear protection makes conversation impossible. We each slide one cup off.

"Could you get me a gig in Orlando?"

"What about your probation?"

"They discharged me. The state doesn't have the money to make me piss in a cup anymore."

He can't help but smile. I know that expression, seen it before—the promise of changed circumstances. I'm worried because I know how these stories can end. On the other hand, I've only gone upstate once. The first six jobs, we got away clean. Then Libby Drouillard got t-boned by a garbage truck.

I wasn't driving that day. I hope maybe that absolves me, but I know it doesn't. I was *there*. Mister Bobby's trusted me. Why, I don't know. Does he deserve to get hit? Do I deserve $20K of unearned cash? Have I scrubbed enough blood off floors, pulled enough half-chewed food from stopped-up U-bends? I remind myself we never hurt anyone. Our guns were pellet jobs painted black. We targeted shops that moved stolen jewelry. The prison psychiatrist called this "rationalization."

"I need to start over," I say to Ernesto.

"Don't we all," he says back.

I arrive late to Rory Dolan's in Yonkers. Parking for Sunday brunch in this section of Yonkers is a nightmare. Off the boat Irish Catholics still attend church. Me, I haven't gone in years.

They've got a table in the back. Dark wood lines the walls, the floors. Brass rails and the scent of sizzling hash crisscrosses the dining room. The four-top doesn't have room for me. I stand there while Steph rearranges the kids.

"There's always space for family," Vic says, sliding to his right.

"Jeremy, get that out of your mouth," Steph says. "That's not food."

Vic swipes at his son. The room is crowded. The waitress brings me a chair she's pulled from a storage closet. It doesn't match the others. I squeeze in between the boys. Tuck my elbows, read the menu. I feel silly sitting here, an afterthought. The waitress fills my cup with coffee I didn't order.

"Anything new with you?" Steph asks.

I take a long time to answer. I know what I'm going to say, the inevitability rising slow in my chest. But it's not real until the words hit air. Next to me, Ryan thumbs the iPhone that distracts him from the world.

"A job came up. This gig down in Florida. I'm thinking about taking it." The statement commits me. I dump sugar into my coffee.

Vic and Steph trade looks. I try to interpret their silence. Decide they'd welcome my relocation. That I'm a weight on their family unit. I figure I'm confirming my biases. Another phrase I lifted from the prison therapist.

"That's ... " Steph glances again at her husband, "that's great. But what about ... "

She doesn't say the word. We're among people whose relatives might not have lost the right to vote. My past embarrasses her. She's not alone.

"I'm getting discharged early." I don't mention the state's budget shortfall.

"Hey, man," Vic says, "that's awesome. Good for you."

His smile reads genuine, but his condescension galls me. I'm the oldest at this table. I'm bracketed by children playing video games and eating plastic. I feel a resentment building. The sensation's familiar. It's pushed bad decisions on me, ones I accepted without fighting.

"I'm proud of you, Joey." Steph smiles, pats my hand.

Forty minutes later I head for the nearest hardware store.

On Monday afternoon I'm dumping used machine oil into a drum a company collects once a month. Mister Bobby swings by, walking fast.

"There he is!" He backslaps me as he passes. "You good? Need anything?"

"All good here."

He gives me a thumbs up and keeps moving. Mister Bobby's a decent man, a kid born into a role I sometimes think he did not want. He does his best and gave me an honest job. The oil I'm disposing of's thick and pours slowly into the funnel.

Later, Ernesto finds me in the lunchroom. I'm eating a sandwich I can't taste.

"Are we on?"

I slip him the copied keys, the alarm code I printed off a library computer. He smiles and pats me on the back. The gesture reminds me of Vic at Rory's. Makes me feel less than. I tell myself the $20K will be worth it.

Miss Jenkins calls that Tuesday. "Do you have a minute, Mr. Rebale?"

Her voice is heavier than usual. I duck into the maintenance closet; slop sink, chemicals in spray bottles, nitrile gloves, masks I never use, a state-mandated eyewash station that I'm pretty sure is supposed to be on out of the floor.

"Yeah," I say.

"I hate to tell you this, but the state pulled some fiscal magic and found the money to fund this office. That means the early discharge program's been, well, discharged. I know I got your hopes up, and I apologize. But listen, you're on the right path. Sixteen months'll go by in an eyeblink. Just keep your nose clean and those pay stubs coming."

I end the call and hunt down Ernesto.

"I need the keys back."

He blinks about a thousand times.

"My probation officer called. They're not cutting me loose."

Ernesto's Adam's apple bobs.

"That means I need this job."

His eyes flash left, then right.

"You can't do this," I say.

"Joey," he says, "Rosie flew the kids down yesterday."

This time I hit the gym hot. Navigate swaying heavy bags and teens whipping double-unders. Giant fans push stagnant air. Long-limbed fighters dance around each other. Their fingerless gloves pop loud, a snapping sound that draws my attention. They trade shots. Kicks to the thigh that I feel twenty feet away. Stubbs is doing pull-ups off a steel bar bolted into the cinderblock. I head to him.

He drops down onto the mat. He looks at my booted feet, then at me. I don't move off. I'm past caring about gym etiquette.

"You can't do it."

He picks a scab off a knuckle. "Ernesto told me about your situation."

I wait. "And?"

"And what? Wheels are in motion, man."

"Fuck your motion."

I press a hand to his chest. It feels like stone. He glares at me. I pull it back.

"You'll still get what's yours," he says softly. "Unless you get stupid."

In one of the rings a fighter shoots in and upends her opponent. In an instant she's straddling the girl, raining punches down. Her fists catch forearm, wrist. And face. A trainer breaks it up. The girl on the mat stays there. The other bounces from one foot to the other. In every fight there's a loser.

"He's gonna know it was me."

"You give that guy too much credit. Nobody's gonna suspect you."

"Fuck with the locks."

Stubbs looks at me. The gash in his head's healed into an ugly line scarring his shaved scalp.

"Make it look like you didn't have the keys."

"Stubbs! You up."

Inside the ring Ray leans on the ropes. I wonder where the girls have gone.

Stubbs starts wrapping his hands.

"You haven't thought this out," I say.

He eyes me direct, and I see in him a flash of the terrible men I've known over the years. "Yes we have."

Saturday, nearing midnight. The crowd's packed in tight. I figure half of them've seen the bookings. Mister Bobby's beaming and bumping fists. These nights have elevated him. He loves playing the heavy.

I'm not afraid to admit I'm terrified.

We'd arranged pallets and lined them with steel sheets, these improvised viewing platforms. They rise three levels high, give fans a stadium-style view of the ring. Which is just high school gym mats velcroed together. No barrier between fighters and crowd. The scene vibes underground and dangerous. That's the draw.

A pair of skinny kids open the card. One's a bleeder and nopes out fast. He staggers back to his cornerman, leaking bad. I swoop in with my mop and smear his blood across the blue vinyl.

The bar trash needs emptying. Mister Bobby's brought in shot girls from the old Sin City. Young Dominican girls who flash ass and move bottles. I move among them unnoticed. It's funny how Mister Bobby runs these illegal romps like they're legit. He doesn't understand he's out of his depth. Maybe Stubbs is right. Maybe Mister Bobby won't make a stink when he finds his safe empty. No matter how hard I try I can't believe that. No man takes a $60,000 hit and doesn't swing back. I corral Ernesto outside the locker rooms.

"Don't do this."

He won't look at me. I grab his forearm.

He reads my fear and says, "I'm sorry, Joey."

I find Stubbs in the makeshift locker room. He's shadowboxing in the corner, weaving low and high kicks into his five-punch combos. He shoots a foot out higher than my head. Ray watches, his hands on his hips. Stubbs's jabs crack the air. Ray says, "Good, good."

I approach. Off Stubbs's *gimme five* look, Ray steps out.

"You do this and I'm fucked."

I've been arrested five times. Ran with three different crews. Survived Rikers and two upstate prisons. In my world, I earned a measure of respect. But that was so long ago, and I was never muscle. Stubbs and Ernesto read me as a reformed striver who'd buried his desperation. They worked what they needed out of me. They won't call the job off now.

"You give him the heads up," Stubbs whispers, mean, "and I will hurt you. You go to the cops, and I will hurt you."

I don't doubt him.

"You said so yourself," Stubbs says, a little looser, knowing I'm in a spot, "the last time you got locked up, you didn't flip. Shut your mouth and tomorrow you'll have twenty grand you didn't have today."

"Pay stubs are a condition of my post-release."

"Then quit. Like there ain't a hundred places with toilets need cleaning?"

I bite my lip. My father spoke about the honor of an honest day's wages. But the world's changed. I'm old and know too much. Namely, money stolen spends better than money earned.

“You’ll be fine,” Stubbs says, “there’s shift foremen that’ve got the keys.”

“They don’t have my record.”

For a long time Stubbs says nothing. Then he snaps a fist out, quick. It brushes my ear and I flinch like I just got shot at. He smiles something ugly.

“Stubbs,” Ray calls from the hall. “We up.”

Stubbs presses a thumb to his nose, looses a wad of snot onto the concrete floor. He rolls his shoulders, heads for the ring. As the door swings slowly shut, I hear the crowd chant and catch the rented lights shining. I squint, and the factory fades, and I’m in a proper casino, not some South Bronx steel factory holding underground MMA matches for local thugs, and I’m not a bit player in a batshit crazy scheme to rob its witless boss. That image quickly fades. With a rag, I wipe Stubbs’s snot off the floor.

Stubbs wins his match. After trading blows upright, he shoots in quick. Worked his opponent into a reluctant tap. I only know this ’cause I heard two guys with diamonds in their teeth describe what was happening as I emptied a trash bin. There’s this ball in my stomach, nerves eating me from the inside. Sweat slickens the back of my neck. I move to the bag of trash—Mister Bobby keeps a clean shop—and I almost vomit into it.

The next fighters enter the ring, two women in sports bras and cornrows. A local DJ spins inter-fight beats and announces names. One’s face is tattooed. The other howls like a wolf.

Ernesto glides by. I grab his arm. He shakes me off. I want to run. To claw back every stupid decision I ever made. But fantasies are for children. In the ring the ref—this guy who lost his accreditation for gambling—rubs his foot over a patch of mat. He calls for me. I hustle over, drop to my knees and scrub the patch of red. I feel like less of a man, hunched over, wiping away another's work.

Tonight's my last shift. I'll collect my share and drive my Matrix upstate. Get a room in a cheap motel for a week or two. Apply for another job. Anything to satisfy the rest of my probation. Then I'll join Ernesto in Orlando. Stubbs is right. Mister Bobby isn't equipped to hunt us down. This can work.

The girls go at it harder than the men who came before. In the third round Face Tattoo mounts Wolfgirl and pummels her with closed fists. Blood and teeth splatter wide. Wolfgirl goes limp. The crowd goes apeshit. It takes three men to pull Face Tattoo off her. The new doctor, Elena, strides into the ring. With gloved hands she tends to Wolfgirl. In the makeshift front row, Mister Bobby stands with Vasin, the fighter who busted Stubbs open, and two suits who I can tell have done time.

I fill my bucket with bleach.

Stubbs is late with the cash. Pushing 7 a.m. and he still hasn't shown. I don't want to call Ernesto, but my discipline fails me. I dial his digits. The call goes right to voicemail. The phone's shut off. He's gone dark.

In my tiny studio I stand, I sit. I stand again. I'd packed a bag—jeans, underwear, socks—and could leave now, but I need my share. I've never been this removed from a job before. I don't care for the disconnect.

When the knock comes, I open the door fast and know, even before I see her in her white suit and gloved hands—the same hands that stitched up Wolfgirl—that the job's blown and I am fucked.

Vasin and one of the ringside suits fill the tiny hallway. None of them speak. We're all experienced enough to map the terrain. They allow me to lock my door. I wonder what Steph will tell Mom.

Mister Bobby won't look at me. Probably because he's no longer in charge. The other suit that was with him ringside stands in the center of the loading dock with his hands in his pockets. Casual, like he's waiting for the valet to bring his ride. Four hours ago, men and women pummeled each other on this spot. Not that anyone'd know; I washed away the blood, broke down the stands. Stacked the mats in a storage room. I got $150 for the extra-hours work. I wish it was enough.

Through windows set high in the walls, sunlight starts to creep in. Rectangles of yellow shoot nearly level across the factory. They remind me of blades. I think I'm going to die here.

The Suit's older and moves little, but vibes hyperaware. I saw his kind in Green Haven. I kept my distance then. I don't have that luxury now. He stands six feet off, half-slouched and casual. Eyeing me like a used car he's considering.

I'm scared, but pride is stubborn and I try to stand tall. I volunteer nothing and hope they'll respect my honor. It's my only righteous trait. Elena and the Suit speak in a close-bodied whisper that tips familiarity. No one asks for Mister Bobby's opinion.

"I'm not going to ask what your share was." His accent's hardened by cigarettes. The fighter throws the Suit a bag—Stubbs's bag from the night he pitched me on this. The Suit unzips it and shows me the cash inside. "Because you don't have it."

My legs go full Jell-O. Somehow I manage to stay upright.

He tosses the bag back. Vasin catches and sets it down. He shrugs himself out of his jacket. Strips off the sweater underneath. I have no tattoos; he's covered in them. I don't exercise; he's shredded.

"Mister Bobby says you have been incarcerated and that you work hard. And, until tonight, you haven't stolen from him. Unfortunately for you, you also stole from me. We both know I cannot let this behavior go uncorrected."

My heart drumrolls. The Suit walks back to Elena. Vasin swings his arms in big windmills. Rotates his hips. Drops to a squat, jumps high, does it again. The whole time he's bouncing on the balls of his feet. He's getting limber. I swallow bile.

Vasin—shirtless and shoeless but still wearing jeans—comes toward me. I instinctively back up. He rolls a shoulder. He doesn't even put his hands up. I'm not a threat. Past him, in a plastic chair meant for the union guys, Mister Bobby turns away.

As I dance in circles I raise my fists. I'm a felon and probationer with seven commercial scores under my belt. But I've been in fewer fights than you'd think. Not every criminal's a hardcore thug.

Flight's got nowhere to go, so I switch to fight. I throw a punch. It glances off Vasin's shoulder. He snaps a kick that catches me in the left thigh. Pain shoots through my leg, like an electrical shock. I almost go down.

I throw another lame punch that he leans away from. I'm so slow. He jabs a hand out and slaps me. Demeaning, yeah, but it still makes my eyes water. As I blink the tears away I swing blind. Then again. Vasin laughs and says something in a language I don't understand.

I drag my forearm across my eyes. The world refocuses. Vasin's got his head turned toward the Suit, and some instinct in me takes over. I throw myself behind my right fist, the one I'm aiming at his jaw, and I feel that fist buckle as it lands square. The jolt travels up my arm, across my shoulders, and I'm still leaning in, still swinging through, and I know as I come out of it and for a moment lose my balance that I have never hit a man that hard.

Vasin spits blood onto the concrete.

He comes at me fast. A kneecap lands in my chest. For a split-second I wonder how he got it that high. Then the air leaves my lungs, and I care only about breathing. A fist catches me on the temple. My head snaps to the right. I feel a molar go flying. His shin bends my right knee toward my left. I hear a snapping sound, and my world goes white. I collapse onto the floor. Shots hit me everywhere: face, skull, torso. A heel plants down hard into my leg. Someone screams, and I realize it's me.

I turtle. Lilly Droulliard appears in the blackness of my shut-tight eyes.

The concrete's cold and hard. I try to disappear into it. It says no. I'm on my stomach. Clawing at the floor, trying to get away. Vasin straddles my hips. He tenderizes my kidneys. Pain overtakes my body. I wonder when I'll pass out.

Then I'm being grabbed at the shoulders and flipped onto my back. I know this by feel; my left eye's swollen shut and through the right, the world's a blurry pink. Blood mixing with my tears. Something hits me in the chest. I worry my heart's exploded.

Then Vasin's hand is in my hair. He lifts my head off the concrete. My damaged brain makes out his fist, cocked high and ready. That's when a voice says something I don't understand. Blood bubbles from my mouth, wets my chin, neck, and chest. My head bounces back onto the floor. I don't move. I *can't* move. To my right, I see a river of blood drifting slowly toward the century-old grate cut into the floor.

Someone drops a mop handle onto my chest.

# About the Authors

**Scott Blackburn**, the editor of this collection, is an English instructor and a graduate of the Mountainview MFA program. His debut novel, *It Dies with You*, was chosen as a summer read by Garden and Gun Magazine, and it was a finalist for the Crook's Corner Book Prize. When Scott is not writing and teaching, he enjoys training in combat sports such as boxing, Muay Thai, and Ju-jitsu, in which he holds a black belt. He lives in North Carolina with his wife and their two children.

**A.M. Adair** draws much of her inspiration from her experiences as a retired Chief Warrant Officer of the U.S. Navy. Specializing in human and counterintelligence, her duty has included conducting numerous tours internationally to countries like Afghanistan and Iraq. Her works range from short stories, novellas, screenplays, and more—becoming multi-alward winning with projects like her most recently completed Elle Anderson thriller series. She spends her days in Tennessee as a wife and mother of two children, along with two golden retrievers.

Bronx-born and raised, **Jason Allison** spent twenty years with the NYPD, mostly as a homicide detective. His debut novel is forthcoming from Crooked Lane Books, and his short fiction has won a regional award and has been featured in multiple volumes of Rock and a Hard

Place and New England's Best Crime Stories. Jason and his wife now live in Massachusetts with a sneering, judgmental Golden Retriever. He is represented by Alec Shane of Writers House.

**Laura Brashear** has lived her entire life on the Front Range of Colorado. She and her family currently reside on a farm with an eclectic assortment of animals. Her lifelong passion for storytelling and a deep interest in the human psyche led her to obtain an MFA in Creative Writing. She also teaches at a local college, where she's able to share her love of writing. Her adventuresome spirit has led her to travel to many interesting destinations, where she can enjoy the location and also observe human behavior. Her fascination with what drives people's actions serves as the foundation for her psychological suspense and crime fiction, where she creates stories that examine the complexities of human nature. When not writing, Laura can be found tending to her garden, chipping away at her massive "To Be Read" list, and cherishing moments with her family and beloved animal companions.

**Ashley Erwin** writes bombastic fiction with a body count, the Southern Pulp writer of *Grit, Black, Blood* and *A Ballad Concerning Black Betty or the Retelling of a Mankiller and Her Machete,* with shorts appearing in Cheap Pop, Shotgun Honey, Switchblade, Revolution John, and Cowboy Jamboree's 'Grotesque Art,' Dark Waters, Vol. 1, Action Spectacle, and many more. An avid reader at Noir at the Bar traveling across the country with some jaunts over the pond for debauchery in England, she is the Woman to a Man and the enabler of a big boy cat and she bides her time peddling bourbon and storytelling for the day job.

Born with less than a one-percent chance of survival and an open-heart surgery survivor, **L.S. Goozdich**'s close relationship with death inspired him to bring his dream of being an author to life. A natural born storyteller since he was kid creating short films with the family camera, narrative has been a powerful force and motivator for why he continues to write. Goozdich is the author of adventure fiction novels such as Vipers, Frozen Wraith, and Retaliation. When not using the pen to inspire people to pursue their dreams, he's hosting the Men's Adventure Fiction Podcast or enjoying the great outdoors.

As a NYC crime and horror fiction author of novels such Boise Longpig Hunting Club and most recently Where the Bones Lie, **Nick Kolakowski** pays homage to his favorite influences like Tim Parks and Joseph Heller. Exploring the imperfections of modern-day life, Nick's works have appeared in magazines and anthologies like Mystery Magazine, House of Gamut, Best American Mystery & Suspense 2024, Shotgun Honey. and more.

**Meredith R. Lyons** grew up in New Orleans, collecting two degrees from Louisiana State University before running away to Chicago to be an actor. In between plays, she got her black belt and made martial arts and yoga her full-time day job. She fought in the Chicago

Golden Gloves, ran the Chicago Marathon, and competed for team USA in the Savate World Championships in Paris. In spite of doing each of these things twice, she couldn't stay warm and relocated to Nashville. She owns several swords, but lives a non-violent life, saving all swashbuckling for the page, knitting scarves, gardening, visiting coffee shops, and cuddling with her husband and two panther-sized cats. Her first novel Ghost Tamer is an Amazon Editor's Pick for Best SciFi Fantasy, an IBPA Benjamin Franklin Gold Winner for Best SciFi Fantasy, an IPPY Award Winner for Best First Book, and a Silver Falchion Winner for Best Book of 2023 and Best Supernatural. A Dagger of Lighting released April 1, 2025, both with CamCat Books.

**David Moloney** is the author of Barker House, a novel that revolves around a number of correctional officers at a fictional county jail in New Hampshire. His short stories and essays have also appeared in Guernica, The Yale Review, AGNI, Joyland, The Common, and elsewhere. His forthcoming novel, Lion in Love, will be released in 2027. David is a graduate of the University of Massachusetts Lowell and earned his masters at the Mountainview MFA (SNHU), where he was awarded the Lynn Safford Memorial Prize for Outstanding Thesis. He now teaches and coordinates the undergraduate creative writing program at Southern New Hampshire University.

**Keith Roysdon** is a former journalist who has won both national and statewide awards for his coverage of criminal activity that has spurred on police investigations and indictments. Using his 40 years of journalism expertise, he now uses his pen to delve into the world of crime fiction, which has won awards such as the 2021 Hugh Holton Award for Best Unpublished Novel from the Mystery Writers of America Midwest and first place for Best Nonfiction Book in 2021 from the Indiana Society of Professional Journalists. The Tennessee resident is the co-author of 4 true crime novels and the author of That October. You can also find Keith's short fiction pieces and pop-culture articles published at CrimeReads, Punk Noir, Shotgun Honey, Hoosier Noir, Rock and a Hard Place, and other sites and anthologies.

After studying at The Citadel to receive his bachelor's degree, **J.B. Stevens** completed his master's at Troy State University. He previously acted as a U.S. Army Infantry Officer and was later honorably discharged under the rank of Captain. J.B. currently lives in the Deep South with his wife, daughter, and Yorkshire Terrier. His literary work— fiction, poetry, nonfiction, and reviews— have gained many nominations, including the Pushcart Prize, and many awards, like Mystery Tribune's inaugural micro-fiction contest. He spends his free time training in Brazilian Jiu-Jitsu, in which he holds a black belt, and he is a former, undefeated mixed martial artist.

www.ingramcontent.com/pod-product-compliance
Lightning Source LLC
LaVergne TN
LVHW100509110826
845146LV00002B/570

* 9 7 9 8 9 9 5 1 3 4 1 0 7 *